SHE SMILED BACK

Suddenly, the benign expression was washed from
his face. His features were contracted in a gaze of
delicious triumph. Heady with the taste of killing,
his lips curled at the sides. A dimple flickered in his
cheek.

In this small dark room, a manic savageness had
gripped him, a desire to inflict pain shone in his
face.

"My, my, you sure have pretty legs . . . I like pretty
girls . . ."

THE SUN place

Ray Connolly

AVON
PUBLISHERS OF BARD, CAMELOT, DISCUS AND FLARE BOOKS

THE SUN PLACE is an original publication of Avon Books.
This work has never before appeared in book form.

AVON BOOKS
A division of
The Hearst Corporation
959 Eighth Avenue
New York, New York 10019

First Avon Printing, December, 1981

AVON TRADEMARK REG. U. S. PAT. OFF. AND IN
OTHER COUNTRIES, MARCA REGISTRADA, HECHO EN
U. S. A.

Printed in the U. S. A.

WFH 10 9 8 7 6 5 4 3 2 1

For Sylvia

_____*PART I*

Delicately resisting the swell, the small white boat nosed curiously along the pink sliver of beach. Curling breakers sucked inwards toward the shore. It was late afternoon and the sun hung limply above the green carpet of bush that dressed most of the small island. A steady breeze fanned kindly from the sea.

The boat was shallow and wedge shaped, a two-seater runabout with a couple of Volvo Penta outboard engines. At the wheel sat a slim, muscular man of about thirty-five. He was alone. On the seat next to him a blue transistor radio sang with the fractured rhythms of reggae. The man mouthed the words as the wind dispersed the song across this quieter corner of the Caribbean.

Carefully the man scanned the long beach, casting cautious glances at a jutting promontory of coral. Suddenly becoming aware of potential danger he accelerated into the security of deeper water sending two jets of foam arcing in his wake. A miscalculation of an inch over a spire of pillar coral and the see-through bottom of the boat could be sliced open.

Satisfied that he was clear of the reef, the man settled back and studied the line of coast intently through heavy binoculars. He was a cautious sailor. Had he not handled his craft so expertly, he might have been mistaken for a tourist down from New York for a couple of weeks jetting around the islands. But his skill, and his sun-bleached, shoulder-length hair and prematurely dry, deeply lined brown skin, identified him as someone who had made the islands his home. His clothes were casual, but almost like a uniform—white tennis shoes, socks, and shorts, and a pale blue V-necked shirt, which bore on the pocket a small red motif of a reclining mermaid and the letters CV. He edged the boat north, moving carefully around a headland and into a small bay, where mangroves tangled with sea grapes along the shore. A partly obscured break in the bush seemed to beckon to him. He looked at his watch. It was nearly five o'clock. "Just one last look and then home," he said aloud, and delicately guided the boat down a narrow channel and into a large crescent-shaped lagoon, a scented, mysterious place overhung with casuarina trees.

Now that he was turned into the late-afternoon sun the man squinted and put a smooth, unworn hand to his eyes. The lagoon looked idyllic, but he could see why it had never been of any use to the islanders and why it would be unsuitable for his purposes. Swamps lined all the shores, beyond which lay apparently impenetrable bush.

He was about to turn away when he caught sight of a flash of steel in the far western corner of the lagoon—a distance of about two hundred yards. Intrigued, he screwed up his eyes, pulled the boat around, and headed into the sun.

Even before he reached the mangroves their insect population began bidding him welcome as squadrons of sharp stinging bugs, disturbed by the noise of his boat, made kamikaze attacks at his skin. Irritated, he pushed open the throttle and sped quickly down the wider channels, sheltering behind the windshield for protection.

Now he could see clearly what had caught his eye. It was a powerboat, identical to the one he was using, right down to the CV emblem and mermaid painted on the stern. The only difference was the name. His was the *Méditerranée*, the other boat was called the *Pacifique*.

He slipped his own boat into neutral and drew alongside the deserted sister craft, which was tethered to a stake driven into the beach, a remnant of what had once been a small landing stage. Threading a length of rope through the fairleads of both craft he secured them and, using the *Pacifique* as a stepping-stone, he jumped down onto the beach. The swamps around him whispered as a slight breeze stole through the leaves. Puzzled, he began to make his way up the path, which led through the undergrowth toward the interior of the island.

He heard the music before he saw the house, a melancholic electric wailing sound, a high-pitched voice of vigorous despair, dipping and soaring above the howling of guitars.

What was left of the house was standing in a clearing that the forest had all but reclaimed. It might once have been an elegant island home, but now it was a broken-down wooden shell from which the shutters hung, torn from their hinges by years of hurricanes, and where the veranda and balcony had fallen away to provide a ramp up to the gap where once there had been a front door. Incongruously, a basket of bougainvillea and jasmine hung above the veranda in full bloom.

Suddenly the music stopped. The man started up the broken steps, making a creaking sound. A lizard skittered up the peeling wall and disappeared into a niche in the window frame.

At the porch the man stopped and peered inside. It was dark. The creepers, which had once been trained to grow in pretty profusion around the walls, had stretched across the window frames and into the house, blocking out the sunlight. He stepped into the house and moved silently along the dark hall. Weeds grew determinedly through the rotting floorboards.

"Hello! Is anyone home?" he called out, more to break the stillness than because he expected an answer.

The silence became deeper, sharper. He held his breath and listened, peering up into the gloom of the staircase.

"Hello," he called again. "Anybody home?"

A low giggle in the darkness behind him made him spin around.

"Just us chickens." The voice was slow and lazily sardonic.

A figuré moved into a shaft of pale light, where some sun had forced its way through a cracked wall. It was a young man, his face grotesquely painted yellow, black, and green into a lizard's mask. A cheap wig of long, straight black hair hung limply beyond his shoulders. He was naked to the waist, his body smooth and tanned, and a floral Tahitian pareo was tied loosely around his hips, falling around his legs like a skirt.

"Jesus God," the man murmured, stepping back, his eyes fixed, almost hypnotized by the grinning, distorted mask of paint.

"Welcome to my house," the boy's voice hissed mockingly from the slash of green that was his mouth. "How did you find me?"

Slowly the man began to back away.

The boy moved toward him. "Don't be frightened, Dick," he cooed. "It's only me."

The man stared. "Who?"

"You don't recognize me? Well, isn't that just neat?" There was a low snicker of amusement.

"My God . . ." Recognition and a kind of relief shredded the man's voice. "Jesus . . . you scared me. What the hell are you doing done up like that?"

"You scared me, Dick." The voice was even and calm, but the grin was gone. "I didn't think anybody knew I was here. Why did you follow me? Why can't you leave me alone?"

"Follow you? Are you crazy? I didn't know you were here. I came by to scout for picnic sites," the man rushed on, but his voice faded as he realized that he wasn't being listened to. The boy was suddenly holding a long, double-bladed knife. And even as the man stared at it, he realized it was already too late.

An hour later, as the sun was giving way to the silver gray of a Bahamian evening, the pilot of a DC-3 Trans Island Airways freight plane noticed a fire far below on one of the Dutch Cays, and banked his orange-and-white plane to get a better view.

"Looks like someone's house caught fire down there," Carl Ellington remarked laconically to his copilot, Aaron Jones.

Jones peered downward. "No one lives on those islands anymore. Probably some Club Village picnickers let their barbecue get out of control," he said.

Ellington banked again, did a circle, and peered down for signs of activity. There was nothing, and even before he had completed his circle the fire began dying. "Better report it to Nassau, anyway" he said as he brought his craft back onto an even keel.

Aaron Jones grunted a reply and made the requested radio call.

Someone in the Nassau control tower probably took his call, and doubtless it was logged in the appropriate place. But if so, it was soon forgotten. And no one, not even Ellington or Jones, gave it further thought. A fire on a tiny, uninhabited island in a remote part of the Bahamas was of no significance to anyone.

"What makes you think I'm looking for an affair with you? What makes you think that your body is so attractive to me, so tantalizing that I would drive four hundred miles from Paris just to taste its delights? Don't you think, James, that you're being just a little presumptuous?" Beta Ullman lifted a carefully etched eyebrow and smiled; standing with her arms buried inside the deep pockets of her fur coat and with her snow goggles perched just above her blond hairline, she possessed a kind of recklessness only the most exquisite, self-confident women enjoy.

James Hardin considered her carefully before answering. He liked her. She had a bantering jokiness that turned every conversation into a sexual game of wits. Not for the first time he found himself regretting that she was the mistress of one of his employers.

"I didn't presume anything of the sort," he countered untruthfully. "I merely wondered aloud why, out of the eighty-three Club Villages scattered around the world, you happened to choose this one."

Beta shrugged, dismissing the question. "Why not here? It's very beautiful. The snow's good. The company is convivial. I even know the *chef de village*. And sometimes I even like him. Besides, I enjoy making Ernst jealous. Don't you?"

Hardin imagined the polished, aquiline features of Ernst Ronay, his managing director. "No," he said, "not really."

9

Beta giggled. "Coward! Anyway, I mustn't monopolize you. I'm sure you have all kinds of interesting and important duties to be getting on with. Perhaps we could have dinner together tonight . . . if you can drag yourself away from your job for just a couple of hours?"

"Perhaps," Hardin repeated.

Again Beta laughed, and, ghosting his cheek with a kiss, she closed one huge gray eye in a provocative and promising wink and began to trudge off through the snow, her slender figure now made chunky by the fur and boots.

Hardin smiled inwardly. She was the kind of woman he could only imagine God creating in a most ungodly moment of high libido. She was wonderful, but fraught with delicious hazard.

Resolving to cast his mind to more serious matters, he turned and, pushing his weight on the soles of his feet, he listened as the thick bank of snow crunched under him. Twenty feet below, the morning's first ski class was returning, coming to startling, calamitous stops as the beginners lost control and tumbled into drifts that banked against the log walls of the ski room. Flurries of fine snow blew sharply into his face. It had been snowing for two days, and no break in the weather was forecast. While it was safe for the beginners to putter about on the easy slopes, Hardin had felt it prudent to ban all intermediate and senior classes. There was nothing to stop the guests from going out by themselves, but Club Village certainly wasn't going to encourage its employees and guests to take their lives into their hands. This particular area of Haute Savoie was renowned for its beauty, but a couple of the higher runs were hazardous in bad conditions.

Nearby a group of children skidded to a halt, shouting and laughing to each other in a polyglot of Western European languages. Club Village had originally been a French organization, and had been established in 1952 as an outdoor sporting society for Parisian health fanatics. But in the past decade the combination of cheap travel, jumbo jets, and a massive investment by four of the biggest banks in Paris and Zurich had turned the club into the second largest holiday organization in the world—just behind the archrival, Club Méditerranée. Now, at any of the vacation villages around the world, less than a third of the guests would be French. Guests came from all over Europe, enticed by clever advertisements that subtly suggested sexual freedom and potential variety, while reassuring those who were not looking for romantic adventures that the club also offered sports, sun, and health. To keep the one-hundred-million-dollar-a-year Club Village turnover in healthy profit the balance between the two types of guests had to be measured very delicately.

As head of the village, Hardin's job was both administrative and symbolic. He was on show the whole time—inspiring confidence, talking to the lonely, watching the staff, and generally keeping in close touch with every facet of village life, from security to after-dinner entertainment. The philosophy of Club Village was that a guest who left with a substantial reason for dissatisfaction could undo thousands of dollars' worth of advertising.

Choosing his footholds carefully, Hardin strode down the bulldozed mountain of snow.

"Well, how did it go this morning?" he asked Solveig, a plump, dimpled milkmaid of a Danish girl who was head of the Children's Club, noting as he did that one small English child was sobbing silently.

"It was very cold up there," said Solveig. "The English always feel it more than anyone else." And, putting a chubby arm around the pink-nosed, weeping child, she bent down and kissed him warmly on his lips. In his embarrassment the boy stopped crying. Solveig winked at Hardin. "That always works on the boys," she whispered wickedly. Then, turning back to her charges, she began shouting orders in French and English.

Hardin smiled and, ruffling the snow-flecked hair of a couple of children, left Solveig and her two French assistants to shepherd their charges in for lunch.

Hardin, thirty-five years old, was a big man, six foot three and handsome in the way of an athlete, his uneven features receiving more than adequate compensation in the strength and grace of his body. He had short, black hair and blue eyes, and a loping, sinewy spring to his step, which gave the illusion of moving in slow motion.

Born in Caracas of a French mother and American father, Hardin's early life had been a blur of half-packed suitcases. He had trekked around the world after his parents while his father rose slowly and unspectacularly through the rungs of the diplomatic trade. Although he had American citizenship he was equally at home virtually anywhere in the world, having had most of his education at the International School in Geneva, spending his vacations at any number of places between Manila and Helsinki. At seventeen he had begun his university education at Trinity College, Dublin, added a little more to it at Northwestern in Illinois, and eventually ended it some four years later with a degree in international relations from the University of New South Wales. Traveling was in his blood, and any excuse to get on to an airplane was all he needed. For a time the excuse had become tennis. He was not a great player, having started to take an interest in the game too late in life, but he was good enough to win some top amateur tournaments. So when he was twenty-three he had walked away from a promising career in the Foreign Service in order to join the pro circuit, where he had been a happy-go-lucky low-ranking player. Then one day he had collided with Club Village, and along had come a third career.

As he made his way through the new drifts around to the front of the club Hardin reflected again that he was lucky to have been given this particular village as his first appointment as *chef de village*. With only 350 guests and 150 staff Val d'Isabelle was small enough for him to keep an eye on everything.

Crossing the polished marble foyer he headed toward the dining room. As he passed through the bar a couple of Lufthansa stewardesses caught his eye and said something to each other. He smiled and walked on. Their ski suits were skin-tight, brand-new, and, so far, untested for warmth since the wearers had scarcely moved from the environs of the bar. They had already been at Val d'Isabelle for nearly a week and their willingness to make new and close friends was already the enthusiastic talk of the staff quarters. Hardin didn't need his name to be added to their list. Every week brought girls like that. The trick was to avoid finding oneself alone with them without being rude.

The dining room was large, high, and airy, but the log beams and massive open fireplace gave a semblance of coziness. Forty tables, each set for twelve and bearing bottles of red and white wine and mineral water, waited for the avalanche of lunch. Hardin's eye passed quickly over everything, seeking out the details, checking that the carnations on every table were fresh, that the tablecloths were spotless, and that all the glasses were polished. Nimbly the waiters, Turkish boys and North Africans, skipped about the room making last-minute preparations.

The chef, a Mateus-colored Parisian with a small goatee, emerged from the kitchens and stood challengingly behind the thirty-yard-long table from which lunch would be served. He had been with the club for nearly twenty years, but still regarded every meal as a personal challenge. Hardin allowed his eyes to travel appreciatively along the table: There was poached turbot in mousseline sauce, trout with almonds, guinea fowl in port, beef in red wine stew, stuffed veal hearts, iced liqueur mousses, rum and lemon sorbet, a virtual orchard of fresh fruit, and a dozen cheeses. The chef waited for the verdict. "Excellent, Charles," Hardin smiled. The chef's eyes twitched momentarily as he absorbed the compliment. Then, like the martinet he was, he turned and began scolding a young Algerian who had inadvertently overfilled a huge tureen and was now in danger of flooding the dining room. Hardin moved away and headed toward the doors to greet the guests. A particularly high management profile was called for at mealtimes.

Suddenly, in a Coppertan deluge, the doors opened and the diners were upon him. Hardin smiled a welcome to all, shook hands when they were offered, and exchanged a multilingual smattering of bonhomie. There was a spinster music teacher from Paris, who, he suspected, had struck up a most unlikely relationship with the Turkish head-waiter; various athletic-looking couples; a German mortician of fifty who had come with his dumpy librarian daughter; all kinds of secretaries from all over Europe; couple of divorced ladies in their thirties who wore too much eye makeup for lunchtime eyelash flutterings; and a dozen or so single men.

"Ladies and gentlemen . . . just one announcement." The voice of Jean-Paul Cartier, the head of indoor entertainments, boomed from a speaker. There was a general wincing at the noise level, and Hardin made a mental note to have the amplifier adjusted. "Tonight's entertainment is a masked ball, to which everybody is invited. If you don't have a mask, ask the CV at your table. Thank you."

Cartier stepped down and moved gracefully toward his table. He had been a dancer before Club Village had seduced him away from his vocation. Now he was that most privileged of Club Village employees, captain of the CVs. The CVs, Club Villagers, as they had originally been known, were the backbone of the club. At Val d'Isabelle there were over seventy, young men and women who worked fourteen hours a day, six days a week, who shared in virtually all the benefits of the guests, and for whom life was one long working holiday.

Hardin had been a CV himself at first. It was a hectic, never-ending job of organizing entertainments, games, expeditions, travel timetables, and the other hundred things required in a village. And it was a dangerously seductive life. After two years as a CV Hardin had begun to realize that he had lost all sense of reality outside the club. He had been in Mexico, Sri Lanka, Corsica, and Yugoslavia, but nothing that happened in the outside world had any relevance to his own life. All decisions about eating and sleeping were made for him, and since the club did not, by policy, encourage guests to buy newspapers or watch television while on vacation, he had found himself becoming alarmingly isolated from the world outside. For a young person, the life of a CV seemed to offer paradise: no money worries, total security, work that seemed more like play, and as much sex as was desired. But the dangers were immense. People who had been CVs too long became prisoners of Club Village, afraid to go out into the world, shy of mixing with people who were not on vacation, increasingly unable to make decisions for themselves, and terrified of being alone. In the club no one was ever alone.

Hardin had been made aware of the dangers when a sudden call to his father's funeral took him back to Washington and he found himself having to cope with the real world. He had stayed away six months, rediscovering the outside world, and when he had rejoined the club, it was to run a booking bureau in Lisbon. The life of a CV was for people who never wanted to grow up. But the club had a way of becoming disenchanted with its perpetual Peter Pans, and Hardin had seen many CVs gradually frozen out of an organization which had outgrown them. An empire built around the promise of endless youth tolerated uneasily those who lingered too long in growing up.

Selecting a small helping of poached turbot, Hardin peered around the room for an empty place. He chose one between an optician from Brussels who was holidaying with his son, and a German-Swiss secretary. She was a healthy, outdoor woman of around thirty-three, with long legs and heavy, muscular shoulders. Her nose was putty-shaped, and looked as though it had been pushed onto her face as an afterthought, and her cheeks were crimson with windburn. Around her eyes were large owlish white patches where her goggles had protected her eyes.

"May I join you?" he said as he laid his plate on the table. It was the duty of the chief of the village to seek out the less integrated guests and make them feel welcome. "We haven't been introduced. I'm James."

"Valerie," the girl grinned back.

"I understand you work for the Bank of America in Zurich," Hardin went on politely.

"Chase Manhattan, actually," she said. Her English was perfect, but somehow accentless, the product of a tape-recorded education. She sounded neither English nor American.

Hardin dug into his fish. "And why did you come on a Club Village vacation?" he asked.

"To be quite honest," said Valerie, leaning forward conspiratorially with a smile as wide as the Alps, "I came to get laid."

Hardin, determined not to show surprise, sipped a glass of mineral water, aware of the conflicting feelings of pity and admiration he was feeling for the girl. He suspected that if they were honest with themselves 90 percent of the single guests would admit that the lure of sex and/or romance had drawn them to the club, and it was refreshing to hear someone actually come out and say it. But looking at her, at the lopsided face and carelessly assembled features, and the ungainly, clownish, pear-shaped body, he knew that she would inevitably be one of the last-chance choices for married men, unsuccessful CVs, and kitchen staff. Every week brought two or three girls like her, and every week they would hang around by themselves, chat to each other at dinner, and be overenthusiastic on the slopes. Until, toward the end of their vacations, their standards would lower, and, desperate not to leave without at least the mirage of romance, they would inevitably accept the attentions of the most unsuitable of companions and spend joyless yet grateful nights having their bodies explored by men frustrated and saddened by their own lack of success with the popular and beautiful.

The lie of romance had an awful lot to answer for, considered Hardin, but he didn't say that. Instead he smiled graciously. "Then I suspect some lucky young man is going to be in for a very nice surprise," he said, trying to sound as though he meant it.

The girl shrugged with an indifference born out of a

lifetime's plainness. "You're lying, James. I'm here to vacuum up the leftovers, and you know it. Don't worry, though. This is my eighth Club Village in five years, and I've no complaints so far. In fact, some of the best nights of my life have been spent in the club. Even the leftovers here can make a pretty incredible team."

In Paris the snow of the afternoon was turning to rain as Quatre Bras climbed into the back seat of his stretched Citroën Prestige for the evening drive from his office in the Club Village headquarters to his apartment near the École Militaire in the Seventh Arrondissement. Around him the sound of pneumatically luxurious French cars rose and fell as they inched forward through the inevitable jam which surrounded the Bourse and stretched out into the avenues and streets of the capital every evening at this time.

Quatre Bras stared calmly through the tinted window of his car. He was a rich and powerful man, some said one of the most insidiously powerful men in France, and others said far too powerful, but nothing he could do would dissolve the metallic congestion which was twining around him like some kind of steel creeper. He shrugged his square shoulders. He had more to worry about than traffic jams, and opening the slim doeskin briefcase he always carried, he pulled out a sheaf of papers.

In the seat in front of him, Michel Girardot negotiated the Place Vendôme and headed for the Rue de Rivoli. Girardot had been with the General, as Girardot liked to call Quatre Bras, for forty years, ever since they had turned what might have been, in other circumstances, considered adolescent delinquency into deeds of daring patriotism as they tormented the occupying German Army with acts of larceny, arson, and eventually violence and terrorism. By the end of the war the two street fighters

19

from Les Halles, instead of being in reform school, had
become exalted public heroes. From then on the career of
Quatre Bras had been a steady, accelerating drive toward
wealth and influence, while Girardot had remained his
faithful lieutenant.

Now Quatre Bras was wholly respectable, and the
details of his early, prewar life of delinquency surfaced
only occasionally in the more salacious French gossip
newspapers. But to Michel Girardot, he and his friend
were both still street boys.

Through the rearview mirror Girardot examined the
traffic. The snarlup was virtually complete. He swore
softly to himself.

Quatre Bras looked up and caught Girardot's eye,
turning the sides of his own mouth down in a comic
expression of fatality. "Don't worry so, Michel," he called
to his driver. "You'll give yourself a coronary."

Girardot didn't answer. Nothing ever seemed to ruffle
Quatre Bras. He had always been like that. Once, when
disturbed by a German foot patrol as they had been
loitering near a gasoline dump, he had calmly walked into
the glaring floodlights and the line of possible fire, and
begun to discuss an exchange of black-market goods with
an astonished German corporal, leaving Girardot to escape. Girardot had expected never to see his friend again,
but within hours Quatre Bras had turned up unharmed,
with a contract to provide girls, liquor, and fresh meat for
his new business partners! For years after, Quatre Bras
boasted that his major contribution to the war effort had
been in infecting half the German garrison in Paris with
gonorrhea and dysentery. The extraordinary deals he
arranged and the facility with which he tricked the Ger-
mans had become legendary throughout the French Resistance and had resulted in his being nicknamed "Quatre
Bras," a name which had become even more appropriate
as his business career had flourished. Now only tax men
and enemies addressed him by his real name—Alain de
Salis.

In the back of the car, Quatre Bras sucked carelessly on

a Gitane, allowing the heavy gray ash to cascade across his navy blue Christian Dior cashmere overcoat. He was a large, heavily built man, with hooded, impassive blue eyes, hair like polished steel, and a thick, powerful bull neck. At fifty-five he was still attractive and his permanent suntan glowed in the twilight of the reflected street lamps.

Always a man of few words, Quatre Bras was unusually quiet tonight. Years earlier, Girardot had given up any attempts to follow the intricate business deals and empire building that had taken Club Village from a few straw huts near Cannes to a massive worldwide vacation institution, but he was always ready whenever his old friend wished to talk about a problem. On such occasions, Girardot would take his cue from his boss, nodding sagely or shaking his head according to the inflection in Quatre Bras' voice. Eventually, after an hour or so of self-examination, Quatre Bras would suddenly jump to his feet and thank his old friend warmly for his wise and loyal advice.

So it was not with any surprise that Girardot felt a gentle tap upon his shoulder and heard a request that they go home. Whenever Quatre Bras spoke of home, he didn't mean the opulent apartment he owned in the exclusive Eiffel Tower area, but one of the small bars around Les Halles which had survived all the rearranging the Paris planners had wrought on the area in the past few years.

"We have a problem," said Quatre Bras to his friend as they hunched over a red checkered tablecloth in a shabby back-street cafe. At the bar a couple of French West African laborers watched a soccer match on a black-and-white television. In a corner, a desolate middle-aged prostitute drank an espresso slowly, sheltering herself meekly from the cold and rain.

Michel Girardot nodded his agreement. Once again, despite their St. Laurent suits and Gucci shoes, they were a couple of street urchins plotting an exploit.

"An American problem—or maybe two or three American problems. Do we go in, or do we stay out? What do you say, Michel?"

Girardot did not say. The question was, of course,

rhetorical. Quatre Bras valued Michel's silence and secrecy, not his advice. It had always been that way.

"My feeling is that we go in. Go in big. Thirty Club Villages spread across the United States in three years, and ten new ones in the Caribbean. Total investment if we move now is, maybe, 350 million francs. Ninety to a hundred million dollars."

Girardot moved his Scotch around in his mouth before swallowing it. Quatre Bras always enjoyed talking in millions.

"Yet the board urges caution. They say we must consolidate before we go American. They say we should do what we know best, that if we Americanize, then the whole concept of Club Village will be bastardized into some kind of summer camp with McDonald's hamburgers and Coca-Cola for dinner." He stopped speaking and examined his nine polished fingernails and the stump of his right little finger, which had been severed in a bobsled accident.

"And you say?" Michel always knew when to prompt. He pushed his black hair away from his forehead and waited.

"I say that if we don't move now, someone else will. Perhaps Club Med, or maybe even Holiday Inn or Sheraton will steal our concept. For twenty-five years we have been growing. If we stop now, we will begin to go backward."

"And the funding?"

"Universal-American Airlines. They're interested in buying into the whole Club Village. They would want 30 percent of the shares."

At last, Girardot began to understand something of the dilemma. The club was already largely owned by a loosely knit consortium of French and Swiss banks. Quatre Bras, the chairman and life president, held a substantial minority of the nonvoting shares, and three out of ten of the voting shares. He had never once been defeated in a boardroom battle. He was known as the man who had started Club Village, and so far his judgment had always been good enough to gain the support of the board when he needed it. To go now into the American zone would require massive American funding. That, in turn, would lead to a further redistribution of the shares and inevitably, to several more seats around the boardroom table. And that meant that his personal power would be reduced. Even Girardot, with his elementary grasp of economics and tribal warfare, could appreciate the delicacy of the situation. But Quatre Bras could never stand still. He had to keep expanding his empire. It was the nature of the club, and it was the nature of Quatre Bras.

"You said there were other problems?" prompted Girardot again.

Quatre Bras shrugged, a huge, expansive movement which seemed to come from deep within his diaphragm. "Unions," he said, as though mentioning an irritating allergy. "In America a week's work is not what we're used to. When did we ever work an eight-hour day, Michel? Never!"

Girardot nodded, watching his friend carefully.

Something else was obviously worrying him. For the first time Girardot wondered whether in fact the board were not right to be wary of the American adventure. The first trial village in the Caribbean had already been the cause of considerable notoriety because of some hyped-up New Yorkers who had chartered down for fifteen days of sun, sex, and illegal substances.

Girardot glanced over at the prostitute. She had finished her espresso, and the barman was suggesting that she find another place to shelter. In a few more years, considered Girardot illogically, such women might be nearly obsolete. The prospect saddened him, but better an honest hooker anytime than a devious little liberated lady.

Quatre Bras had also noticed the altercation. Standing up he walked with dignity and authority across to the prostitute. "Madam," he said, with the air of a man who has spent a lifetime charming women, "my colleague and I would be flattered if you would care to join us."

The woman looked up warily, ready for the double cross, the cruel insult. Then, suddenly recognizing Quatre

Bras from the thousands of newspaper photographs and television appearances, her lips cracked open in a smile, revealing a jagged array of decaying and broken teeth. Girardot winced, but Quatre Bras kept his smile, holding his arm out kindly, "We would be very flattered . . ."

Overcoming her bashfulness, the woman joined them and bathed herself in whiskey, freely poured for a good hour, as she, Quatre Bras, and Girardot recalled the old days in Les Halles. Finally Quatre Bras made polite murmurs of regret and, standing, slid a couple of thousand-franc bills across the table to the protesting lady and insisted that she treat herself to a new outfit as a gift from an old boyfriend. Despite her affectation of pride, she was pleased to accept.

It wasn't until Girardot was parking the Citroën outside Quatre Bras' apartment in the Avenue Frederick Le Play, pulling onto the cobbles and under the bare, knobbed chestnut trees, that he picked up their conversation.

"And the other problem, General?" he asked as Quatre Bras swung his long legs out onto the shining pavement. "The *real* problem."

"The real problem . . . I don't know. Perhaps I'm imagining it, Michel, but the *chef de village* at Elixir is missing. He disappeared yesterday afternoon while out in one of the outboards. There's an air-and-sea search out for him, but . . . I don't know. He's too experienced to get lost. Something is wrong. I don't know what it is, but I sense it."

forming some kin
lovers and abo
position that
she saw h
The
tion

If Quatre Bras was worried, Sharon Kennedy was approaching desperation as she sat alone in the office she shared with the chief of the village of Elixir. It was now late afternoon in the Caribbean, just a day since Dick Pagett had failed to return from what he had described as a "quiet afternoon's tour around the cays." There was no word from him. Since dawn the Bahamian Coast Guard and the local U.S. Navy Air Base on Eleuthera had been flying sorties over the area, but in a part of the world speckled with cays, rocks, and uninhabited islands, it was not unusual for small boats to be missing. What was unusual was for someone of Pagett's experience to run into difficulty.

Sharon stared silently at the telephone, willing it to ring. She was a tall, all-American, fair-haired girl from Kentucky, one of life's natural cheerleaders, with a smile seemingly crammed with too many Pepsodent white teeth, and a tan of pure honey brown. But on this particular day, the tan looked yellow with worry and the teeth gnawed anxiously on the end of a pencil.

Sharon and Pagett had been lovers for just three weeks, and although neither had suggested that they set up house in his bungalow, the thought had crossed Sharon's mind.

Marriage between CVs was not common, but a serial monogamy inevitably developed on a seasonal basis. During her ten years with Club Village, Sharon had rarely stayed at any one village for more than a season without

of relationship. She had had seven
a dozen casual affairs. For a girl in her
was hardly considered promiscuous. Indeed,
erself as one of the older, more sedate CVs.

sharp ringing of the telephone bit into her distrac-
. It was the Coast Guard at Freeport. A yacht had
een sighted drifting off Bimini, but there was no sign of
the missing powerboat. Sharon thanked them for this
unnecessary information and replaced the phone.

The door from the outer office opened and Homer
Wolford loped into the room carrying a Telex message.
"Paris want more details," he said simply, sprawling his
six-feet-five frame around a bamboo rocking chair. Homer
was the director of sports, a black giant from South
Carolina who had given up a promising pro football career
to be a penniless nomad with the club.

Sharon took the Telex. It was a cold, impersonal request
for details of when and where Pagett had last been seen,
and any information he had left about his plans for the
day. She thought bitterly that the message had all the
markings of some officious time server in the Bourse who
wanted everything done by the book. Behind the paternalistic affection of Quatre Bras stretched a huge bureaucracy
of computers, efficiency, and impersonality.

"What do you think, Homer?" she asked.

"What can I think? Dick decides to take a powerboat
out to scout locations. He often does that. But this time he
doesn't come back. No one remembers seeing him after he
left the harbor. But he was too old a hand to be caught out
or hijacked or any of those things. I just don't understand."

Sharon stared at the Telex again. "Do you think Paris
thinks he was into something?"

Homer shook his head. "They can think what they like.
I know that guy. I've done five seasons with him. He was
straight. Maybe eccentric sometimes, maybe too easy-
going sometimes. But he was straight."

"Paris wants us to keep it a secret from the guests until
we get more details," said Sharon.

"Wouldn't they just?" Homer shook his head wearily. "It's too late for that. Keeping a secret in a village like this is about as possible as staying celibate. The CVs have been gossiping around the bar all day."

"Saying what?" Sharon demanded.

Homer shook his head. He wasn't going to tell her the wild stories he'd overheard, the stories that Pagett was involved in a dope-running deal, that he'd fallen out with his bosses and paid the inevitable penalty, or that his body had already been fished out of Nassau Harbor. Club Villages saw a great deal of gossip, like every small community. People there could be warm and loving, but they could also be vicious. Dick Pagett had always joked that just by sitting at a Club Village pool you would see all aspects of human behavior.

And Homer knew only too well that behind many gracious smiles lay cruelty and envy.

The evening in Val d'Isabelle began well and got better. The six-o'clock weather forecast on ORTF brought a promise of an end to the blizzard, and fine days for skiing ahead. Cheered by this news, Hardin decided to celebrate by ordering a bottle of champagne for every table. The head of food and beverages argued that Paris would have something to say about that.

"Paris will have a lot more to say if we send 350 people home having had a lousy vacation for the sake of a few thousand francs," Hardin replied irritably. "Later in the season we'll find some way of making a saving if it's possible, okay, Georges?" And with that he dismissed the argument.

Dinner was usually followed by a show performed by the CVs, a series of mime acts to well-known records, or sometimes amateur revues. But Hardin's idea of a masked ball had quickly become a weekly favorite at Val d'Isabelle.

He had noticed that there is something romantic and yet anonymous about a mask. It breaks down barriers between the more reserved guests, and draws together the most unlikely couples.

The masked ball was an occasion for which everyone was expected to dress and, apart from the inevitable few scruffy young Dutch, everyone did. In keeping with the tradition of European balls, Hardin had devised a program of music, played by an amateur band who worked farther down the valley. The band took the waltz time from Strauss and played it through a four-stringed electric bass.

As a final incentive for couples to split, Hardin, acting as master of ceremonies, directed the men to one side of the assembly hall, now decorated with an assortment of lascivious masks, and the women to the other.

"And there is one final rule," he called out as masks were pulled over the eyes of the guests, blotting out the white rings that distinguished the keen sports from the frivolous sun-seekers, "For the first three dances, no one is allowed to dance with his wife, fiancée, or girl friend. This is a ball for getting to know new people."

Despite her beauty, or perhaps because of her beauty, Beta Ullman was not the first person to be asked to dance. Indeed, she was a wallflower as guests and CVs raced to bag the prettiest of girls. Beta, aloof in her black Valentino dress, was intimidatingly beautiful, but it was the huge Swiss girl, Valerie, whom Hardin invited to dance first.

On the dance floor Hardin felt Valerie hook herself onto his loins and hang on. Apparently the notion of subtlety had never been one she had found very useful.

"This is a great way of getting to know people," said Valerie, as her pelvis crushed farther into him.

Hardin smiled wanly as he felt a flicker of automatic interest and tried gently, and uselessly, to ease his body away from this all-devouring woman. He had asked her to dance because he had not wanted her to suffer further the indignity of being forever a last choice, but he had not been prepared for such an open attack.

"We find that the masks allow people to behave in a way they normally would not," he said. "It lets their inhibitions fall a little bit farther." If Valerie had any inhibitions she was keeping them very secret. Gripping him tighter, she moved him around in a circle so that she could observe the rest of the room.

"Who's the very beautiful girl who never takes her eyes off you?" she asked.

Hardin shot a quick look across to the solitary figure of Beta, watching from the sidelines. "A friend," he answered, and turned back to Valerie. He was glad no one had asked Beta to dance. He had purposely ignored her invitation to dinner, not because he wished to be rude but because he had a feeling that girls like Beta always had everything too easy in life. Remembering the times in his youth when he had had the door slammed in his face by women like Beta, he took pleasure in neglecting her.

Valerie crunched her thighs closer to his. "You must be very sure of yourself," she said with half a smile.

"What do you mean?" He tried again to prise some space between their locked lower limbs. She responded by swiveling herself deeper into him.

"Aren't you afraid one of your staff will get to her first?"

Hardin shook his head. "No."

"Were you always so arrogant?"

"It isn't arrogance," he answered after a moment's consideration. "That lady is the girl friend of one of the people I work for."

"And where is he?"

"In Paris."

"So?"

Hardin could not answer. Valerie was smiling at him. "So?" he repeated lamely.

"So if I were you I'd stop worrying about my job and enjoy myself."

"You don't understand," Hardin replied.

"Don't I?"

At last Hardin smiled back. Looking over his shoulder, he saw Beta watching them with astonishment. No one who cared to look could be unaware of what Valerie was doing to the chief of the village out there on the dance floor, but almost everyone was enjoying himself in a similar, if less obvious, manner.

Suddenly the music stopped and couples began rearranging. Valerie at last unbuttoned her body from Hardin's. He could see her eyes glinting mischievously behind her mask. "If I were you, *monsieur chef de village*, I would claim the lady while I go away and do my vacuuming," she said. And with a slight tilt of her head she kissed him cheekily on the lips and moved away. Hardin watched her go. One of the CVs who had been watching her manipulation of Hardin immediately asked her to dance, and as the music struck up she once again went straight into a clutch.

Awkwardly, Hardin made his way toward Beta.

"Shall we dance?" asked Hardin.

Beta smiled at him. "After that little exhibition I wouldn't think you'd have the energy, James," she said sweetly.

He held out his arms and she moved into them. Now there was no provocative squirming. Beta kept her distance, and he was grateful to her, as together they waltzed sedately around the room. Above them a spotlight played on the inevitable spinning globe, reflecting a dappled light across the masked dancers.

"Why do you like making Ernst jealous?" Hardin asked as they moved out of earshot of the other dancers.

Beta frowned and gazed reflectively at the band. "Because it's my nature," she said. "He uses me like he uses his wife and everybody else. The only defense I have is to make him jealous."

"You don't have to stay with him. Why don't you find someone who doesn't use you?"

Beta swung Hardin around on the floor, and pressed her lips against his ear. "I suppose I must love him, if you want to know. And now can we stop this silly conversation, and grab a bottle of champagne and go and amuse ourselves somewhere in private? Or do I have to throw myself all over you like your big Swiss friend?"

Hardin hung on for one more minute. "I don't understand you," he said.

"Do you understand your own reflection?" Beta retorted. "I'm like you. I want the best of all worlds. Now can I have the best of this particular one, please?"

With that Hardin capitulated, just like he'd always known he would. Leading Beta from the floor he slipped the key to his suite into her hand, and leaving her to go on ahead, he crossed to the bar, signed for a bottle of Moët

exalted in her fragrancy and bathed in the warmth of her body. And when finally they turned once more to face each other their lips met in a mutual celebration of ecstasy and their bodies dissolved together as Beta pulled him ever deeper into her. It was so good neither of them wished it to end. But when at last he felt Beta's body stiffen and convulse into that final arcing series of spasms, Hardin finally allowed himself the freedom he had been fighting and, with a murmur of relief, he pushed his head into the nape of her neck and, gasping, found himself bleeding freely and warmly into her, while their final desire melted together.

Hardin had liked Beta from the moment they had met fleetingly at a party in St. Tropez nine months earlier, a dusk-until-dawn affair called to celebrate Quatre Bras' fifty-fifth birthday. Hardin, who had been working in Club Village headquarters in Paris at the time, had been surprised and almost flattered to be asked to such an august occasion. Gossip and rumor in Paris had it that Quatre Bras had taken a particular affection to him because he admired Hardin's cavalier attitude to some of the club rules. But if that affection was real it certainly was not in evidence at St. Tropez, where Quatre Bras had gone blithely through the evening bathed in a glow of power, glamor, and film camera lights, never even noticing Hardin's presence among the two thousand guests.

As a party it had been aimed as much at grabbing every gossip column in Europe as celebrating a birthday. Quatre Bras had learned early in his career that the best form of advertising always comes free, and so the undead of Europe's night spots and private beaches had been jetted in like a flock of vampires, all anxious for their fix on the wine of notoriety. Most important among the guests, however, were the board, the nine men who together represented the various interests that governed the financial structure of Club Village, powerful middle-aged men accompanied by their wives or mistresses and, in the case of Ernst Ronay, by the Finnish beauty Beta Ullman.

At that time Ernst Ronay was the newly appointed

managing director of Club Village, a supremely confident
and handsome man in his late forties whose career had
been a series of glittering successes in banking, property,
and latterly, publishing. Ronay was what might have been
described as the complete man for a united Europe, since
although his passport was French, his family stretched
across several frontiers, while his upbringing and education had been conducted in both France and England,
making him a snob in both countries. He had begun life
rich and worked ceaselessly to grow richer, following in
the steps of his father, who had died young but had had the
admirable foresight to invest heavily in London property.

The young Ernst had also shown splendid foresight,
particularly in his choice of bride, Lady Sarah Sloane, the
only child of the Duke of Buckham, who, although he had
disapproved of his daughter's choice, had done the decent
thing by Ronay and fallen under his horse at a polo match
in Windsor Great Park shortly after the wedding. The
funeral had been a very grand affair, and Ronay's sadness
at losing a father-in-law had been relieved to some extent
by the knowledge that his wife had inherited considerable
areas of Norfolk as well as prime parts of the Royal
Borough of Kensington and Chelsea.

From then on, everything Ronay did added to his
wealth, with the exception of his hobby, which was beautiful women. Had Ronay been less conservative and Lady
Sarah less Catholic, they might have reached a comfortable accommodation in the divorce courts. But that avenue was closed to Ronay, who grew increasingly attractive
with middle age while his wife simply became homely. She
retreated to the country and her dogs and horses, leaving
her errant husband to float through Europe as he pleased.

"What are you thinking about?" Beta's voice broke the
silence. Hardin had thought she was sleeping.

"I was wondering why women as beautiful as you ask
dumb questions," he said, and bit her earlobe gently.

She laughed. "Don't you know that there are only four
apres-coitus questions in the entire world?" she said.

"Four?"

"Four. The first is, 'Was it as good for you as it was for me?' The second is, 'What are you thinking about?' The third is, 'Do you love me?' and . . ."

"And what?"

"And the fourth is, 'Why don't we do it again?' "

Hardin groaned and slipped his hands beneath her. "I thought you'd never ask," he murmured softly.

Quatre Bras had never been a jogger. He played tennis and squash like a demon of thirty, but in the morning he liked to walk, a regular brisk half-an-hour's march across his tiny patch of lawn and on to the Place Joffre, which stood bare in front of the École Militaire, and then once around the perimeter of the Parc du Champ de Mars, the geometrically dissected city garden created by Monsieur Eiffel for the greater glory of his tower. This morning, Quatre Bras walked with greater vengeance than usual.

He had awoken at six, as always. Leaving the sleeping Madame Quatre Bras in their elegant calico, chrome, and glass bedroom overlooking the park, he had gone immediately to his study to examine the night's Telex messages. He had never liked the telephone, and shunned it as much as possible. People used the telephone to lie, he would say. But the Telex was different. People had to think before they wrote, and over the years he found himself saving countless hours of wasted conversation by insisting that everything possible be communicated to him in writing.

All night long, as his worldwide empire went about its multimillion-dollar business, the Telex messages had been flowing into the Bourse, where a twenty-four-hour team of specially trusted employees sorted them for the various departments and retransmitted the most interesting items across Paris to the home of Quatre Bras.

There had been fourteen items that morning, ranging from an outbreak of gastroenteritis in Liberia to a shortage of *vin ordinaire* in Fiji and the fatal heart attack of a sixty-year-old Japanese teacher while swimming in the pool at the Singapore club. Quatre Bras flicked through them all carelessly until he read the message from Elixir, sent by Sharon Kennedy. Any bad publicity now could ruin all his plans for the American adventure.

He knew that the biggest problem facing the Bahamian government, as well as regimes on other islands, came from organized crime. Sharon Kennedy's message confirmed everything he had already heard about the missing Dick Pagett.

Had he been a younger man, Quatre Bras would have taken the first flight to Elixir and set himself up as caretaker chief of the village, going through the place until he found exactly where the problem lay. At fifty-five he was hardly an old man, but the club had always prided itself on being a place *for* young people run *by* young people. He might not be old, but he certainly wasn't young either. Besides, how could he leave Paris? Ever since Ronay had joined the board he had been looking for ways to extend his sphere of influence. Quatre Bras on sabbatical would leave the gate wide open for a Ronay takeover, and inevitably end his own plans for the Quatre Bras assault on America.

He had crossed beneath the Eiffel Tower and was beginning his walk home when suddenly he felt a presence at his side. At first, he took the shadow to be another jogger, and ignored it. But the shadow refused to be ignored. At last Quatre Bras turned to acknowledge his companion. He was a small, dark man with coiffured curly black hair that rose to a point across the top of his head.

"Monsieur Quatre Bras?" The accent was pure Marseilles.

Quatre Bras kept his pace, turning his eyes slowly toward the little man, carefully taking in the rest of the avenue. It was empty.

"Monsieur Quatre Bras, I wondered if I could have a few words with you in a business connection." The man had the cockiness of a small-time hood—smart but cheap.

"I talk business only at the office," grunted Quatre Bras, and kept on walking.

"This is business of a delicate nature," continued the stranger. "My friends in Bonifaccio think we should have a little talk."

That did it. The little creep had established his area of interest, one of the Corsican villages. Quatre Bras might have guessed. Ever since Corsican independence had resurfaced in the sixties, every company operating from Paris had been subjected to all kinds of blackmail and threats from people claiming to "represent the freedom of the Corsicans."

"We can't talk here," Quatre Bras stalled. "People might see us."

The little man raised an eyebrow. Quatre Bras continued walking.

"Where do you suggest then?"

Quatre Bras shrugged. Clearly his companion was not even a good amateur. "You know the Café de Liberation in Les Halles? Tonight. Ten o'clock."

"Ten o'clock," repeated the man. Putting a hand to his head, he saluted good-bye and turned abruptly away toward one of the intersecting pathways.

Quatre Bras watched him go. Another job for Girardot, he thought. Just a warning would be sufficient. Girardot was good at that. The little man wouldn't need too much pressure. Not like some of the others.

Quatre Bras continued back to his home and the coffee which his wife, Francine, would have prepared for him. Club Village had steered a straight path for twenty-five years now. Nothing was going to change that. Nothing and no one.

Valerie the Vacuum was late for breakfast. She slopped down shortly before nine-thirty just as the last of the skiers were hurrying off on this most glorious of crisp and sunny alpine days. The Algerian kitchen staff eyed her grumpily as she helped herself to fruit juice, croissants, and coffee. But she did not see their expressions. She hardly saw anything, certainly not the dazzling blues and reds of the skiers as they slalomed down the slopes nearest to the club. Valerie saw nothing other than her own reflection in her eyes, and felt again the pain of being plain.

Once a year she would come to the club, telling herself that romance lay around the corner or that sex was worth it just for itself; and she tried to convince herself by convincing others. But it didn't work that way. Last night had been an exercise in self-degredation to which she had more than contributed. To Hardin she had pretended to be self-confident and brash, but the truth was that she was desperate: desperately lonely. She had always been lonely. At school and then college she was always the jolly one who got the leftovers at parties and dances. She was popular but not because of her body, her face, or her personality. Other girls liked her because she presented no competition, and men liked her because they usually saw her as a sexless frump, until they were hard up or drunk, when anything was better than nothing. Why, she wondered, as every plain girl in the world wondered every day of her life, had God chosen to form her in this cloddish manner? She should be grateful for having her health and intelligence, she told herself. And she was. But why had she been born so plain? In the books she read lovemaking was some wondrous, mystical act performed between svelte-limbed women and kind, attractive, handsome men. But in all her experience it had been a series of grimy acts with men she hardly knew, men she had aroused purposely to fill the void of her loneliness. This morning her body ached, and her conscience sneered at her. She was grateful that she would be going home tomorrow. Last night, how many had there been . . . three, or was it four? They had pretended to form a line, and she had tried to stay deaf to their sneering insults. The memory sickened her. She forced her mind away from the thought. It didn't matter. No one in Zurich would know her secret. Once she was on the airplane she would again be anonymous. Just another plain girl, facing the inevitable loneliness of middle age and hating it; just another lumpy girl who had come to Club Village looking for romance when romance was forever reserved for the pretty and pert. And she wondered, as she always did the morning after, whether she would be taking a Club Village vacation next year.

There were always a lot of girls like Valerie at Club Village.

_____ *EIGHT*

"You really sure you want to do this thing, Myron?" Rodney Calthrop was wearing his most insincere expression of kind solicitude. *Now* he sounded that way, now that it was too late.

Myron Bloomberg scratched the matted black hairs on his thighs, and nodded his large head vigorously. "Of course I want to!" he lied.

To admit that he would rather spend the day lying in the sun reading, or sleeping, or indeed doing anything except fooling around forty miles out into the ocean and thirty feet down would have been an admission of cowardice, something the last honestly committed Freudian practicing in New York City was not prepared to admit. So Myron just smiled . . . and prayed.

Today was to be his first experience scuba diving. Rodney Calthrop was his brother-in-law, a dentist by trade but a cowboy by temperament. The vacation in the rented house on Great Exuma had, of course, been all Rodney's idea. Rodney liked what he called "action" vacations.

In the front seat of the hired Viking cruiser, Myron's wife, Rosa, exchanged glances with her husband. She knows I'm terrified, thought Myron. Rodney's second childhood was getting to *her*, too. But she wouldn't betray Myron.

Suddenly Rodney was talking again. "Remember, we're a team. You and me. Okay? Just stay close and you'll have the biggest trip since Fellini's *Roma*. Jesus . . . what a movie! Okay?"

Bloomberg nodded, not knowing whether he was agreeing with Rodney's estimation of Fellini or his advice for the dive. "Okay," he said, dully.

"And remember—" added Rodney, "don't panic. No matter what happens . . . and nothing will happen . . . no matter what happens, we don't panic. . . . Okay? The only thing to panic about is panic. Okay?"

Rodney had been through it all a thousand times. Myron knew that sharks were nothing to be frightened of, that there were lots of them and they'd probably come to take a look, but that they were just being curious and all you had to do was keep circling. Same thing with barracudas and stingray and grouper and every other kind of beast lurking down there around that reef. But Myron had read those Peter Benchley books, and cable television never seemed to stop showing movies where mad cellists accompanied great whites at thirty miles an hour forty feet down. Jesus, even the angelfish floating around down there looked menacing.

"Ready to go," Rodney grinned, and with that the masks were pulled down and over they went.

At first the only thing Myron could think was how light it seemed to be, bright as day, really. And as he became familiar with the way he could move his arms and legs he began to feel like a spaceman sailing around outside his capsule. Looking up, he saw the belly of his boat, a secure refuge above. He looked over toward Rodney, who appeared to be smiling at him and was pointing toward the coral, a series of elkhorn formations tied together like a string of runner beans growing out of a drift of sand. Kicking with his flippers, Myron propelled himself toward the rocks. He looked over his shoulder. There were no signs of sea monsters. He kicked again, and watched the bubbles darting away behind him. Now enjoying his weightlessness, he moved closer to the elkhorn coral. Rodney was a little way ahead of him and to the right, gripping his underwater camera and looking for the find which would get him those elusive pages in *National Geographic.* Myron approached the elkhorn without fear. At this depth, with the boat right above him, he was actually beginning to feel almost confident.

Then he saw something that intrigued him. It didn't look like anything for the *National Geographic,* more like a few rags bundled together, caught on one of the antlers of coral. Even here they had litter problems, he thought, and he moved closer for a better look so that his paddling flippers sent a current of water swirling around the rags. Slowly the bundle turned toward him. Gradually, almost as though his mind had gone into low gear, Myron Bloomberg realized that he was staring at the ragged, white corner of a gnarled hip bone. What he had taken for rags were articles of clothing hanging from the remains of a human body, casually caught up on this piece of rock, drifting backward and forward in a lazy, eddying motion as the current caught it. It was half a body actually, half eaten and torn apart and then left to float by the replete diners; half a body, with only half its face intact.

At that point Myron decided it was okay to panic.

The Bahamian Coast Guard came out to collect the body and to transport Myron Bloomberg to the Great Exuma hospital. Myron was suffering from shock. Even Rodney was in shock.

At two in the afternoon, as the sun baked hotter and hotter, the Coast Guard pulled alongside, four immaculately uniformed officers and two divers, all smiling happily as though pulling bodies off the coral were just another kind of scuba diving. But by two forty-five, when the bits and pieces of body had been collected and put into a plastic bag and then into a refrigerator on board the boat, the smiles had faded.

The Coast Guard had expected to find the remains of another Haitian illegal immigrant whose boat had not made it. They found them every week. But this was a white man, wearing what remained of Club Village shorts and T-shirt. They could throw Haitians into a hole and forget about them. But now there would have to be a postmortem and an inquest. As Myron was taken away, it occurred to Rodney that the Coast Guard were sorry the corpse had been discovered at all. Another day and there would hardly have been anything left to find.

Hardin got his traveling orders by Telex that same night. The message was simple. From midnight Jean-Paul Cartier was the new *chef de village* at Val d'Isabelle, with salary commensurate with his new responsibilities. Hardin was to report to Quatre Bras in his offices at the Bourse at noon the next day. A reservation on the nine-thirty Air France flight from Geneva had already been booked.

"What's going on?" demanded Beta as she opened the door of Hardin's room to find him packing.

He passed her the Telex.

"Do you think Ernst found out?" she asked.

He shook his head. "Don't worry. I'll deny everything. Your piggy banker won't ever know."

"I'm not worried about Ernst knowing anything," she snapped. "I'm just sorry that our moment was so brief."

"Me too," he sighed. As he picked up his suitcase, he kissed her cheek.

"Will we see each other again, James?" she asked.

He hesitated, and then nodded. "But who knows where or when?"

Only later that night, when Beta lay sleeping by his side did Hardin have time to consider his sudden recall. Jean-Paul Cartier had been delighted by his sudden promotion, but there was a genuine sadness among the CVs and ski instructors over Hardin's leaving. He was a popular *chef de village*.

At thirty-five, James Hardin felt he was at another

crossroad, in his life. Not for the first time, he wondered whether Club Village was the life he really wanted. Years earlier, it had seemed an improvement over the gypsy life of the tennis circuit. But he had been in charge of Val d'Isabelle for only two months, and now he was being moved again.

He turned over and pushed his head deeper into his pillow. Quatre Bras had better have a good reason for fooling around with his life like this, he thought.

"Push . . . push . . . push . . ." Cassandra Mallinson forced her aching arms and legs onward through the pale green water. Her New Year's resolution had been to swim twenty lengths every morning before breakfast at London's Kensington New Pools, but she had not reckoned on the competitive spirits of the male bathers who also chose that time and that pool for training. As she pushed on valiantly, mountainous waves made by the bullet-headed human torpedos alongside forced her to gulp and lift her head higher to avoid getting a lungful of water. It was twenty-five past eight, according to the large pool clock, and she was on her last length. This morning was going to be a slow time.

Reaching the end of the pool, she stood up and walked unsteadily to the steps. Perhaps twenty-nine was too old to start all this, she mused. In the pool, one of the bullet-heads watched her leave, with evident disappointment. She was aware of him, but purposely avoided giving any clue that she had noticed. She had better things to do than encourage young men along flights of fancy.

Recovering her bundle of clothes, she entered a changing cubicle and, stepping out of her simple black bathing suit, she rubbed her body vigorously with a towel. She was a lithe, slim woman, green-eyed, fair-skinned, and long-legged. Taking off her black bathing cap, she shook her long, subtly tinted brown hair to her shoulders. She dressed quickly in clothes too elegant for this run-down part of London and, shoving her wet towel and suit into a Piero de Monzi shopping bag, headed toward her black Renault 5, parked in a side street.

Her timetable never changed. Hurrying through the cold, wet streets to her basement flat in St. Petersburgh Place, Bayswater, she made herself a breakfast of Swiss müesli, toast, and coffee while listening to the news on the BBC.

To the observer she seemed a strong, apparently well-off, self-contained woman. She was pretty, even beautiful in an English kind of way, but she wore a remote expression. She was single and worked, and her life was a selfish one. Without commitments of any kind, she lived for herself and her work. Her parents, now in their midsixties, had retired to an English colony in the Algarve, after a lifetime's devotion to Queen and country, and no man had come along with whom she had fancied setting up house.

For eight years, since coming down from Cambridge with a middling degree in English, she had been working as a journalist, first on a London daily newspaper, and more recently as a European staff writer on *Night and Day*, a weekly magazine. *Night and Day* was the latest attempt by New York publishing interests to steal some prestige and revenue from *Time* and *Newsweek*. She was paid well, and courted frequently, and her life ran on the smooth wheels of the successful single woman, very discreet, short-lived affairs being interspersed with successions of men ever eager to take her to dinner.

The telephone rang at nine-thirty. It was Kurtz, the London editor.

"Cassandra, how do you feel about a vacation in the Bahamas?"

"If it's with you . . . no, thank you."

Kurtz laughed. He was in the middle of a divorce and had been trying to get Cassandra into bed for months. "No such luck. New York wants you to go on a Club Village vacation. They keep hearing rumors about a place called Elixir, and they think you should investigate."

"Why don't they send someone from New York office?" asked Cassandra. It seemed silly to fly her all the way from London when the Bahamas were so near America.

"They know your French is pretty good, and it's a French organization. Apparently there's no one available in New York now with good French. That's a sign of the times, isn't it?"

"What's the angle?" Cassandra was staring out of her basement kitchen at the domed Greek Orthodox Church across the road. A stream of water sprayed across the glass from a broken gutter.

"It seems that there are all kinds of fun and games going on, sex and drugs parties, people missing . . . all that stuff. They want you to turn up as a regular girl on vacation and see what you can find out."

"Since when do I work for the *National Enquirer?*"

"Come on, it isn't like that. Club Village are expected to link up with one of the U.S. airlines soon and go American. New York want you to tell the people what they'll be getting if they go on a Club Village vacation."

"Sounds like a nice way to pay the rent."

"Right. Book yourself a couple of weeks in the sun. There's a Club Village office in Bond Street. Don't tell them you're a journalist unless you have to. Okay?"

"Right. Do I get a couple of new bikinis on expenses?"

"If I say no, you'll do it anyway and I'll never know. So I guess the answer is yes. But don't forget it's a *working* vacation. They want a five-thousand-word piece about life in a Club Village."

"No problem. Let's hope they use it," said Cassandra. Bidding Kurtz good-bye, she hung up.

She drove the couple of miles to the Club Village booking office, where a French woman in elegant wire-thin silver necklace and bracelets greeted her.

"Fifteen days in Elixir . . . yes. That should be all right. We'll get confirmation from Paris this afternoon, so leave me your telephone number. I'm afraid you must pay in full today . . . if you want to leave tomorrow."

Cassandra passed her American Express card, and the booking clerk went to check on her credit.

Cassandra looked around. The office had a twenty-first-century chrome-and-comfort Gallic elegance. On the walls huge pictures of beautiful creatures with batteries of white, even teeth and end-of-vacation tans, smiled and surfed in exotic settings.

"You must understand that we don't have single rooms in Club Village," said the booking clerk as she sashayed back into the room. "We put all single guests in with someone with whom we think they will be compatible."

Cassandra's eyebrows rose. "You mean I have to share?"

"Yes."

"Why don't you do single rooms? You must have a great many single people on vacation."

"It is our policy to encourage single people to make friends. Of course, sometimes people don't like their roommates, or they meet someone else they would rather spend their vacation with . . . and then you can change rooms."

Cassandra shrugged and signed her bill. Nine hundred and thirty-five pounds, and she was going to have to share a room with a stranger.

ELEVEN

It was a busy morning as Quatre Bras waited for Hardin to arrive from Geneva. Girardot telephoned to explain that he had dealt quietly and effectively with the Corsican threat on the previous evening.

"I told him that if one hair of a Club Village guest or employee was hurt we'd have his balls for the bourguignon," he told Quatre Bras. Then Ernst Ronay burst in to demand a full explanation of the rumors going around the Bourse and Wall Street that Quatre Bras had already discussed a deal with Universal-American Airlines.

"That is not true, Ernst," said Quatre Bras, wishing to God that his prospective investors could learn to keep quiet.

"But you have been involved in discussions."

"I have talked about the potential of the American zone," Quatre Bras said guardedly.

"Don't you ever think that you owe your board the courtesy of knowing to whom you are talking?" replied Ronay.

"No," said Quatre Bras. "If we decide to go into the United States, then it will be a board decision. I don't need a board decision to tell me to whom I may and may not talk."

Ronay shrugged his thin, high shoulders and strode out of the room, every inch of him displaying the unconscious class revulsion with which he regarded Quatre Bras.

At precisely midday, Quatre Bras' dark, plump, pretty

secretary, showed Hardin into the room. Quatre Bras did not rise. Hardin did not offer his hand. He simply smiled and waited.

"Sit down, James," said Quatre Bras.

Quatre Bras always insisted on calling his staff by their first names. Hardin looked him straight in the eye, not smiling. Quatre Bras liked that. He was uncomfortable with men who felt intimidated by him.

"We have a problem, James, and I want you to solve it. Furthermore, I want you to solve it with the utmost discretion. Take your orders directly from me, and report only to me. Understand?"

Hardin nodded. He had been noticing again the vast size of the older man's shoulders.

Blinking, Hardin tried to concentrate. Beta's appetites during the night had robbed him of sleep, and it had been a two-hour drive that morning to catch the Paris plane. He had had a couple of midmorning Scotches on the flight, and was feeling a little light-headed. He hoped the secretary had not smelled the Scotch. If so, she would certainly report it to Quatre Bras. She was his eyes and ears, not because she was officially a spy, but becaused she loved her boss with a passion no wife could ever maintain—the passion of the sexually dispossessed.

Quatre Bras was talking. Briefly he outlined the mysterious death of Pagett and the need for a *chef de village* who was completely unknown to all the CVs working in that village. The season files told him that Hardin had never worked with any of the Elixir people before, although it was possible he had run into one or two somewhere along the way.

He handed Hardin a list of the Elixir staff. Quickly Hardin went through it. As always, Quatre Bras had done his homework. Hardin had never worked with any of them before.

"What I want you to do, James, is to find out what is wrong at Elixir and put it right. I want you to clean it up. At the moment the Bahamian authorities are not too interested in what happened to Pagett. But if there is any more trouble, a lot of people will begin to take a close look at the village."

"Have you any ideas at all about what I might be facing?"

Quatre Bras drummed his fingers on the table. "No, James. All I can ask you to do is to take care of yourself. Watch out. When a village goes bad it can get very sick before the cure is found."

Quatre Bras stood up. "I'm depending on you, James," he said, and finally pushed out a hand to be shaken.

Hardin pretended he hadn't noticed. He was damned if he was going to shake hands with a man who was doing his best to place him in acute danger.

_____*PART II*

The island of Elixir had been more or less overlooked for the best part of five hundred years. Columbus did not discover it in 1492, although Bahamians claim he bumped into San Salvador, which is about a hundred miles east, and neither the Spanish nor the British ever bothered to use it for anything more than a marker on their journeys to and from the larger islands of the West Indies. Just seventy miles north of the Tropic of Cancer, exactly halfway between the Exuma Cays and Conception Island, it was named through the misfortune of an epileptic from Bristol, who had been cast away there in 1595 and amazed the world by being rediscovered in 1655 by a ship of Cromwell's fleet. "Truly this place is possessed of the Elixir of life," the rescuing captain wrote in his log, ordering that the unfortunate, and now very feeble, old man be taken on board and given a hearty share of rations and rum . . . a diet that killed him instantly.

Like most of the other islands in the Bahamas, Elixir was, until recently, of little obvious practical value. There was no natural harbor for large vessels, and the thin soil could hardly support a decent potato crop. Just five miles long and a mile and a half wide, it was in fact just a large overgrown coral reef. The local population of fewer than a thousand was made up largely of old people and women with their legions of children. Then, in 1977, one of the bright boys from forward planning at Club Village had suggested that with the cooperation being given to tourist operators by the Bahamian government, Elixir was ideal for an up-market village aimed specifically at the North American market. Within three years the club had become a reality, and Elixir began to enter the twentieth century.

The news that Hardin was to replace Pagett did not fall on altogether welcome ears in Elixir. The chief accountant, Eugene Waterman, saw the Telex first, and relayed the news to Sharon Kennedy, whom he found in the boutique.

"He's that tennis player, isn't he?" said Waterman, recognizing Hardin's name. "This will give the tennis coaches something to think about."

Sharon Kennedy didn't answer. She did not know how to respond. Death in a vacation village was an embarrassment, something which did not fit into the projected schemes. An hour after the news of the discovery of Pagett's body, the CVs had been organizing games and races, giving dancing lessons, rehearsing entertainments, and exchanging pleasantries with the guests. Pagett was already history, and his successor on his way.

Of course there would be an inquest, but that was a mere formality. The sharks had left little to investigate, and the story now circulating was that Pagett had fallen victim to a boating accident. And that, it seemed, was that. So what was Sharon to say?

_____ *THIRTEEN*

Hardin noticed Cassandra when the plane touched down at Bermuda. There were forty minutes to spare while refueling, loading, and unloading were carried out, and passengers were invited to stretch their legs in the passenger terminal.

"Are you going on to Nassau or Kingston?" he asked the pretty, green-eyed elegant woman sitting beside him in the waiting room. He had been late for the flight at London, and had not had his usual opportunity of surveying the women before boarding.

The woman turned to him. Her nose was short and straight and her eyes were bright against her pale English skin.

"Nassau," she replied without a hint of encouragement. Then she turned back and examined the paper cup from which she was sipping water.

Ordinarily that would have been enough of a warning off for Hardin. But, perhaps because he was bored by the long flight, he began to see this cold English woman as a challenge. So he persisted.

"You're going on business?" he asked. She looked extremely businesslike.

"Vacation." The reply was offered without a glance.

"My name's Hardin," he said. And smiled a very broad grin.

"Of course it is," she replied, and looked him straight in the eye.

63

He faltered. He didn't like being made fun of. But he kept the smile. "And your name is . . . ?"

"Cassandra Mallinson," she answered, after a long-suffering pause.

"Well, Cassandra Mallinson," he said, "you are not easy to talk to."

"Mr. Hardin . . . isn't that what you said your name was? . . . Mr. Hardin, every time I take an airplane anywhere in the world I am accosted by men in terminals, in transit lounges, and in customs. And, Mr. Hardin, I do not enjoy being chatted up by strange men, nor do I understand why they attempt it."

Hardin gazed at her for a long moment. "In your case," he said slowly, "neither do I." Then he turned away.

If Cassandra had been honest with herself she would have admitted that she found him attractive, and had actually noticed Hardin as he sat down on the plane in London. Although he had not been aware of her, she had cast him several examining looks during the flight. Like a silly ingenue, she had felt herself physically drawn to him from the moment she first saw him. Her abruptness was the only barrier she could find. Why she should wish to hide behind any barrier at all was a mystery even to Cassandra, but when she felt an attraction as strong as this it was always her initial response.

Only when she was eventually back on board the plane did Cassandra realize that this time her brittleness had been a professional mistake. Hanging from one of the buckles of Hardin's leather saddlebag was a Club Village baggage tag. Cassandra made up her mind quickly. She might have been able to fight her emotions, but she was not prepared to dispute her professionalism. Getting up, she moved down the aisle to the empty seat next to him.

"I wanted to say I was sorry for being so rude," she said. "Can I buy you a drink to make up for it?"

It is nearly a thousand miles from Bermuda to Nassau, which is far enough for two people to get to know each other. After the shaky start Hardin and Cassandra got along famously, although, of course, they both told less than the truth. She told him she was an editor with a publishing company in London, while he admitted that he worked for Club Village but neglected to add that he was the new chief.

Cassandra was fascinated by Hardin's gypsy life. It was exactly the opposite of hers. Her own life was tied up in security and possessions and her home. The willful way Hardin had already jettisoned two careers appealed to her.

Hardin, for his part, was drawn to her because of her independence. She had no man in her life, nor, apparently, did she need one. Her sudden change in attitude toward him was hard to understand but, as she had a pretty smile and seemed genuinely interested in him, he let it pass with no more than a small mental question mark.

As Hardin collected his bags to pass through customs in Nassau, it occurred to him that he was facing a situation fraught with romance and mischief. He looked at Cassandra. Her suit was crumpled and she looked tired. But she was gamely hurling her suitcase off the conveyor belt and onto a trolley.

"We're too late to get across to Elixir tonight. I'm going to try to book a room here through the tourist agent. Do you want me to get one for you, too?"

Cassandra nodded. "Thank you," she said, thinking to herself, "and thank God."

Getting two rooms for the night was easy. Within half an hour of arriving in Nassau, Hardin and Cassandra were sitting side by side in the back of a voluptuous old Lincoln, being driven to the Balmoral Beach Hotel by a huge singing black man.

The hotel was a large, pastel-colored, classically styled Colonial building, complete with tinkling cocktail pianist, British expatriates drinking gin, and middle-aged Americans on safari. A boy of about fifteen showed them to two adjacent suites in a bougainvillea-covered bungalow. Outside was a floodlit tennis court where a couple of near-geriatrics lobbed balls to each other at a mutually respectful rhythm.

Hardin watched them with envy. He had hardly been on a court since giving up professional tennis. To him, tennis had been a way of making a living, and eventually all the enjoyment had gone out of it. Every shot had counted, every hour of training was hard preparation. These two gentle, elderly people, who hardly moved their feet, were enjoying themselves far more than he ever had.

"Are we too late to eat?" Cassandra asked the boy porter.

"If you're quick, they'll probably fix you a sandwich in the dining room."

Hardin passed the boy a five-dollar bill. "We'll be quick," he said. "Can you let them know we're on the way?"

The boy smiled and skipped off toward the dining room while Hardin and Cassandra went to their respective rooms for a quick wash and change.

The sandwich was not exceptional, but neither of them was particularly hungry, and they soon left the dining room for a stroll along the beach.

As they walked along a small wooden pier, lit by a chain of lamps, Hardin wondered whether he should put out a supportive arm toward Cassandra and add a physical element to their relationship, but he didn't; while Cassandra wondered whether he would, and, if so, what the most suitable reaction from her should be. They were both guarded in one another's presence, a factor which added dignity to their relationship.

When they arrived back at the bungalow there was the inevitable pause before they said good night. By now jet lag was beginning to smother them both, but they each clung to the illusion of a romantic evening. They needed to. Tomorrow would be different. It always was.

"If I'd known they gave such wonderful after-flight service I'd always have flown British Airways," said Hardin.

Cassandra smiled. "Perhaps you'll be able to give me some tennis coaching when we get to the village," she said.

"I'd love to," said Hardin, "but I believe they have a

couple of coaches there. You may do better with them. I was never a very good teacher."

"That's okay. I was never a very good student. We'll complement each other."

Hardin grinned. "Okay. It's a deal," he said.

"Well . . . good night." Cassandra lingered at her door.

Hardin waited a moment longer, nearly leaned forward to kiss her, checked himself, and then pushed out his hand. Cassandra took it and then with another "good night" they withdrew into their separate bedrooms.

Some things are better saved and then savored. They both knew that.

Cassandra saw Elixir for the first time the following morning from five thousand feet as the Bahamasair DC-3 banked to approach the runway built especially for Club Village. It was a smaller island than she had expected, just a scythe-shaped coral reef covered in light bush and surrounded by a wash of pale green, shallow sea. Alongside her, Hardin stared down in rapt concentration. She did not disturb him.

The airport terminal was a white, one-room building, around which had gathered a group of local people waiting for relatives and friends. Quite separate from them stood a group of golden-tanned, pareo-wearing sophisticated natives, beautiful girls with flowers in their fair hair, and young men with garlands around their necks, holding skin drums and guitars.

As soon as Hardin stepped down from the plane the performance began. At first it was just drumming, but then, as the guitar players joined in, the assembled group began a Tahitian welcome song, much to the amusement of the local people and their scampering children.

"What is this?"

"It's an old Club Village custom," Hardin explained. "They are saying hello to you and welcoming their new chief."

"Which chief?" asked Cassandra, laughing.

Hardin walked on down the tarmac toward the advancing musicians. "I'm their new chief," he said. "Sounds silly, doesn't it?"

Cassandra stopped laughing. She was both surprised and impressed. By all accounts chiefs of villages were gods within their domains.

By now the troupe of musical CVs had begun to surround Hardin and Cassandra, throwing chains of flowers around their necks. A pretty dark-haired girl in the briefest of bikinis leaned forward and kissed Hardin, open-mouthed, on the mouth.

Hardin didn't even look at her. His face was set in a dark cast as he surveyed the group. Finally he put up his arm. The music stopped.

"Okay, thank you. I want this young lady driven straight to the village." He gestured toward Cassandra.

A couple of men broke away from the group. One put out an arm to take Cassandra's hand luggage. The other moved toward where suitcases were being unloaded from the plane. Cassandra followed the welcoming hand toward a small, open, red Citroën.

"I'll see you later," Hardin called after her.

She smiled back. But her smile was not returned. Hardin's expression was cold and hard.

"How long is it since Dick Pagett died?" he asked.

There was an embarrassed silence. No one attempted to answer.

"Listen," said Hardin, "I know Club Village policy is that everything carries on as normal no matter what happens . . . but so far as I'm concerned that's bullshit. Keep your smiles and your hula-hula welcomes for the guests, but remember I'm here because one of your colleagues is dead, and even may have been murdered. I didn't know Dick Pagett, but you people did. I think he deserves a little more respect."

With that Hardin pushed a way through the group to the CV Land Rover. At the wheel sat a fair-haired boy. As Hardin approached, the boy climbed out and loaded Hardin's hand luggage into the back seat.

"Hi. My name's Sacha," he said quietly. "Sorry about all that."

Hardin climbed into the vacant passenger seat. "Let's go, shall we?" he said. "Those guys can follow on with the luggage."

Sacha nodded and, putting the car into gear, pulled quickly away from the airport building, leaving the welcoming committee looking at each other dismally.

The new chief of the village was obviously a bastard.

He had started as he meant to go on, Hardin reflected as the Land Rover charged up the dirt road toward the village. He had not known any of the CVs who had met him at the airport, but he had instantly recognized the type. They were the self-selecting beautiful group of which every village attracts its share. They would be the group with the highest profile, the ones who would have the star parts in the entertainments, who would be best known (although not necessarily best liked) by the guests, who could invariably be found looking decorative around the bar, and inevitably, considering the amount of time they devoted to looking pretty and being on display, they would be the ones who did the least work.

Hardin looked toward the driver. "I understand Sharon Kennedy and Dick Pagett were close," he said.

Sacha gave a slight shrug, as if to imply that he didn't feel that he ought to be gossiping with the new chief.

Hardin let it pass. There would be time enough to work out all the relationships and rivalries. He remembered reading a dossier in Quatre Bras' office about someone called Sacha, a good-looking CV whom Pagett had hired that season. He had, Pagett had written, shown considerable ability and flair. No wonder Sacha had been keeping a discreet distance between himself and the golden people, thought Hardin, and silently commended Sacha for his good sense. Sacha had managed to make an immediate impression on the new chief without performing fawning capers on the runway. Pagett had obviously been a very good judge of character.

After the welcome at the airport the euphoria evaporated for Cassandra's new companions. Driven by a surly Dutchman called Willem Brummer, the small Citroën chased up the road toward the village at an alarming speed. In the back with the cases sat Matt Hillman, a lean, lanky youth from New York. Willem looked strong and dour. Matt was wearing a pareo tied around his waist.

"If you go to the reservations bureau someone will show you where your room is," said Willem as the Citroën screeched to a halt. Instantly Matt began to unload Cassandra's two suitcases.

"You carry your own cases on a Club Village vacation," said Matt spitefully.

Cassandra nodded and climbed out, and immediately the Citroën skidded away down a track.

Picking up her suitcases, she turned toward the reception area. It reminded her of a sophisticated, air-conditioned temple. Moving between two Doric columns that held up the ornate Grecian-style roof, she stepped out of the bush of a small, poor Bahamian island into a world of perfumed affluence. From hidden speakers the theme from the movie "A Man and a Woman" played quietly. On the walls, huge line drawings depicted classically beautiful men and women, naked and in repose. The entrance was large, bare, and cool. Cassandra carried her cases up a flight of low steps, and found herself in a short arcade, along the sides of which were offices, a small

73

boutique, and a pharmacy. In the center of the arcade a
dozen tanned people were discussing whether or not to go
on that day's picnic. She moved across to the reservations
bureau, where an alarmingly beautiful girl sat at a low
desk.

"Can I help you?" The girl spoke with a strong French
accent. Her eyes were brown and her hair was dark and
razor-cut close to her head. She was stunning.

Cassandra produced her club membership form and her
reservation.

The girl smiled. "Welcome to Club Village," she said.
"I think you will have a very happy time here. My name is
Chloe. There will be a welcome by the new *chef de village*
tomorrow evening, when everything will be explained.
Most of our guests join us over the weekend. You should
leave your valuables in the safe here, because there are no
locks on the doors here. Also, we do not use money at the
bar. Our way in Club Village is to use plastic shells. You
can sign for those from the girl who sits in the large shell by
the bar at any time between eight in the morning and
midnight. There is another shell in the discotheque. In the
boutiques you sign for everything you want and then pay
on your last day. We take most credit cards."

"Will I be sharing with anyone?" asked Cassandra.

"Not tonight. But I think we will be full from tomorrow
onward . . . so I'm afraid . . ." Chloe shrugged. "I'm sure
it will be no problem. All our guests are very nice people."

Cassandra looked doubtful.

"It will be all right," Chloe repeated. And then, producing a small map of the village, she pointed the way to
Cassandra's cabin.

"You are on the top floor, overlooking the central
village area. Room B23. There are many events going on
today, you are still in time to go on the picnic. But perhaps
you would rather stay by the pool?"

Cassandra looked at the map, and then thanking Chloe
for her help headed toward the center of the village,
passing down the arcade and out into a large theater,
covered like a Dutch barn so that three sides were open.

Skirting around the edge of the theater she found herself walking between the pool and the bar, a large concourse area for sunbathing, talking, and drinking. Now she felt as though she were walking a tightrope, so keenly did the variously assembled men regard her arrival. And because she was pale and tired alongside so many beautifully tanned and athletically topless girls, she felt awkward and ugly. She hurried on, anxious not to be examined too closely, stunned by the number of beautiful women and the tonnage of attractive men.

The living accommodations were made up of several discreetly disguised blocks of apartments, three stories high, and boasting long balconies which faced the sun. With little difficulty she found B Block and, carrying her suitcases with some difficulty, climbed the steps. B23 was at the far end of the balcony. Reaching it, she pushed open the door, threw her suitcases inside, and flopped down on the nearer of the two beds.

It was a small, practical room, with a minimum of furniture and a small adjoining bathroom. She was grateful that her roommate would not be arriving until the next day. Cassandra needed time to become accustomed to this place.

Soon her thoughts drifted to Hardin. Would he have his pick of all the CVs and lady guests? Of course he would, she thought, and reminded herself that she was a professional, here on assignment.

Hardin could hardly have been kinder to Sharon Kennedy. He had been sent out from Paris to clean up Elixir, but nothing in the personnel dossier he had read on Sharon suggested that she was anything other than a good, hard-working, willing employee, loyal to the club, and a woman whose only failing was that she was just inclined to let her latest lover hold too much sway over her. In many ways Hardin saw her as a casualty of the club. She had risen through the ranks as far as she was ever likely to go, and now faced a long slide downhill to where she would once again be a regular CV, before her fading smile prompted someone in Paris to suggest that she look elsewhere for employment.

"It must have been very difficult for you, Sharon," said Hardin as soon as the two were alone in his office. "I didn't know Dick, but I heard a lot of nice things about him."

"If you heard he pushed dope it wasn't true," said Sharon defensively.

"No one in Paris believed those rumors," said Hardin soothingly. "Anyone who runs a village in this part of the world is certain to have that kind of allegation made against him."

Sharon looked at Hardin, wondering whether to believe that this quietly spoken man could be the same tyrant who had bawled out the welcoming group at the airport earlier that morning.

"I believe the . . . the remains are being flown back to Delaware for burial," Hardin found himself stammering.

Sharon nodded.

"If you feel you'd like to take a vacation . . . just get away for a while . . . take a rest . . . that's okay. Maybe you'd like to go home or to one of the other villages. . . ."

Sharon shook her head. "Thanks, but I'll stay. This is my home until my next posting comes along. I'd be like a fish out of water back in Louisville, Kentucky. I've been with the club a long time now."

Hardin smiled. "I know what you mean," he said. "I hope we get along very well, Sharon. There are certain to be some changes, and some of the things I want to say to the CVs tonight may sound like criticisms of the way Dick was running this village. But believe me, it isn't intended to be that way. You know as well as I do that Elixir has had more than its share of trouble, and I've been sent out here to try to sort it out."

"And to find out what happened to Dick?"

"Yes, if possible. But that's really a police job."

"But you will *try* to find out?"

"Of course."

"Than I want to stay and help you."

"Thank you," said Hardin. "And now, if it's okay with you, perhaps we could go on a tour of the club and see what everyone does here."

"Sure," said Sharon, and led the way from the office.

The village was one of the most luxurious Hardin had ever seen, partly because it was so new, but also because it was aimed almost exclusively at the North American market—and Americans insisted on creature comforts that Europeans could live without. In the Mediterranean villages guests made jokes about the bugs that fell out of the straw-roofed huts, and the primitive washing conditions. Americans would never have stood for that.

On this first tour of the village Hardin did no more than note where everything was and how efficiently the facilities were being used. He was pleased to see all twelve tennis courts in use and a couple of enthusiastic coaches handling beginners and intermediate lessons. Alongside the courts a dozen guests were doing calisthenics, while on the dance floor in front of the open theater the rudiments of modern ballet were being impressed on a most unlikely group of students. At all these places, Hardin was certain that he was being observed as much as he was the observer. He was, as the saying goes, putting his mark on the village.

There was no doubt that on Elixir the CVs enjoyed themselves thoroughly. There were as many employees around the bar as there were guests—even during the daytime. Dick Pagett, popular chief that he was, had obviously not been firm enough with his staff.

Willem Brummer and Matt Hillman sat thoughtfully in the front seats of the red Citroën. Nominally, they were CVs, but everything they did showed contempt for the sunshine fellows. They had been at the airport that morning for one good reason—to get a good look at the new chief. Once they had seen Hardin, and his anger, they had taken the first opportunity to absent themselves from the scene.

Willem and Matt were men apart. To them the village was no vacation but part of a rich vein to be mined and then abandoned. They worked hard, twice as hard as anyone else in the village. But then, their rewards were high, too. A hundred, maybe a thousand times as high as the other CVs . . . providing they never got caught.

Unlike the rest of the village staff, neither had worked in other villages. They had joined the club when the Elixir village was in the construction stage. Matt had been loafing in Miami, occasionally working for small airline companies. Willem had, after ten years in the Dutch merchant navy, been a common sight around the marinas of the Bahamas and the West Indies. When a skipper wanted an extra crew hand, Willem had been available.

The shortage of manpower on Elixir brought in all kinds of specialist creatures from Florida and the islands, including Matt and Willem. They knew everything there was to know about sea and air transportation in that area. They did outstanding work, and when the village was finished and ready for occupation they were put in charge of organizing the sea and air charters that brought in the twenty tons of supplies from Florida and Nassau every week. Of all the jobs in the village, this was one of the least glamorous, and could involve all kinds of unsociable hours loading and unloading cargo planes and flying to Florida to check supplies. But it was a job that offered more freedom than anything else in the village. And the umbrella of respectability that the club offered suited them both very nicely.

Dick Pagett had never particularly liked either of them. Indeed, no one actually *liked* Willem or Matt, but they were good at their jobs.

The arrival of Hardin was potentially more of a problem to them than to anybody else in the village. From a high point at the end of the island, the two men stared down on the village to the left, and the marina to the right. It was a natural vantage point, and one they had chosen whenever they needed to be alone, *really* alone. The notion of privacy was despised in Club Village.

"We could cut him in," said Matt, but it wasn't really a serious suggestion.

Willem examined the end of his thin panatella and flicked the ash over the side of the car. "Cut him in and they'll cut us out . . . in more ways than one."

There was a ruminative silence. "How far are we ahead?" asked Matt. He knew, but he wanted it confirmed.

"Forty thousand."

"We could quit now."

There was another silence. They both knew that they were in too deep simply to walk away. But at some point, there had to be an escape for them. Willem took another draw on his panatella. "And close down the route? Try to explain that in Jackson Heights and Bogotá."

"You're assuming that this guy is going to find out." Matt was fidgeting with a shell necklace tied around his neck. He was a thin, long-faced boy with a receding chin.

"No," said Willem. "But you can be sure he'll be

walking around with his eyeballs on sticks after what happened to Pagett."

"So what do we do?"

"We carry on, very discreetly and very carefully."

"The next pickup is on Saturday night. Isn't that too soon?" There was a nervous cracking in Matt's voice.

"We don't have any choice. It's on the way. They're using St. Anne Cay again. Twenty pounds of snow. It's expected in Miami by Tuesday at the latest. It has a train to catch."

Matt gazed down at the island thoughtfully. "It's always bigger, isn't it? They keep upping the load every time, as though they're willing us to get caught."

"They recognize a good route," Willem shrugged.

Matt finally broke. "Listen, I don't like it. I say we take a walk. Remember Barias . . . his face got caught in a propeller."

"Barias got into trouble because he wanted more than his share. If we stay cool, keep our noses clean, give no cause for suspicion, and do the job, we're okay. Another six months of this and you'll be able to retire to Sausalito and live like a queen."

Matt didn't answer. When Willem began his *macho,* baiting stuff he knew it was time to stop arguing. Besides, Willem was right. There was no good reason to pull out now, when things were going so well, just because the new chief of the village looked like a difficult son-of-a-bitch.

At last he said, "I get nervous when I think about what happened to Pagett."

"Accident," said Willem, gazing at the marina where boats were being filled with picnic cases.

"Do you really believe that?" asked Matt.

Willem shrugged indifferently. "What else can I believe?" he said. "We didn't kill him, did we?"

Normally Cassandra would have left the picnic for another day, but the early start, coupled with the intimidation of tans around the pool, left her, at eleven-thirty, not knowing quite what to do with herself. Surely, she reasoned, a picnic would be as good a way of getting to know the other guests as any other. And so, changing into a Calvin Klein wrap dress, under which she wore her briefest bikini, she assembled her sun creams, camera, and tissues for the day and went down to join the rest of the picnickers.

"You're only just in time," smiled a large beefy man with a paunch, "Psi Upsilon" written across his T-shirt. About forty-five, he was accompanied by a short, wide-hipped woman with heavy breasts that hung unsupported inside a Club Village T-shirt. Like nearly everyone else, he was carrying an expensive camera.

"I only just arrived," Cassandra said.

"Our last day," Psi Upsilon replied. "Best vacation we ever had. Right, Myrna?" He turned, grinning, to his wife.

"The very best." Myrna nodded enthusiastically. "Are you from England?"

"Yes," Cassandra nodded.

"You've heard about Club Village picnics in England then, too, have you?" said Psi Upsilon, and suddenly both he and Myrna began to guffaw.

"I'm sorry . . . ?"

Psi Upsilon shook his head, smiling. "I'm sorry," he said, "just a joke. I'm Andy . . . this is Myrna."

"I'm Cassandra."

"My . . . Cassandra . . . that's a pretty name. Isn't that a pretty name, Andy?" Myrna enthused. "Don't people have pretty names at Club Village? You know what we had here last week? There was a Pandora, and there was an Imogen. Aren't they pretty names, now?"

Cassandra smiled and extricated herself from Myrna's flattery.

Suddenly a large CV in a pair of minuscule shorts and a baseball cap began to shout instructions. "Okay, everybody, for those who haven't been on a picnic before, this is what happens. We all walk down to the marina, where you will find a whole bunch of boats to take us on our mystery picnic. Everything has been arranged by Lucien and there are enough boats and drinks and eats for everyone. The journey will take about forty-five minutes in the outboards, and we'll be back at about four. So if any of you want to change your minds, now is the time. Any questions?"

There were no questions, and with that the whole company, about fifty people, set off along a short cart track toward the marina. Already Cassandra was beginning to feel less like a stranger as first one person and then another commented on not having seen her before.

"Hi . . . I'm Chuck." A rotund fellow of around fifty offered his hand. He had pale blue eyes, and a moustache that drooped like a tired geranium.

"This is the first picnic I've been on," he confided quietly, apparently afraid he might be overheard.

"Me too," Cassandra replied slowly and thoughtfully. There seemed to be something almost furtive about this picnic. What could make her feel that way? It was really all quite puzzling, but, since it was such a beautiful day and everybody else was in high spirits, she allowed the small questions in her mind to evaporate.

As they started toward the marina, she glanced around

at the other picnickers. Surprisingly there were no children. The party included two teenage girls, Jenny and Cathy from Washington; a French couple from Limoges who owned a couple of boutiques; a young dentist from New York called John-John, and his girlfriend, Mary, who looked like a model but was actually a speech therapist. There was an extremely tanned young Mexican called Miguel, and a boy of twenty-three, who was already a hit with Cathy and Jenny.

The site chosen for the picnic was a small island, hardly more than a heap of sand with some bush and pine and palm trees, about ten miles west of Elixir. It was so small that it reminded Cassandra of the cartoonist's idea of a castaway's island. By the time the boat in which she was traveling reached it, the rest of the party were wading through limpid waves up the dazzling white sand to the shelter of the pines.

"They say no Club Village holiday in Elixir is complete without taking part in one of the picnics," said Mournful Chuck as, holding his Nikon aloft, he splashed down into the sea and headed for shore. Wondering whether she ought to have left the experience for the last week of her vacation, Cassandra followed.

The games began even before lunch. While the *sous-chef* unloaded refrigerated hampers from one of the boats, and half a dozen CVs began to erect small trestle tables in the shade of the palm trees, Hector, a large CV, dressed grotesquely in only a loincloth, began to organize them into groups of twenty.

Cassandra found herself in a group with Psi Upsilon, Myrna, Jenny, and Cathy, some young investment bankers, dentists, and their wives or companions. A couple of girl CVs she had come to recognize as Lydia and Barbara passed around large glasses filled with Planter's Punch. Cassandra sipped hers. It was 90 percent rum, she realized as she watched the others knock theirs back as quickly as possible.

"Okay . . . is everybody ready?" Hector with the loincloth was striding around among the groups. "I want you to arrange yourselves guy, gal, guy, gal . . . know what I mean?"

There was a general shuffling across the hot sand as the groups arranged themselves. Cassandra stayed where she was. The rotund Chuck and Psi Upsilon sat on either side of her.

"Now we're gonna play a game called finger in the hole, okay?"

Everybody giggled.

"Now . . . you each have a finger, right?" Hector held up his right middle finger. "And you each have a hole . . ." There was more snickering. "No, not that hole . . . this hole," Hector shouted, and proceeded to make a ring with his thumb and the first finger of his left hand. "Now I want you all to put your hole down on the sand . . . come on, everyone." Obediently the groups put their left hands on the ground. "Now when I shout out 'Finger in your own hole,' you have to put your finger into the hole of your left hand. But when I shout out 'Finger in someone else's hole,' you have to find the hole of one of your neighbors. Understand?" And he demonstrated by putting his finger cozily into the small circle made by one of the dentists' wives. She laughed with mock embarrassment. "The only trouble is that, as in life, there will not be enough holes to go around, because I only have a finger, and no hole. Understand? It's a game of elimination, and as you are eliminated you have to pay à penalty." He paused for effect. "And the penalty I've chosen for today is that as you are eliminated you have to take off your clothes. Okay?"

There was a loud yell of agreement from several men. Some of the women giggled. More drinks were passed around, and then it was time to start the game.

At last Cassandra realized why children were not taken on Elixir picnics, and why so much alcohol was consumed. She wished desperately that she had stayed in the village, but it was too late to run away. The best she could do was try to brazen it out and just watch the others.

"Okay . . ." Hector was standing in the middle of the circle. "Finger in . . . wait for it . . . finger in your own hole." With screams and shouts, the participants carried out the instruction. "Now finger in . . . someone else's hole." In a sudden flurry of excitement everyone looked desperately around for a vacant hole. A young man of about twenty was left without a partner.

"Okay, Donald, you're out first. Come on, you know the rules," Hector shouted. Donald looked awkward. Alongside him, his girl friend, a pretty, plump girl with chestnut hair wearing a full-length beach robe, began to giggle nervously. Someone else began to sing "The Stripper." "Come on, Donald . . ." Hector repeated, grinning.

Donald began to take off his shorts, slowly at first and then with a rush, until, naked, he lay down just outside the circle, where he helped himself to another drink.

Cassandra averted her eyes, the chestnut-haired girl friend kissed Donald, and there was a hearty round of applause.

"Now," shouted Hector, "who will be the next lucky person?" He grinned around at the girls. Cassandra looked to both sides of her. She was going to have to be pretty quick not to be eliminated. She could already feel the attentions of Chuck and Psi Upsilon on her. "Finger in . . . your own hole." Again there was confusion, and then a relieved giggle. "Finger in . . . your own hole." This time several people dived onto their neighbors, only to laugh again as they realized the mistake they had made. And just then, as they were dragging themselves back to sitting positions, came the next order: "Finger in someone else's hole." That was it. With people still off balance, pandemonium set in. Two or three desperate people looked around for vacant holes. Throwing themselves across the sand in exaggerated desperation, they clambered over bodies. Again, inevitably, someone was left out.

This time it was Cathy. She was wearing a bikini. Casually she threw the top half into the circle, and then wriggled sensually out of the bottom half, turning slowly around to give everyone a good look. Then, picking up her drink, she went to join the unfortunate Donald, who was now trying to rub suntan cream across the white cheeks of his bottom. Taking the tube from him, she squirted some onto the palm of her hand and then began delicately to massage it into his skin, leaning over him and sliding her fingers tantalizingly between his thighs. The girl with the chestnut hair watched without saying anything. Then the game began again, moving quickly. Only two people refused to take their clothes off—Mary, the beautiful speech therapist, and Cassandra. At first she felt like a spoilsport, and wondered whether she would be ostracized during the rest of the vacation. But no one seemed upset. Everyone else was too busy with himself to care much about her.

"Don't worry if you're shy at first, Sandra," said Myrna, who was now quite naked, drunk, saggy, and stretch-marked. "I was really embarrassed the first time, but by the end of the second week you'll feel more at home."

Cassandra smiled. "How often do they hold picnics?" she asked, deliberately keeping her eyes away from Myrna's body.

"Just twice a week. Tuesdays and Thursdays. Most people here are into their second week. The first picnic took a lot longer to get going, if you know what I mean."

The naked picnickers were now tucking into a huge lunch of *poulet en gelée,* cold lobster in scallop shells, iced leek soup, tuna, lots of fruit, and lots of wine. Watching them eating there, naked on the beach, Cassandra felt rather overclothed and, since it was now burning hot, she waded out into the sea and swam. The water was surprisingly cold, and she quickly hurried back to the beach, where she pulled on her sundress and discreetly took off her bikini.

By the time lunch was finished more and more couples were pairing off to sneak away into the bush together or lie alongside each other at the edge of the beach, necking as the surf broke over them.

Suddenly Hector announced another game. "Okay

. . . you all know what the next game is . . . it's the fruit
game. Can I have twelve ladies . . ." he looked around.
"Come on . . . Cathy . . . Sue . . . yes . . . what about
you?" he pointed at Cassandra. She shook her head. He
carried on until half a dozen women had climbed to their
feet and were wandering a little drunkenly into the center
of the group. Eventually he had his twelve.

"And now I want twelve guys . . . okay?" In moments
fifteen or twenty men had joined him. "Okay . . . maybe
we'll have a few more . . ." he said, and called for more
girls. "Now I want all the guys to lie in the sand on your
backs, with your legs open and your knees up. Right?
Then we're gonna put some fruit on your stomachs . . .
and you, ladies, you have to eat the fruit off the men's
tummies without using your hands to help. Okay?" The
girls nodded and giggled. Clearly, they had played the
game before.

"For God's sake . . ." Cassandra murmured.

The men lay down in a circle, and Hector, with the help
of a couple of CVs and two or three of the guests, began
ladling out ice-cold fruit cocktail onto their bare stomachs.
Even before the women got near, some of the men began
to grow excited.

"Okay, you guys, what's your hurry?" called Hector.
Some of the onlookers cheered. The sense of sexual
expectation had taken over, and the atmosphere was
tense. Cassandra began to feel uncharacteristically excited, and she found herself digging her fingernails into her
hands as she watched the women, all naked, begin to crawl
on their hands and knees toward the men.

Psi Upsilon was not a player, but his wife, Myrna, was,
and had been paired with a handsome youth across whose
body slices of oranges, grapes, and apples had been
placed. Even as Myrna leaned over him to lick at the juice
dribbling across his skin, the youth began to grow excited.

Suddenly Pentaxes and Nikons were grabbed as amateur
photographers began burrowing themselves into the
ground all around the couples, pointing zoom lenses at
hanging breasts and fruit-covered male stomachs. As the

cameras clicked and silence fell over the watchers, the
women began to withdraw their interest from the fruit in
favor of other things. Allowing long, loose hair to hang
like curtains below their faces, they slowly went down on
partners chosen at random.

Then gradually, as the cloud of eroticism passed among
the onlookers, people began to fall on their neighbors, and
the aroma of sexuality mingled with the wine and rum. All
across the beach, men and women were making love,
thrusting, entwining bodies in couples and threesomes and
foursomes until quickly a whole area of the beach looked
as though it were made up of dozens of adults indulging in
some frenzied game of Twister.

Cassandra tiptoed quietly away. She had never once
taken her camera from its case. She could hardly believe
what she had seen. She approached the sea, where a
number of people had congregated by the water's edge,
refugees from the orgy.

"Welcome to Club Village," whispered Mary, the
speech therapist from New York.

Cassandra remembered that she had seen Mary's boyfriend just a few minutes earlier, lying drunk in the sand
while Cathy worked on him with her mouth.

She could see the speech therapist crying quietly. On
days like this there were certain to be a lot of casualties,
Cassandra thought. She wondered how she could explain
all this in prose suitable for family reading.

Hamlet Yablans considered his porridge-white face in the small mirror propped on the flimsy dressing table in his bleak, sunless room. His expression was empty, almost vacant. He observed the black eyebrow crescents, which rose over his eyes in perpetual surprise, and then delicately added a touch of mascara. His face was moon-shaped, yet lugubrious, and his hair was dull, dyed black and brushed straight back from his forehead. He rubbed a dusting of white powder into his cheeks, and then, taking a lipstick from a makeup case, he very carefully accentuated the line of his thin lips until they were bright red and mean.

He was naked to the waist. His body was small and muscular and slightly bent. His waist was slim, but half an inch of slack flesh below his armpits at the extremity of his ribs reminded Hamlet that he was not a young man. He was sitting in a pair of black tights and wearing black moccasins. Satisfied that his face was as doleful as he could make it, he stood up and took one of several black silk blouses from a plastic hanging wardrobe.

Outside he could hear people splashing in the pool as a game of water polo reached its climax. Moving to his window, he gazed sorrowfully at the fun. He checked the cheap digital watch on his wrist. It was ten past four, almost time for his afternoon's siesta to end. As always, he had spent the two hours' break lying on his bed and reading. It was the only private time he had. He was working his way slowly through the Russian classics. But

93

he was a slow reader, and he had already been involved with *War and Peace* for six months.

A last look in the mirror assured him that he looked totally miserable, and, picking up a bucket, he opened his door and stepped out into the sunny village to begin his evening's clowning.

As the resident clown at Elixir, Hamlet's job was to provide continuous diversion. In the Mediterranean villages this could usually be achieved by banal slapstick, in which the clowns made sure that they ended every day by covering themselves in custard pie, or carelessly dropping a dozen dinner plates after they had performed tricks of balance with them. But the American zone was different.

Dick Pagett had recruited Hamlet after the antics of the village's first clown, a traditional Yugoslav buffoon, had met with stony silence. He had found Hamlet doing mime in a dinner theater in Tampa, and been struck by the man's anarchic sense of humor, and the challenge with which he approached his audience. The supper crowd had been confused by his act, but they had not ignored him. No one could ignore Hamlet. He had a way of confronting people with their own prejudices. In Paris there had been a bemused reaction to his recruitment to the village, but although the occasional bourgeois French complaint had found its way to the Bourse, the reports from the American guests had been nearly all good. Hamlet was weird and he was ugly. But he was never dull.

It was not difficult for Hamlet to assume the role of the mourning Prince of Denmark. He was now fifty, and his life had been all failure. Sadness and black humor had overcome him during two years in Korea, and he had never quite got started after that. He had been a singer, a dancer, a bit player in TV shows, and had hung around off-Broadway for the best part of twenty years. But it had been twenty years of loneliness until his metamorphosis, when someone asked him to step in as Hamlet in a summer-stock company in the Catskills.

It was the first time he had played Shakespeare, and though he had played the part as seriously as he was able, the audiences began to chuckle the moment he took the stage. And by the time the curtain fell at the end of the fifth act they were in hysterics. It was unfathomable. All that week he tried to get the proper reaction. But the more serious he became, the more audiences laughed. By the end of the run he had discovered a new performing identity and a new name. Unfortunately, not many directors were looking for Hamlet as farce, and the Tampa supper theater attended by Dick Pagett had been Hamlet's first gig in months.

Like a shadow, Hamlet moved stealthily around the edge of the pool and bar area. He was instantly the focus of all attention. Near the bar, Hardin was being briefed on beverage affairs by Lieberson, the head of wines and beverages. "I don't believe you've met Hamlet yet, have you, James?" he asked.

Hardin turned to see Hamlet make his way slowly up a ladder, which was propped at the side of the stage and which led to a trapeze. "I understand he's funny," he said.

"Weird," said Lieberson, "but the guests like him. It's like having your own resident lunatic hunchback."

Hardin turned his attention to Hamlet, who was now unfastening the trapeze from the theater roof. Very nimbly, Hamlet pulled himself onto the bar and, pushing himself out, began to swing gently backward and forward, making long swooping runs across the bar just above the heads of the drinkers.

Hardin watched in amazement. Slowly he heard the clown begin to speak. "How all occasions do inform against me, and spur my dull revenge!" said Hamlet. "What is a man, if his chief good and marker of his time be but to sleep and feed? A beast, no more."

Around the bar people began to giggle. Hamlet was swinging on his trapeze, cuddling the skull of Yorick and intoning Shakespeare in a voice as theatrically melancholy as doom, but spiced with the intonation of a New York cabbie, all gravel and adenoids.

Hardin looked around the bar. "Is this all he does?" he asked Lieberson.

"Sometimes he climbs to the top of a pole and does speeches, other times he hangs from the ceiling and speaks. . . ."

"And that's funny?"

"The guests like it."

Hardin shook his head. He couldn't see anything funny in this. He looked back at Hamlet. With his long, skinny legs and enormous codpiece, he looked like a broken spider.

Suddenly Hamlet caught Hardin's eye and winked slowly, deliberately, and lasciviously.

Hardin looked quickly away. Instinctively, he didn't like the man. Hamlet was more than weird. He was sick.

Cassandra began making notes the moment she got back to her room. She was, she imagined, in some kind of shock. She had never seen another couple making love before, and certainly never expected to witness a pageant of group sex. Before the details blurred in her mind she wanted to record them. She was not sure how she felt. She was certainly shocked, alarmed maybe, and astonished. But also she knew that a part of her had been thoroughly turned on. She had not been a participant, only a bewildered voyeur, but all the way back in the boat, as couples regrouped and more rum was dispatched, she found herself wondering what might have happened if she had been drunk, if she had been relaxed, and if she were just a little less prudish.

Lost in thought, she dressed for dinner. Wishing not in any way to be provocative, bearing in mind the events of the day, she chose a very pale green silk suit that she had bought at Ralph Lauren during one of her editorial briefing trips to New York. Already her skin was glowing from the first sun of her vacation, and, with her hair newly washed, she felt as though she had expelled the cobwebs of a European winter from her entire system.

Making her way down to the bar before dinner, she suddenly began to feel a lightness she had not experienced in years. The fragrance of hibiscus and jacaranda lay heavily on the air, and the lights around the pool and bar threw a Technicolor glamor onto the waiting diners, who were grouped at tables talking and laughing. Every man looked tanned and handsome, while all the women were competing in displays of glamor.

Cassandra made straight for the large pink plastic shell where a pretty Eurasian girl was dealing in the Club Village currency of multicolored plastic bar shells.

"Five, ten, or twenty dollars?" asked the girl as Cassandra approached.

Cassandra shrugged. She didn't know the cost of drinks. How could she know how much she would need?

"If it's your first day I'll give you twenty. You can always come back for more when you've spent it," the girl said.

Cassandra nodded.

"Name and room number?"

Cassandra gave the required information, signed a piece of paper that told her she would be charged the required amount at the end of her stay, and was handed a string of interlocking pink, gold, and navy blue shells.

"The pinks are one dollar, the golds two dollars, and the blues are five," said the girl.

Cassandra thanked her and shouldering her way to the bar ordered herself a Campari and soda.

"That'll be two golds or four pinks," said Alex, the bartender, as he pushed the drink, a tiny Campari with a very large slice of lemon, an avalanche of ice, and a flood of soda, across the bar.

Cassandra handed him the chain of shells so that he might take what he needed.

Two golds or four pinks, she repeated to herself. Was that four dollars? She couldn't remember what the girl in the shell had told her. Could one minute Campari really cost four dollars? She felt she ought to make a note for her story and her expenses. The shell system of money had to be the simplest and most open con trick ever worked. There was no sensation of spending when you were dealing in colored toy shells. She had already forgotten the exchange rate. She remembered reading in the brochures the shells encouraged people to forget their money problems and had a leveling social effect. But that was nonsense. It may be a moneyless society so far as the vacationers were concerned, she decided, but it was a maximum-profit place for Club Village. And taking her Campari to a nearby empty table she resolved to make a special effort to remember in the future what she paid.

Through the crowd of people Alex, the bartender, watched Cassandra sullenly. Although Alex did not know her, he did not like her. He did not like anyone in Club Village. No decent girl would ever be found in a place like this. No *clean* girl. Scrupulously he wiped the top of the bar, his eyes taking in the guests who assembled there every evening. They disgusted him. The mating rituals of two hundred people on the make almost made him shudder with nausea. Sometimes he imagined he could smell the semen as they leaned across his bar to buy the drinks that would stoke their desires. One day God would punish them, he told himself a hundred times a day.

At twenty-eight Alex, with the dull, brooding eyes, and lank, brown hair, was a born-again. God had shown him the way and led him out of the depths of the depravity he had known since he was fourteen. Now he was repaying God by spitting in the face of daily temptation which was flaunted before him. Jesus loves me, he repeated to himself, as his eyes found again the figure of Cassandra. Jesus loves me. . . . Jesus loves me. . . . Jesus loves me. . . .

"May I sit with you?" A very fair, extremely handsome boy in washed-out jeans, sandals, and white sweat shirt was smiling at Cassandra through pale blue eyes. He looked no more than twenty.

Cassandra gestured to an empty table near by.

"You arrived today, didn't you?" the boy said after they were seated. He was sipping a Coke through a long straw. "I was at the airport. Sorry about the welcome. My name is Sacha."

Cassandra offered her name.

"I expect you're still feeling a little like a stranger," said Sacha, still smiling. He was, thought Cassandra, one of the most beautiful and charming young men she had ever met, and she was embarrassed to be so overcome by a man so much her junior.

"I'm picking things up," she said, and then laughed.

Sacha laughed easily, but did not, as another man might have done, make an obvious joke.

"Tell me, Sacha, do you work here?"

"I'm a CV," Sacha explained. "I'm in charge of things like set designs for entertainments, and some of the games. I generally help out wherever they need me."

"I didn't see you at the picnic today."

Sacha looked surprised. "You went on the picnic?"

"Well . . . yes. I heard it was an experience not to be missed," Cassandra explained lamely, hoping for a response.

"I guess it depends on the kind of experience you're looking for," said Sacha. "You don't strike me as a picnic type. Did you enjoy it?"

Cassandra found herself blushing for the first time all day. This beautiful boy had a way of staring straight at her, demanding that she answer truthfully.

"I was surprised," she confessed. "I hadn't any idea what would happen. I didn't want to become involved in the games. I won't be going again, I can tell you *that.*"

Sacha laughed softly. "Don't worry. That's the way a lot of people feel. Some of those guys running the picnic, and most of the people who play the games . . . they're freaks, real lunatic freaks. Most of the CVs won't take part."

"I can't believe it's Club Village policy. Is it?" asked Cassandra. "Do they have the same games at all the other villages?"

Sacha shook his head. "Not from what I hear. For some reason Elixir seems to be the capital of group sex. I don't know why. Maybe Dick . . . he was the last chief of the village . . . should have discouraged it. But I think perhaps he believed in giving the customers what they wanted, and there are always some who want that. He was a nice guy. A really nice man."

"He was the man who was drowned, wasn't he?" asked Cassandra.

Sacha nodded, but didn't answer.

Aware that she might have intruded into private grief, and careful not to behave like a reporter, Cassandra changed the subject. "Where are you from, Sacha?"

"The Midwest . . . I'm a Midwest farmer's son. Place called Summitville, Indiana, about seventy-five miles north of Indianapolis."

Cassandra considered the flowing golden hair, the delicate features, and clear, bronzed skin. "You don't look much like a farmer to me," she said, hoping she didn't sound too admiring.

"When I got out of high school I was off that farm faster than a Le Mans start. I went to school in California . . . theater arts, design."

Cassandra nodded. This boy had a way of talking that was instantly intimate. Somehow all the people around her having drinks before dinner faded completely. He was so pretty, so sympathetic. He could recount the most banal details and make them fascinating. It was, Cassandra thought, a most uncanny gift. And while she scorned herself for being taken in by it, she could not help admiring him.

At that moment they were joined by a couple of girls—Chloe, the beautiful short-haired French girl from reception, and a vivacious green-eyed beauty from the boutique whom Sacha introduced as Florinda. This boy certainly attracted the best that Club Village has to offer, conceded Cassandra, as Sacha went off to buy all of them drinks from the bar. She was grateful to meet some of the more normal members of the village after her traumatic afternoon.

Beyond the ridge of bush that ran like a spine down the curve of the island, the sun was setting, but not in a blaze of red. Instead it appeared to have already been lost in a deep sea of aquamarine. It was quite the most unusual sunset Cassandra had ever seen, leaving the palm trees standing sturdy and back-lit, like black paper cutouts.

"Hello, everything okay?" Hardin asked as he joined them. Sacha and the two girl CVs moved deferentially to one side to allow him in. He acknowledged this with a curt smile. "Did you play tennis?" he asked Cassandra.

"I went on the picnic."

His face fell. "Yes? What did you think?" he asked cagily.

"I didn't know *what* to think."

Hardin glared down at his hands. "Well, I do," he said. "And so will some of those CVs when I've finished talking to them."

The three CVs present exchanged glances.

"Were any of you there?" he asked.

They all shook their heads.

"Wise."

There was a silence. Then Sacha and the girls slipped quietly away.

"How did you know about the picnic?" asked Cassandra.

Hardin groaned. "I learned about it because some people came and complained. I was told before I left Paris that some of the picnics got out of hand, but the stories I heard today took some believing."

"They were true," said Cassandra. "I thought Club Village had invented a new kind of vacation sport. I wouldn't have believed so much copulating could go on in the whole of the Bahamas."

Hardin shook his head. "I'm sorry. It can't have been a very pleasant first day for you."

"Don't apologize. I'm not antisex. To each his own."

"By the time I've finished, this place will be cleaner than Disneyland."

"I didn't take you for a prude," said Cassandra.

Hardin shook his head. "I'm no prude. Anything anyone wants to do privately is okay with me. In fact, the more they do the happier I'll be, because I'll know they're having a good time. But public performances are out. If the Bahamian police ever came around during one of those exhibitions they'd be able to close us down."

"Could they afford to? Don't they need you as much as you need them?"

Hardin stared hard at Cassandra. "What kind of books do you edit?" he asked suddenly.

Cassandra thought quickly, realizing she had been too inquisitive. "Art and religious."

Hardin nodded. "Which publisher?"

Her mind went blank until she thought of the last two men to buy her lunch. "Sissons . . ." she said. "Sissons and Jones. Why?"

Hardin grinned. "I was just thinking what nice ears you have," he said playfully, changing the subject. Then before she could respond he stood up. "I'm afraid I have to have dinner with the senior staff tonight, but perhaps you'd care to join me some other time?"

"That would be very nice," said Cassandra. "I'll look forward to it." And, getting up, she joined the line of people making their way into the dining hall.

By ten o'clock Hardin was well prepared for his meeting with the staff. He had spent the entire first day examining the workings of the Elixir village, and he was a thorough man.

It had become clear that this village was not being run as Quatre Bras would expect. There was a casual attitude in most of the staff that would never have been tolerated in the European villages. While it did not bother him much that the reputation of the organization was at risk, it infuriated him to realize that so many guests were not getting full value for their money.

He also suspected that the prevailing sloppiness could be dangerous in all kinds of ways, because it encouraged people to take risks and cut corners. Hardin did not know what had happened to Pagett, but it was possible that he might not have met with his accident had he run a tighter ship. And Hardin was determined not to meet with an accident himself.

He had called the meeting purposely for ten o'clock, since it was the time of evening when virtually all the staff would be off duty, when guests were generally sitting around the bar drinking, or dancing.

The meeting place was in a wing of the dining hall, which had purposely been cleared early. At exactly one minute to ten Hardin left the small bungalow he had inherited from Pagett and walked across the lawn, now

damp with dew. From the dance floor he could hear the
sounds of a local reggae band. A canopy of stars was slung
across the sky, their different colors as bright as lights on a
Christmas tree.

As he entered the dining hall a hush fell over the
assembled staff. His behavior at the airport that morning
had been thoroughly reported.

He made his way through the crowd to a low stage which
was there for occasional dinner-hour entertainments. He
looked at his audience. Counting tennis coaches, diving
team, men to look after the boats, transportation staff,
and the non-Bahamian kitchen workers, there were almost
one hundred employees.

Stepping up onto the stage, he smiled at his staff, but it
was a smile without warmth. He took a deep breath and
began. "I think most of you will have seen me around the
village at some time today," he said, aware that the palms
of his hands were damp, "but for those who didn't meet
me—my name is James Hardin, and I have come here as
replacement for Dick Pagett. I would like to say a formal
'hello' to all of you. I hope we're all going to get along
well."

A murmur of agreement ran around the staff. Someone
shouted an ironic "Hear, hear." Hardin turned his eyes in
the direction of the caller. The way to handle sarcasm was
to top it.

"I'm glad you all agree, then," he said, "because that is
one of the few things we are going to agree on this
evening. Let me make one thing very clear right from the
start. I don't like a great many things I've heard about this
village, and I like even less some of the things I've seen
today. So if any of you want to leave, you can pack your
bags. First thing tomorrow, we'll put you on a flight to
Nassau."

No one moved. Hardin's eyes flicked around the CVs.
They were, he had to admit, a particularly attractive lot.
Quickly his eyes picked up Florinda, the pretty girl from
the boutique, who was sitting with Chloe and Sacha.

Farther toward the back sat Lieberson, the head of wines and beverages, with Eugene Waterman, the chief accountant. Waterman did not deserve the verbal roasting, since the village was extremely profitable, and that was rare for a new village. Homer Wolford, the head of sports, was standing alongside Sharon Kennedy. Both had been very close to Pagett, and Hardin could see the resentment in their eyes as he began his tirade.

"I was sent out here to take over from Dick Pagett," explained Hardin. "But I'm not much like Dick. I don't know what he expected from CVs, but I certainly don't expect them to behave as though it is they who are on vacation. You and I are here for one reason only, and that is to work. Okay, so we also get to have a good time, but that is only by the way. So far I've seen a lot of CVs having a great time, and a lot of guests being ignored.

"Of course, there are exceptions to this. The tennis coaching looked excellent and I've every reason to believe most of the sporting activities are carried out with a lot of enthusiasm. But there are areas that need tightening up."

Hardin's eyes passed around the CVs. Willem Brummer and Matt Hillman were watching him silently. Over in a far corner, leaning against a pillar, stood Hamlet Yablans, playing casually with a Yo-Yo, almost as though willing Hardin to reprimand him. Hardin did not rise to the bait.

"Let's start by reminding you of some of the basic rules about being a CV, shall we?" said Hardin, feeling increasingly like a schoolmaster. "First, it isn't *your* vacation. You all have to be available at all times for whatever is required of you.

"Tomorrow we have virtually a complete change of guest list. I don't want a single one of those people to go home complaining that the CVs spent all their time around the bar and they had to look after themselves. Understood? Also, while I was in Paris I heard some weird stories about CVs encouraging sex parties during the picnics. Well, I didn't believe those stories, but since I've been here today I've discovered that I heard only about a fraction of what went on. Now, I'm not blaming anyone in particular for this. I'm saying that from today we start discouraging those games at picnics. I know a lot of people come down here in order to do a little wife-swapping, but as of now we don't help them. If they want to do that, let them do it in their own cabins. Okay?"

Hector, the chief picnic organizer, smiled sardonically to himself as heads turned to look at him.

"Now, I want to talk about drugs. The Bahamian government does not approve of buying, selling, or taking drugs, including marijuana. They have very stiff sentences down here for that. But I hadn't been in this village for more than an hour before I realized that this is a pusher's paradise. So let's get this clear. I don't want the Bahamian police raiding this place while I'm chief of the village. To be honest, I don't have any opinions either way on grass or coke, but I've got lots of opinions on keeping the law. So if you have your own little cache stowed away somewhere, I suggest you flush it down the toilet, because if I ever come across it you'll be out of this village instantly. Okay?"

He looked around for responses. Nearly one hundred blank faces met his. That was apparently the most unwelcome news for the staff. At the back of the crowd, Matt Hillman looked anxiously toward Willem Brummer, but Willem stared straight ahead, his face expressionless.

"Well, that's all I want to say to you tonight," went on Hardin. "If you don't think any of the criticisms apply to you, then I hope you won't mind me making them to the others. But for those who can see a trace of truth in what I've just said, may I suggest you pay attention to my suggestions. I shall be getting to know all of you in the next few days, and I hope things are going to improve immediately, and that we're all going to be very happy here for the rest of the season."

With that Hardin stepped down from the low stage and walked quickly toward the door. No one spoke. It was as though he were a spoilsport parent who had just announced it was time for homework.

Once outside, Hardin breathed freely for the first time since he had been on Elixir.

Cassandra would have preferred an early night, but no attractive woman is ever allowed to disappear by herself at ten o'clock at Club Village, and it was midnight before she was able to draw herself away from the agreeable banter of late-night talk taking place around the wide and open bar.

Dinner had been a culinary masterpiece. Because she was alone, a hostess placed her with a group of Canadians and Americans. They were all in their late twenties and early thirties and had come down to the Bahamas strictly for the scuba diving, and Cassandra listened with awe as a skinny little woman from Bronxville described nonchalantly her meeting with a couple of sharks out near one of the Exuma cays.

It came as a shock to Cassandra to realize that her fellow vacationers were so little upset by Dick Pagett's death. Without newspapers or television, a day in a Club Village seemed an eternity. But still, there was something odd about it. The fact that life in the village carried on without mourning was unreal, as though the guests had been anesthetized. Elixir, she thought, was so removed from reality that normal emotions were suspended.

At midnight, after dancing a couple of times with a scuba freak from Toronto, Cassandra excused herself. She was very tired. Crossing the pool area, she headed toward her room. Although there were lights attached to trees, it suddenly seemed much darker than she had expected and she found herself hurrying across the open lawn toward the bedrooms. The dance music had stopped and been replaced by a steady bass thump from the basement discotheque.

She hurried up the steps back toward her room, and began to walk along the long balcony. For some reason she had the overwhelming sensation that she was being followed. She looked over her shoulder. There was no one.

At last she reached her door. Since Club Village did not issue keys, it was open. Very quickly she stepped inside and turned on the lights. All was as she had left it. She slipped the lock across the door. There were locks on the inside, but not on the outside. She didn't like that, but there was not much to steal, anyway, since all of her credit cards and valuables had been lodged with the bank earlier. Telling herself that her imagination was playing tricks with her, she undressed quickly, slipped into her nightdress, and climbed into bed.

Suddenly she felt cold sweat sweep through her body. Again she had the sensation of being watched. In the far distance she could hear music, but there was also something much closer, a slight rapping, a rustling noise. Timidly, she pulled herself up and looked around the room. Everything was still. Had she locked the door properly? She crossed the room. The door was secure. Now she had the feeling that there was someone on the outside, someone who wanted to come in. Half laughing at herself for her silly imaginings, she suddenly pulled open the venetian blinds that covered the window to the balcony.

The blinds were open for only five seconds before Cassandra screamed and dropped them. But those five seconds were long enough to terrify her. There, facing her on the far side of the glass, was a ghoulishly painted, grinning witch with long black hair and a reptile face, in green and black and yellow, a face that was distorted by madness. As she screamed, the face turned and fled into the night.

PART III

_____ *TWENTY-THREE*

John Arrowsmith lay cozily under the blue patchwork of the quilt listening to the exertions of his wife, Ruth, as she went through her early-morning routine. Physical torture was, she believed, the only way to the prolongation of youth. He could not see her except during the sit-ups, since she had selected the foot of their bed as her training territory, but he knew that she would be naked except for a tiny pair of white cotton pants. Fifteen years ago such a performance would have had him high on arousal, and would undoubtedly have ended prematurely when he would have hauled her back under the sheets. But in those days there would have been no reason for Ruth to worry about her figure. Ironically, fifteen years earlier Ruth would have worn a bra for any kind of workout.

Ruth's dark, pretty head popped up from the foot of the bed. "Twenty," she gasped, and immediately flopped over onto her stomach to begin her series of twelve pushups.

Arrowsmith didn't even look at her. Unconsciously, his hand gripped the layer of flab which was spreading comfortably just below his ribs. He really ought to do something about that, he thought, and then just as quickly dismissed the idea. At forty a little bit of flesh was acceptable, even attractive on a man, he thought. Quite honestly, he wouldn't have objected to it on Ruth, either.

Pulling himself out of bed, he went into the bathroom, locked the door, and turned on the shower.

Forty years old, he told himself. If this was the beginning of middle age then old age had to be unthinkable. He gasped as the water ran over his hair. When he had first married he had had masses of thick, black hair. Now he had thinning gray hair, and a skin which seemed just that bit less polished than he remembered it.

The door handle was turned from the outside.

"John . . . how long are you going to be?" Ruth's voice was already impatient, and these were her first words of the day.

"For Christ's sake . . . I only just got in here," he retorted, and regretted his abruptness instantly.

"Only asking," came an airy response. "I'll use the children's."

Fifteen years married and conversation was so often needlessly barbed and laced with irritation. "Stalemate," someone had said to him recently. "Marriage is a couple of stale mates." He frowned. He didn't like to think like that.

Maybe Ruth was right. Maybe a vacation would do him good. The vacation had been her idea, or at least an idea dreamed up by her and her racquetball friend Joanna Roeg. Normally when the Arrowsmiths took midwinter vacations they trekked out to Colorado or to upstate New York for the skiing. But this year, because of Joanna, four places had been booked at the Club Village, Elixir, for the Roegs and the Arrowsmiths.

The whole thing seemed to suit Ruth admirably. She was already well into the vacation spirit, and had surprised him the previous evening by in one breath admitting exhaustion from all the packing and then in the next suggesting almost girlishly they should celebrate the start of their vacation with a little lovemaking, a sort of hors d'oeuvres for Elixir, she had said. It had been successful, as it nearly always was, in that they both declared themselves satisfied. But afterward, as Ruth lay snoring quietly, Arrowsmith lay awake and gazed at the pattern of lights shining on the curtains, wondering why he was not the happiest man in the world.

He should have been happy, he told himself. Everything he could possibly once have wished for had become his.

He had married the only girl he had ever loved. He had been successful in his profession, which was law, and which therefore carried a certain degree of blighted respectability. He was reasonably well off, and his three children, aged twelve, ten, and six, were happy, well adjusted, and healthy. He still loved his wife. At least he thought he did. Certainly, he did not love anyone else. But over and over his mind said to him, "So what?" So what if he was now a senior partner? So what if he owned the best house in the neighborhood? So what if they could afford to run three cars and had a gardener? So what?

Once upon a time, he had had a two-room apartment on East Eleventh Street, a wonderful, vibrant place of Puerto Rican colors and Phil Spector records. Sometimes he had been too broke to eat. But he had been happy there. He had been happy when he had married, and he was overjoyed with his children. But somewhere along the line, all the fun had gone out of life.

Ruth tried to sympathize with his predicament, but she could do no more than try. She really didn't understand, and he could see that. For her these were the best years of her life. The early years of sacrifice and make-do had been hard on her, but she had borne them silently and valiantly, and now that she was thirty-six, she was suddenly free to do all the things she had always wanted and felt were important to her.

As he watched his wife move happily through classes, sports, and societies, ever bent on pursuing every moment of life as usefully as possible, Arrowsmith had begun to feel an indefinable alienation creeping over him, a distancing of himself from what he was, what he had become, and what he really wanted out of life. He was not sure what the mystery of self-fulfillment was for him, only that he knew that work, a degree of affluence, and a stable home life had not provided it. Once when he had tried stumblingly to articulate this mild panic into which he found himself slipping Ruth had listened, at first consolingly, but then she had made a flip comment about the onset of the male menopause.

He had not confided in her after that. She had locked herself into the orderliness of suburban society and he had withdrawn to an imaginary world where such gibes did not hurt him; a world that allowed him to go through the motions of fatherhood and good neighborliness, but which left him alone in his mental desert, watching everything as though seeing it on television, a state of mind that he sometimes thought must be madness.

And as he watched the rest of the world, he found himself looking at himself, and hating what he saw. He had been a particularly faithful husband, much to the amazement of many of his friends and colleagues, but now he suddenly found himself drawn to other women. He did not wish to be unfaithful, but neither did he wish to stay faithful. Sometimes in bleak moments he would look back over the fifteen years of his married life and wonder why he had not strayed, what the mystical secret had been that had kept him locked in the same bed every night. He felt pretty sure that Ruth had also been faithful, but where, he wondered, was the virtue in that? Surely she desired other men. He certainly desired other women. He didn't even feel jealous when he imagined her having an affair. It somehow didn't matter. Nothing mattered, only the fact that he was now forty, and unless things changed soon his life would have been a boring stroll through affluence toward death—always completely devoid of the poetry of excitement.

"Kaopectate . . . I forgot the Kaopectate," said Ruth as he entered the kitchen. She was already looking like midsummer's day in her jeans and matelot shirt, with a navy blue silk scarf tied rakishly just below her Adam's apple. Fifteen years ago she wouldn't even have mentioned the possibility of diarrhea. Proximity bred indifference. Could romance and Kaopectate flourish in the same suitcase? he asked himself.

"For someone going on vacation you don't look very happy," said Ruth as she poured the coffee.

Arrowsmith didn't reply.

"You'll enjoy it when you get there," said Ruth without looking at him. "You always do."

That was the killer line. Arrowsmith felt his being shrink a little inside himself. She was treating him like a mother, and he, because of all his uncertainties, was allowing it to happen.

Ruth hurried on "Besides, you'll be able to ogle Joanna in a bikini for a full two weeks, and there won't be a thing I'll be able to do about it."

Arrowsmith changed the subject. "Did you remember to give Mark enough hydrocortisone? he asked. Their eldest child suffered from an unpredictable form of eczema.

"I remembered to do *everything,*" said Ruth, amused by his refusal to discuss Joanna.

She was right, of course. The only bright spot on his horizon was the expectation of seeing Joanna without most of her clothes. Fifteen years earlier Ruth and Joanna had been roommates at Wellesley, but had lost sight of each other until a chance meeting at a tennis court a few months earlier. Now they were emotionally joined at the hip, and he often wondered whether Joanna had ever told Ruth about the night in 1965 when a mix-up in arrangements had led him to take Joanna to a movie while Ruth had been at home celebrating her grandparents' diamond anniversary. It had, in retrospect, been one of the most deliciously naughty nights of his life, although the guilt when an unsuspecting Ruth had returned had been vicious. Consequently he had not been dismayed when, shortly afterward, Joanna flunked her exams and left Wellesley to take a job in Washington, and the two girls had lost contact.

Like most girls attached to the political world, Joanna's career had gone at the foxtrot rate of slow, slow, quick, quick, slow. A number of affairs had been followed by an unhappy marriage to an economics professor, and then she had moved back to New York, where a rich realtor had offered her a country-club, color-magazine life in return for unlimited boredom, although obviously he hadn't quite phrased it in that way. Six months after their marriage, five months after Joanna had realized just what she had let herself in for, she and Ruth had met at the tennis tournament.

At that moment the front door bell rang. "That'll be the cab. He's early," said Ruth and got up to answer the door, while her husband began to clear away the breakfast things.

Two weeks in the sun with Ruth and Joanna, thought Arrowsmith, wondering why an awful feeling of trepidation hung over him.

They met the Roegs in the departure lounge at Kennedy International Airport. As always when Ruth and Joanna met, they rushed to each other like a couple of kids, giggling and kissing and chattering, while the two husbands approached each other with the weary gloom of opposites.

"So they finally got this thing sorted out," said Michael Roeg, as he handed the porter a five-dollar bill.

Arrowsmith gazed at him. He was a short, bulk-chested man with fine brown hair, which looked as though it was regularly back-combed and blow-dried in an attempt to give him the appearance of being taller than he was. He was wearing a pair of mustard-colored plaid slacks, which folded around his bulging paunch like a tent, and a navy blue blazer complete with polished chrome buttons. Around his neck was a yellow cravat. He looked ridiculous. What Joanna could have been thinking of when she married this creature Arrowsmith could not possibly imagine.

"How are you, Michael?" he asked, wondering if he would care if the little man said he had a terminal disease.

"Raring to go," said Roeg, rubbing his hands together with anticipation.

Jesus God, thought Arrowsmith. He said, "Joanna looks very attractive."

That was true. Joanna looked wonderful, to be honest. Arrowsmith would not know it, but she was wearing a pair of Giorgio Armani dogstooth trousers and a collarless Italian jacket. Her hair, which had been long and wayward when he shared his night of delight with her all those years ago, was now short, combed back at the sides, and left swooping down across her forehead at the front. Alongside her, Ruth looked like the good, wholesome, all-American, unsophisticated mother she was. Ruth was pretty, all right, but since being kicked out of college Joanna had acquired a sophistication which Ruth had missed.

"Hello, John, I like your ice-cream jacket," grinned Joanna as she and Ruth pried themselves apart.

Arrowsmith flinched uncomfortably. There was always a bantering sexuality to all of Joanna's exchanges with him. She couldn't even be mildly, playfully insulting without fixing him with a look that said, "Do you remember that night?"

"Listen, why don't you guys go and have coffee while I check our bags," said Arrowsmith.

"We already checked ours," said Roeg, as though scoring a point.

Arrowsmith began to push his baggage trolley to the back of the line. Although they were over an hour early for the flight, at least a hundred people for the Continental charter to Nassau were already milling around the departure lounge. There seemed to be a fair number of attractive young women, and muscular, flat-stomached young men.

Alongside him in line stood a girl of about twenty. Her hair had once been permed, and once dyed blond, but now both processes had grown out, giving her a piebald look, straight dark hair reaching to her neck and then turning into a mass of blond frizz. She was wearing a pair of scuffed Calvin Klein jeans, and a pretty white lace blouse under an olive linen jacket. Around her neck hung a thin silver band. She looked straight, gone scruffy.

With embarrassment, Arrowsmith found that she was returning his gaze.

"You going to Elixir, too?" he asked, realizing that the girl was probably half his age.

Grinning widely, she said, "Did you ever fly on amyl nitrite?"

"Excuse me?" Arrowsmith wondered if he had heard right. He decided to joke his way through it. "Is that a Middle Eastern airline?"

"Better than Quaaludes."

Arrowsmith edged nearer to the check-in counter. The girl followed him.

"I wouldn't know," he said lamely.

The girl thought for a moment and then smiled. "I used to hate flying," she said. "I was a stewardess with American Airlines, and every time the pilot talked about *'final* approach' and the *'terminal* building' I used to go shitless. All the words they use . . . they're just another way of saying, 'Prepare yourself for the big D.'"

Arrowsmith looked again at the girl. She was actually very pretty, in a used and abused kind of way. She had the hallucinogenic smile of a Hare Krishna freak. He tried a reassuring smile. "A lot of people are afraid of flying," he said.

"Especially people who fly a lot," she replied, still wearing the inane grin. "Do you know that the highest level of alcoholism in any profession is among airline pilots?"

"Is that so?" said Arrowsmith, trying to sound as though he believed her.

"You know why? Because they know that the fucking planes they fly aren't safe."

Together they edged nearer the check-in counter again.

Arrowsmith tried again. "Come on, now, planes these days are very safe," he said.

She looked at him knowingly, and then she gave him a long, sly wink. "Okay," she said, "if that's what you want to believe, but don't say I didn't warn you."

Still grinning happily, she turned to the couple in line behind her and extended the conversation to include them.

Arrowsmith lifted his bags on to the weigh-in scales. Club Village certainly had to be complimented in sorting out the kooks from the crowd, he thought.

Cassandra barely slept at all during that first night in Elixir. Her glimpse of the smirking reptile face at her window had banished the possibility. Surprisingly, no one heard her scream, so no one rushed to her aid.

Her first thought was to summon help by telephone, until she remembered that Club Village did not provide telephones in the rooms. So instead she armed herself with a heavy glass ashtray, turned on all the lights in the room, and then, huddling under the sheets, waited for the security that morning light would bring.

From time to time she heard the whispers and footsteps of late-night revelers as they made their way back to their rooms, but she did not call out. As the hours passed she began to wonder whether the face had been merely a cruel joke. Perhaps Club Village encouraged the CVs to play Halloween pranks on newcomers.

But the cruel delight she had seen in the face told her that if it was a joke, it was very sick. Although she had seen the face for only a moment, she had recognized irrational malevolence there, a spiteful desire to frighten and hurt.

Morning came suddenly, without the grayness of warning with which she was familiar in Europe. There were few birds to sing a welcome in this isolated corner of the Caribbean. But the sun saturated everything in color, turning the hanging wisteria blossom which twined around her cabin window into delicate bunches of petaled mauve grapes. They gave her a reassuring welcome when she finally worked up the courage to raise the blind.

Feeling safe again, she ventured out and wandered alone through the village. Early morning in the Caribbean has its own delicately washed freshness, and in January, when the nights are cold, the new sun is crisp and cleansing. For the first time, Cassandra was fully able to appreciate the careful planning that had gone into the village. All the buildings, the sleeping blocks, the chief's bungalow, the infirmary, theater, and restaurant had been arranged in a semicircle on the top of a hill, so that no one need ever be more than a hundred yards from the pool and its adjacent bar and boutiques. Down one side of the hill lay the path which ran to the marina, while the track in the opposite direction led through a fifty-yard screen of pine forest to the beach. At this point the island could have been no more than a half a mile wide, half a mile separating the Caribbean from the Atlantic.

Once out of her room, Cassandra's confidence began to return. She still thought she ought to report the intruder, but not yet. She could hardly go hammering on the door of the chief of the village at six in the morning to tell him that six hours earlier she had been frightened out of her wits by a face at her window.

Leaving the village, with its white buildings and red tiled roofs, she picked a cautious way through the spongy, needle-covered, sparse pine forest, and headed down to the beach. It was, she thought, probably the most perfectly proportioned and unspoiled beach she had ever seen, a full mile of pink and white sand running in a huge arc into which the waters of the Atlantic washed.

She explored the beach for an hour, and returned to the village at seven o'clock to swim in the pool. If she did twenty lengths in the Olympic-size pool in London she would need to do at least forty here. She worked hard for thirty minutes, until the pool got too crowded. Then she headed back to her room to dry and change for breakfast.

"How are you today?" a quiet voice asked at her side as she turned to climb the steps to her room. It was Hamlet

Yablans, the white-faced, black-bloused comic with bad breath. Cassandra shuddered. The paleness of Hamlet's complexion and the thin-sliced lips were repulsive. She had seen him the previous evening at dinner, when he had moved from table to table with an empty box, asking in his high-pitched, feminine voice whether anybody had seen Yorick in his ghost's disguise. For some reason, Hamlet amused most of the guests, but he did not amuse Cassandra.

"I'm just fine, thank you," she said, and hurried on past him. Hobgoblins in the night had been enough.

By the time the new guests arrived from New York at four in the afternoon, Cassandra had decided not to report the face at her window, not officially at any rate. She was there as a working journalist, and she did not wish to draw attention to herself. The bright, sunny atmosphere of the day, the two sets of tennis she had played, and the charming, diffident manners of the boy Sacha, with whom she had played a round of chess before lunch (he won), all persuaded her that the events of the previous night had been some kind of joke. She resolved to push the encounter to the back of her mind until she could have a quiet word with Hardin.

The first busload of new guests to arrive from the airport contained the Arrowsmiths, the Roegs, the piebald girl, and about another twenty self-conscious New Yorkers. From behind a long cool glass of Planter's Punch, Cassandra watched herself appraise the new arrivals, much as she had been appraised just a day earlier. Was it really only two days since she had left London? she asked herself. All that seemed so far away.

Although guests were expected to carry their own suitcases, Cassandra could not help noticing that some of the prettier girls already seemed to have made friends with some of the male CVs, who were clambering over each other in their enthusiasm to help the newcomers to their rooms. They were, Cassandra recognized, the same bunch of beautiful layabouts who had serenaded Hardin at the airport the previous morning. On consideration, she reached the conclusion that meeting the prettiest guests off the planes, and hopefully cementing instant relationships with them, had to be one of the more delightful perks of the job. And wickedly she wondered for a second whether the infirmary would have sufficient supplies of penicillin to cope with an epidemic of lovers' infections.

"May I join you?" Cassandra had not seen Hardin approach the pool. He was wearing a pair of Club Village white swimming shorts and a pale blue T-shirt with the red mermaid motif.

Cassandra pulled her sunglasses and towels from an adjacent chair and smiled a welcome. "How's your day been?" she asked.

"Busy." He shook his head. "Sometimes I don't think anyone works around here. There's a carefree attitude that bothers me."

For a moment Cassandra debated telling him about the previous night. The sensible side of her won, and she quickly recounted the details, with a suggestion that it might not be the best game to be played on nervous, single women.

Hardin listened in astonished silence. "If that was a game," he said, "it's a game that no one on the senior staff knows anything about. We don't go in for anything like that. And we certainly don't try to frighten the women." Then, very carefully, he made her recall in as much detail as possible everything she could remember about the encounter.

"I only wish to God I'd known about this last night," he said.

"You don't think it was a hoax?" asked Cassandra, once again feeling chilled.

Hardin smiled reassuringly. "Probably," he said, "but those kind of hoaxes can backfire, and we don't need them here. Don't worry about it. I'll scout around and box a few ears."

Cassandra was not impressed with his lighthearted denials. The incident had obviously worried him.

"Someone at dinner last night was telling me that you came out to replace a chief who was killed," she said.

"He drowned," said Hardin, rather too quickly.

Cassandra said nothing.

Hardin was quiet for a moment. Then he changed the subject. "Will you be entering the tennis tournament, or the pareo-tying competition, or the ladies' volleyball championship, or . . . ?"

Cassandra laughed and shook her head. "I'm not really very competitive, not in sport, anyway."

"This must be a strange place to come on vacation," retorted Hardin. "Club Village is all about enjoying competition."

"I enjoy being a spectator to competition," returned Cassandra. "Right now I'm enjoying watching the competition among the CVs to get off with the best-looking new arrivals. Aren't you afraid you'll miss your place in the queue, or does the chief of the village practice a kind of *droit du seigneur?*"

Without her intending it, Cassandra's manner had again become brusque. This time Hardin didn't wait to be insulted.

"I suppose you could say something like that," he said, and, getting up, he made an excuse about having to talk to the chef before dinner. He wandered away toward a group of young women, recent arrivals who were trying out the pool.

Cassandra watched him, angry with herself, and a murmur of jealousy ran through her as she noticed how easily he joked with the girls. All were younger and prettier than she was.

There was something about Hardin that always brought out her sharp rebukes and silly, rude replies. "You know your trouble, Cassandra Mallinson," she told herself. "Your trouble is that you are attracted to him and are afraid to show it, in case you make yourself look silly." That *was* her trouble, all right. It usually was.

It was after eleven when Matt Hillman slipped quietly away from the bar and made a reluctant way down to the marina. He was sorry to leave for two reasons. One was that he felt that the odds against the continuation of the business he and Willem Brummer had built up had increased drastically since the arrival of Hardin.

The other reason was personal. For the third time since he had been on Elixir, he had fallen in love, or at least into a state of infatuation. The object of his attentions was an elfin-looking boy from Quebec, an urchin of a fellow with gypsy looks. He was a rogue, Matt could see that instantly, but he found himself compelled to seek his presence, mesmerized by his capricious flirting with girls and boys alike. His name was Michel, and he had arrived that afternoon with a charter load of Canadians. As soon as Matt saw him he felt an awkward, gnawing, and yet exhilarating attraction.

Matt was not a handsome man. He was too tall and too thin, and the bones of his chest protruded like railings under his gaunt skin. But he made the best of himself. His deep tan disguised the acne on his shoulders, and he washed his long hair daily. He knew that Michel was playing with him, probably even mocking him behind his back, but somehow it had to be worthwhile. They had picked out each other at the bar with a series of looks and alternating displays of interest, and conversation had

flown freely and easily. Michel was everything Matt would
wish for himself: a pretty puppy dog of a boy who sparkled
with a teasing humor and possessed a lithe grace.

All evening long Matt had bathed in Michel's wit and
banter. Michel had quickly attracted a little posse of
admiring girls, and when it came time for Matt to keep his
rendezvous with Willem Brummer, Matt found himself
violently jealous of the girls who would have the gypsy's
sole attentions. Not for the first time did Matt Hillman
wish he had never become involved in his illegal trade.

Brummer was waiting for him in a small copse of fern
trees behind the marina restaurant. The marina lay on the
only part of the Elixir coastline which resembled anything
approaching a natural harbor, a small semicircle of high
coral cliffs which faced westward, toward the Caribbean.

"You're sure you weren't followed?" asked Brummer,
staring edgily back up the path toward the village. He was
chewing nervously on a matchstick.

Hillman shook his head, somewhat relieved to discover
that Brummer was more tense than usual. Perhaps they
would be able to avoid the meeting that night after all.

"We're taking the *Bayliner*," said Brummer. He toyed
with a set of keys in his hand. Since he was in charge of all
transport in the village, he had access to the keys of every
vehicle.

"You know . . . I'm really not sure anymore," Hillman
began to stammer.

Brummer spat his matchstick from his teeth. "You told
me. We've been through it all already, but you knew what
you were getting into when we started. All we have to do
is carry on delivering. They'll close us down before long
and we'll be out of it and a fucking sight richer."

"How can you be so sure they'll close us down before
the Coast Guard or the Bahamian police get to us?" asked
Hillman, although it was Hardin's face that swam in his
mind.

Brummer shrugged. "Listen, our friends out there in
Bogotá have a big investment in their little cruises around
the islands. We're only a small part of it. They don't want

us to get caught any more than we do. They'll stop our line well before it gets too dangerous. Right now all we have to do is keep our heads and do the job.''

Hillman shrugged his thin shoulders. He was still scared.

Satisfied that he had dealt with Hillman's little show of emotion, Brummer led the way down the dock. The *Bayliner* was lying in the deepest water at the end of the floating boardwalk. Stealthily, the two men clambered aboard. From the village came the music of the local reggae band. This was always a good time to go out, because the band covered the sound of the engine. As Brummer started the motor, Hillman quickly untied the rope and pushed the boat away from the jetty. A pale moon shone through the cumulus clouds, and a cold light fell on the marina. Carefully, the boat was steered away from the island and made its way out into the bay. All the time Hillman scanned the shoreline for any signs that they were being observed. But he saw nothing.

This was the eighth time the two men had borrowed a boat to make a pickup. When they had each become involved in Club Village two years earlier, a dope-smuggling connection had not been part of their plan. When they met, they had not liked each other, but they had both quickly realized that with their combined knowledge of boats and airplanes, and the street wisdom of men who knew how to get jobs done quickly and cheaply, they would make a formidable team.

Then, just as the Elixir village was nearing completion, along had come an offer. One day, when they were in Nassau together loading a cargo boat, they were approached by a suave gentleman of Latin appearance and invited for a drink. The man, who refused to give his name, suggested a business deal. Once every two months a trawler set off from Barranquilla on the northeastern coast of Colombia for a cruise among the islands. On its way it made numerous calls on friendly entrepreneurs. The task of the entrepreneurs was to ferry the cargo over to the States, where it would be recovered and distributed by a well-organized network of eager ancillaries. The rate for the job was 2 percent of the street price. In addition, said the businessman, there would be a nice little cache of goodies for home consumption. For Matt Hillman, that had settled the matter.

Willem Brummer had been less certain, and very carefully went over the details of the pickup and drop-off points with the stranger until Brummer was satisfied that the degree of risk was acceptable.

Neither Brummer nor Hillman had any idea how many other units were involved in the ferrying process, but by the size of the trawler they guessed it was considerable. In this way the shippers maximized their chances of success, and minimized the risk of losing the whole cargo to some exceptionally zealous narcotics agent.

Once the *Bayliner* was well clear of the harbor Brummer opened the throttle and set off in a southwesterly direction. Hillman took a quiet toot from the end of last month's supplies, and, feeling thus invigorated, went back to musing about his new friend Michel.

The rendezvous point selected for the pickup was thirteen miles north, northeast of Pink Cay, one of the most southerly of the Great Exuma Cays. It was so titled because it boasted hardly a blade of grass on its entire horseshoe-shaped mile length, and appeared to sailors as a pink mound floating on the surface of the water.

Brummer saw the trawler first, waiting, as ever, with only a couple of weak fishing lights to point it out. It was a long, low vessel, which might easily be mistaken for a legitimate fishing boat.

As the *Bayliner* neared the mother ship Hillman felt a grip of panic. The death of Pagett had frightened him. Was it possible that Pagett had fallen foul of the syndicate in some way? Nervously, he squeezed a pimple on his left shoulder, enjoying the moment of pain as it exploded into his T-shirt.

Neither man spoke as Brummer cut the engine and allowed the boat to drift alongside the ship. Suddenly a rope ladder was hurled down from the darkness of the deck above, together with a couple of mooring ropes. This was the way it always was. They had both learned not to expect conviviality from their business associates. Quickly, a figure clambered down the ladder and jumped onto the deck of the *Bayliner*. He was a dark, unshaven Colombian with a dirty sweatshirt and a two-thousand-dollar watch. They didn't even know his name, although they saw him every time they made a pickup.

"Okay?" the man asked, his eyes darting sharply around the deck of the *Bayliner*. Hillman glanced upward at the trawler. He knew they would have been watched ever since they came into sight.

"Ready when you are," said Brummer.

The Colombian took one last look around and then shouted something which might have been garbled Spanish or even an Indian dialect. Within seconds six five-pound bags of cocaine were lowered to the deck of the *Bayliner*. Last came a small plastic bag, which Hillman knew would be his own personal supply. He reached up and grabbed it, then gave himself a bit of pleasure.

Brummer watched him with disdain. Hillman's fondness for coke was the one major danger area in their whole venture. He would have preferred giving the whole consignment over to the distributors in Miami. As long as Hillman kept tooting up in the village, there was always the chance of someone finding out. Brummer even suspected that Hillman used his endless supply of coke as a way of currying favor with those he wished to impress. He had tried to dissuade the suppliers from giving Hillman his little monthly treat, but without success. The Colombians expected their runners to like dope, and in this way they were able to ensure that no one was tempted to pilfer from the main cargo.

Within a few minutes the loading was complete and the Colombian shinned quickly up the rope ladder, which was hauled up after him. Hillman unfastened the mooring ropes and he and Brummer sailed away.

"So far, so good," said Brummer, as he started the engine and pulled the *Bayliner* away from the trawler.

"The load is too big," said Hillman, viewing the cargo with consternation.

Brummer pulled a panatella out of his pocket and lit it. Now he was thoughtful. "Maybe you're right, fella," he said. "Maybe this should be our last trip."

"You're going to tell them?" Hillman saw danger lurking.

"Let me think about it. We'll get rid of this lot tomorrow when the meat shipment comes in. Then we'll figure a way of extricating ourselves and getting the hell out of here."

Hillman breathed a sigh of relief. Brummer was a much more positive person than he was, a natural leader. If Brummer was beginning to feel uneasy, then it sure as hell was time they began to think of their escape route.

A piebald junkie from New York was not Cassandra Mallinson's idea of the perfect roommate.

It had taken the piebald girl several hours of stumbling around the village before she had finally decided that B23 was her room. But it was not until late in the evening that Cassandra returned to her cabin and met the girl.

It was not a happy surprise. When Cassandra had left the room at around six it had been neat and organized, with her clothes all tucked neatly into the shallow drawers and her dresses hanging smartly in the closet. But her first thought on opening her door was that she had entered the wrong room. She was about to apologize and leave when she noticed that the strange girl with the two-tone hair was wearing a suit that looked suspiciously like one of hers.

"Excuse me," Cassandra said.

The girl was standing in front of the single six-foot mirror, her fingers across her eyes, peeping at herself in a gesture which was both self-adulatory and coy, as though she were watching another person in the mirror. Spread around her were all of Cassandra's dresses, bikinis, slips, and shoes.

Cassandra stepped into the room. "What the hell are you doing in my clothes?" she shouted.

The girl's beatific expression never left her eyes as she slowly panned to face Cassandra. "Hi," she said. "I'm Jane. You know," Jane continued, scooping up her hair at the nape of her neck so that the blond ends fell forward over her pretty, pale face, "you know, if you were about five inches smaller, you would have been the perfect roommate. Nothing you have fits me. But the style is wonderful. You have wonderful taste . . . er, I don't think you told me your name."

"Will you please take off my suit," said Cassandra, beginning to clear up her clothes. There was something casually friendly, almost warm, about this lunatic of a girl, and Cassandra could feel her temper subsiding into bewilderment even as she stood there.

"Sure. It's really very pretty, you know. Are you English?"

"Yes," said Cassandra.

"And your name?"

"Cassandra."

"Great. You know, I can tell we're gonna be great friends. I just have that feeling that we were put together for a purpose. I think it was fate. Pity you're so tall, though."

"Yes," Cassandra said.

"My sister was tall like you, but they had to remove her gallstones."

"What?" Cassandra couldn't follow.

"It left a great long scar right down her middle . . . she can't ever wear a bikini now," the piebald girl rambled. "She's still tall, though. She looks great in a one-piece. Black's her favorite color, scooped away at the thighs, right up to the hips. You have a suit like that . . . me, I always wear bikinis."

Cassandra picked up her one-piece blue bathing suit from the floor and shoved it into the drawer. She hated to think of this strange girl trying it on and she resolved to wash it first thing in the morning. Picking up three pairs of her shoes, she pushed them into the closet.

"If there's anything of mine you'd like to try . . ." Jane was smiling at her.

"No, thank you," said Cassandra haughtily.

Jane smiled. "Don't blame you," she said, and then, without warning, she suddenly stepped out of the suit she had been wearing and handed the clothes back to Cassandra to put away. She was naked now, her body small and round, her breasts disproportionately large.

Cassandra looked away in embarrassment. There was something disturbingly intimate about this small room and the presence of a strange naked girl.

Jane didn't notice Cassandra's awkwardness. Still naked she sat down on the edge of her bed and searched through a pair of jeans for a stick of chewing gum. "You know," Jane said casually and with disarming friendliness, "when I was told I'd have to share a room here with another woman, I almost canceled my reservation. I mean, I've always liked men for roommates. This is a new experience."

Cassandra was about to come back with some tart reply, but she was beaten to it by Jane's candor.

"I think I'm going to like it. I know I'm going to like you," said Jane, and, climbing over her bed, slipped between the sheets, leaving Cassandra to do all the tidying up. "Do you think you're going to like me?"

Cassandra stared at the strange little piebald head which lay, like a chipmunk, on the pillow. "I'm sure we're going to get along famously," she said wearily, but whether Jane recognized the sarcasm she had no way of knowing, because by this time the blue-coated eyelids had closed and the pale little face was expressionless.

Tomorrow, Cassandra thought, I'll go and see Hardin and demand a single room. Fifteen days of this and I'll be begging to be taken out of this Technicolor concentration camp.

_____ TWENTY-EIGHT

Trouble for Willem Brummer and Matt Hillman began almost immediately. In the early hours of Sunday morning they slipped the *Bayliner* back into the marina unobserved and, before dawn, installed some of their bags of cocaine in the false bottom of a refrigerated metal box used to transport meat from Florida. The system had worked before, but both men were now unnerved by the very size of the load they were being asked to ship. It was possible to hide ten or twenty pounds, but thirty pounds was too much, and there was only one container in which it could be concealed. When they had finished there were still two bags left over.

"We'll have to find some place to store this, and make another run later in the month," said Brummer, now staring anxiously at the plastic covers that protected the heavy white sacks.

"We should have told them it was too much," said Hillman, cursing himself.

"Too late now," said Brummer.

Hillman delved into his personal supply, and, with the aid of a crisp bill, tooted up.

Brummer watched him scornfully. "I hope to God you're going to keep that stuff well hidden," he said.

Hillman sniffed, and then rubbed his nose, which was numb. He wanted to giggle at Brummer's steadfast, old-fashioned attitude. "What about hiding the rest of it?" he asked.

Brummer frowned. The trouble with Club Village was that everything was so open.

"The best place is the library," said Hillman. "No one ever goes in there . . . under one of those big cupboards where they keep the books no one ever reads."

Since this was actually the first bright idea Hillman had ever had, Brummer was almost congratulatory.

"Not bad, little fairy, not bad," he said.

Hillman winced. He did not like being reminded of his homosexuality. "Let's go take a look," he spat. "One bag each."

Brummer grinned to himself. He enjoyed getting a rise out of Hillman. It disguised his own fears and reestablished his command over the younger man.

One at a time, they slipped out of the kitchen warehouse and crossed to the wooden, boxlike building. Carefully, Brummer opened the screen door to the library. Hillman followed.

By the light of the new day they stared at the rows of French and English paperbacks, books bought at foreign airports and left behind by readers who did not wish to add to their luggage.

"There's a whole lot of wasted effort here," said Hillman, surveying the banks of pulp literature. He was not a reader, and could never understand the obsession that forced some people to write and others to read.

Brummer grunted and began examining the shelves and floorboards. After a few moments he felt a floorboard creak just below an electric plug. It had obviously been lifted at some time in the recent past when rewiring had been necessary, and was never screwed down again. Taking a penknife from his pocket, he prised a two-foot length of board upward. Carefully Brummer dropped his bag into the hole and pushed the bag under the floor. Hillman waited for him to step aside, and then dropped his bag into the hole. Together they replaced the plank.

"I'll go to Miami on the Tuesday flight and explain what's happened," said Brummer. "We'll be able to get it out next week sometime."

Hillman nodded. "And then?" he asked.

"And then I think we should take our winnings and get the fuck off this island before that bastard Hardin starts asking too many questions."

Hillman nodded and made for the door. For the moment, danger was past. His mind was now back on the young gypsy-looking boy, Michel. Hillman was wondering whether he had scored with one of the young girls, and a pang of jealousy and hate lanced him. He had to think of some way of getting Michel's affection.

John Arrowsmith woke at seven o'clock on Sunday morning, with a hangover, a laser beam of a headache, and a decidedly delicate stomach. Disorientation befuddled him. No sounds came from the bathroom, so, pulling himself clear of the bed, he stumbled toward Alka-Seltzer and a shower.

He couldn't imagine where Ruth was so early in the morning. The previous night she had complained of tiredness after dinner and she and Joanna had retired early, leaving Arrowsmith and Roeg sitting at the outside bar watching the dancers, drinking, and listening to the reggae band. Despite himself, Arrowsmith was beginning to see how this summer camp for grown-ups could actually be enjoyable. In New York he felt like forty going on fifty, a middle-aged lawyer, but here in the Bahamas he suddenly had the enthusiasm of a twenty-five-year-old.

Stepping out of the shower, he slipped into his jeans and sweatshirt just as Ruth came panting in through the cabin door. She was wearing her white Adidas track suit and had a white band around her dark hair. She was, he had to admit, still a very handsome woman.

"Where've you been?" he asked as she flopped down on the bed.

"Running along the beach. It's beautiful at this time. You should try it, John."

"Maybe tomorrow. I had a skinful last night. Did Joanna go with you?"

Ruth nodded.

"I was just about to go down to breakfast . . . I'll wait while you shower," he said.

"No. That's okay. You go ahead. I'll come on later."

"No, I don't mind," he insisted. "I'll just sit here and read the Club Village rules and regulations again."

"I might be half an hour."

"So I'll read them twice."

Slowly Ruth stretched and sat up. "What I'm trying to say, John, is that I want you to go to breakfast now. And I want to go later. Do you understand? I don't think we should be each other's watchdogs in a place like this. I think we both should have our own space while we're here. Do you understand? I don't want to be an imposition on you, and I don't want to have to feel responsible for you every hour of the day. That's the only way a vacation like this can work. You do your thing, and I'll do mine, and I think we'll probably both enjoy ourselves a lot more if we don't hang around each other the whole time."

Arrowsmith sat down suddenly. This most certainly did not sound like his Ruth. "You mean you want us to behave like a couple of geriatric singles?" he asked.

"Don't be silly. Joanna and I were talking about it last night, and we decided that there was nothing as boring as married couples hanging onto each other all through a vacation. You want to get to know more people, new people, and so do I. Every vacation we've ever had we've spent the whole time with each other or with the children. Now let's do something different."

Arrowsmith was already agreeing with her. There were all kinds of people here he would like to get to know—the piebald girl, the boutique queen called Florinda. A man could have a wonderful time just flirting. All the same, he was surprised to have this thrown at him on his first day on vacation. "Why didn't you tell me all this before we got out here?" he asked.

"It didn't really hit me until last night, if you want to know," she said. "I think we probably miss a lot in life when we stick so close together."

Arrowsmith pulled himself to his feet. By now Ruth had begun to do her exercises, pulling her legs back over her head and then releasing them again. She was determined to grow old as slowly and gracefully as possible. "Okay, it's a deal," he said. "See you later . . . maybe."

"See you later, for sure," said Ruth and gave him a wide grin.

Arrowsmith grinned back. Years of reading his wife's smiles told him that before the day was out, he was going to be rewarded for being so understanding. But instantly he was saddened again. Fifteen years earlier he would not have considered it a reward.

_____ *THIRTY*

A trough of low pressure centered just south of Miami
swung the winds around to the west that Sunday afternoon, and the newcomers to Elixir found themselves
sunbathing on a beach whipped by brisk winds and flying
spray. The Bahamas look even more beautiful in a wind,
palm trees bowing gracefully and whitecaps chasing the
waves to shore, the sand on the beach gathering in white
drifts.

Joanna Roeg and Ruth Arrowsmith sunbathed together
by the pool. At first Ruth had refused to take off her bra,
but after most of the other women went topless she joined
them. Joanna, of course, had been topless and bottomless
since breakfast.

John Arrowsmith and Michael Roeg were amusing
themselves in quite different ways. Roeg was hanging
around the bar, chatting to anyone who would listen, and
leaning over for a quick, furtive grope whenever the
opportunity presented itself. Arrowsmith had joined the
New York soccer team and was training under the guid-
ance of an instructor from Yonkers. Ever since Pele had
gone to New York, Arrowsmith had fancied himself as
something of a soccer player and had become an enthusiastic Cosmos supporter. But the reality of ball control,
trapping, and tackling was giving difficulty to his forty-
year-old limbs.

Hardin's first Sunday as head of Elixir was spent rein-
forcing the hard line he had already begun. He was

everywhere, watching everyone, rebuking CVs he thought had not taken his warnings seriously enough, prowling the kitchens for signs of dirt or waste, demanding that CV quarters be tidied up, viewing the boats in the marina with the stern eyes of an admiral, and arranging the entertainments and games departments. He was, it seemed to the CVs, in five places at the same time, snooping into their work and homes. The lazy good-timers hated him, but the old Club Village employees and the enthusiastic young workers were grateful.

Hardin made discreet inquiries regarding the face Cassandra had seen at her window, but he learned nothing.

"She must have imagined it," Sharon Kennedy said unhelpfully, and others expressed similar opinions.

But Hardin did not believe that Cassandra Mallinson was the sort of girl to imagine things. In the back of his mind the death of Pagett and the reptile face were linked somehow, but he had no idea how to find that link. He gave CVs lectures on protecting guests from mishaps, but nobody betrayed any sign of guilt.

Cassandra had been determined to ask for a change of roommate, but there was something oddly appealing about Piebald Jane. She was so obviously dizzy, and subject only to her own whims. She was a silly, self-indulgent, thoughtless girl, but totally without rancor or guile. Cassandra's life, on the other hand, was complex and organized, and her career ruled everything. The butterfly flights that Jane took fascinated Cassandra.

"Did you know I was born again two years ago?" Jane asked Cassandra as the English girl was dressing.

"I didn't even know you'd died two years ago," said Cassandra tartly.

Jane snickered at the comment. "Oh yes, my soul was dead, and then I was born again during a stopover in Phoenix, Arizona."

Cassandra brushed her hair. "So what happened?" she asked.

"What always happens happens. I met a good-looking guy in the airport Holiday Inn in Denver who sold IBM self-correcting typewriters, and I couldn't wait to get unborn again as quickly as possible." She paused thoughtfully for a minute, then added, "Wonder Woman is born again. Lynda Carter. Did you have that show in England? She was born again, but her legs still didn't meet at the top."

Finally Cassandra had to laugh. "You mean you had an affair in a Holiday Inn, and you felt you'd fallen from grace. Is that so bad?"

"Well . . ." By now Piebald Jane was wandering around the room in a pair of Snoopy pajamas, picking up items of clothing and then dropping them again, and causing complete chaos wherever she turned. "Well, it wouldn't have been so bad if I hadn't enjoyed it so much. I think affairs are okay if they're no fun. Then the Good Lord doesn't mind too much. But this guy was just too delicious. He was called Wayne . . . no, I think it was Wade. Anyway, he was hung like a goddamn stallion."

"How terribly uncomfortable for him," said Cassandra, and began to laugh. Now that Piebald Jane wasn't stoned, she made eccentrically convivial company. So, despite her earlier misgivings, Cassandra found herself spending the day with her extraordinary roommate.

Piebald Jane loved the way Cassandra swam and the way she spoke, her tall, slim figure, and her apparent wealth of confidence. Cassandra had poise and education. Cassandra had always worked, even during her university days. When Jane had been short of funds she had ripped off an entire wardrobe from Bloomingdale's, which, she assured Cassandra with some pride, took more than a little skill.

As the two of them were about to go in for lunch at twelve-thirty, a plane swooped low over the beach.

"The pilot's trying to see how many of us are nude," said Jane, pulling a T-shirt over her breasts, which were now becoming sunburned.

"Big thrill for him," said Cassandra.

"You know what men are like," said Jane. "They only do it to amuse each other. If they couldn't talk to their friends about it I don't think most men would ever even get around to doing it. Up there in that plane now, all the crew will be telling each other what they think they saw. Little boys, that's all they are . . . apart from the big ones."

"What are the big ones like?" asked Cassandra.

Piebald Jane grinned. "Something like that big chief of the village who can't take his eyes off you," she said. "God knows what he's hung like."

Cassandra laughed. "And I suspect only God cares, too."

Piebald Jane shrugged. "To know him is to love him."

"What?"

"The Teddy Bears sang it. It was the first record I ever stole," said Piebald Jane with what sounded like a touching honesty.

The airplane which Piebald Jane had imagined to be a talent spotter was, in fact, the weekly meat plane, flying in from Miami with its refrigerated cargo. Because Elixir was a new village, with only limited refrigerated space, warehouses in Florida had to be used.

As always, Hillman and Brummer were at the airstrip to meet the consignment. They had brought the empty containers and a couple of trailers.

Around the small white building that served as a control tower and air terminal, a group of local Bahamians dressed in their Sunday finery waited for the next passenger plane. The two men sat and waited as the yellow-and-white DC-3 of Trans Island Airways taxied down the single runway toward them.

"Everything all right?" A voice behind them on the runway made them both start. It was Hardin.

Brummer recovered first. "Everything's normal," he said.

Hillman's eyes flickered nervously toward the first container on the second trailer. Did Hardin know something? At that moment a police car drew up at the control tower. This was not unusual, since one of the two policemen on the island tried to make it a habit to meet all incoming planes. Hillman was unnerved nonetheless.

The airplane taxied to a halt. The engines were turned off. Behind them, a forklift truck began to rev up, ready to lift the full containers off the plane.

Hillman stared straight ahead, unable to face Hardin's unblinking, scrutinizing stare. Then, without another word, Hardin began to walk across to the pilot and copilot, who were coming down the plane steps.

"What the fuck does he want?" Hillman hissed.

"Keep calm. He's just nosing around. He doesn't know anything."

"Pagett never came down here on a Sunday morning."

"Pagett never got up on a Sunday morning."

Silently the two men watched Hardin cross to the pilot, introduce himself, and shake hands. At the terminal building the police car had stationed itself right along the large wooden signpost that announced the Bahamian laws against illegal drugs.

"I swear to God if we get through this one I'll never do another run," Hillman was mumbling to himself.

Brummer stared straight ahead.

Quickly, the forklift truck drew up a couple of trailers by the freight doors of the plane.

"Come on, we'd better give a hand," said Brummer.

Silently, Hillman put the car into gear and drove carefully around to the far side of the plane, opposite to where Hardin was standing.

Hardin watched them go with a sense of unease. According to Pagett's reports these men were the best operators in the islands, but Hardin found them hostile and boorish. Putting them out of his mind, he turned back to the pilot.

"Saw you swooping down over the beach, so I thought I'd come down and say hello," he said.

The pilot, a young bearded man with flowing brown hair who looked like a refugee from Woodstock, smiled at Hardin. "We were just doing a tit count. Hope we didn't disturb anyone. You know, you get better women in Club Village than anywhere else in the islands."

Hardin nodded. "The trouble is that most of them know it," he said. "Listen, next time, instead of scaring the natives half to death with the Waldo Pepper act, why don't you stay over for a while and have a closer look at what

Club Village has to offer? Be my guest. You never know, you might even get lucky."

"Okay . . . that's a nice offer! We'll do that next week. Today's one of those busy ones. Thanks a lot."

"I'll look forward to seeing you," said Hardin. It hardly hurt to extend himself a little to a couple of pilots, and it was always useful to cultivate friends.

Brummer and Hillman watched as Hardin made his way across to the police car, chatted with the police driver, and then climbed in beside him.

"What *is* that guy up to?" said Hillman again, his hands resting nervously on the container containing the coke which the unknowing pilots were about to fly to the States for them.

"Maybe he's just getting acquainted," sighed Brummer.

That was the truth, but neither of them could believe it.

Michel, the gypsy-looking boy, attracted everyone who was young and beautiful and quite a few who were neither. He held court frequently in the evening, by the bar, and he was an immediate Club Village personality. He even brought his guitar and sang from time to time. Dozens of listeners longed to devour him. His voice was plaintive and sad, not unlike Jim Croce's, whose songs he sang.

Ruth and Joanna watched the engaging boy from the periphery of the crowd. Sharon Kennedy, who had so lately been mourning the death of Dick Pagett, leaned against an upright roof support and felt romantic. Cassandra and Piebald Jane lounged at the bar and pretended indifference while each admired the animal allure of the boy.

Among the CVs Michel was both lionized and hated. Florinda and Chloe watched admiringly, and for the first time in months the beautiful Sacha appeared to have real competition. He accepted this with his usual equanimity. Hamlet Yablans hated Michel because he stole attention from him and his act. Chief of Sports Homer Wolford liked the songs, but thought the singer might be gay. Matt Hillman was simply in love.

"If I were a romantic I would say this looked something like paradise," said Michael Roeg.

"But you aren't a romantic, are you, Michael?" replied Arrowsmith.

Roeg chuckled. "Shit, did you see the ass on that girl in

the boutique? I'd give all my credit cards for a night with her."

Arrowsmith had in fact noticed the mouth-watering physical attributes of Florinda. It was impossible not to, since she spent most of every day wearing a tiny clingy little bikini that seemed to display more of her body than any garment he had ever seen on any woman. And it was true, despite his skepticism about Roeg's finer nature, Elixir did look like paradise, or at least like the glossy brochure version of paradise which Club Village liked to promote. The sky was blood red and a warm glow fell across the whole pool and bar area, deepening tans and bathing everyone in rosiness. It was a rich, colorful scene of palm trees, shrubs ablaze with blossoms, and people made beautiful by happiness.

At eight-thirty Michel's audience reluctantly began to break up and head into the restaurant for dinner. By nine o'clock only Hillman and a couple of plain and desperate teenage girls were left behind. By now an affair of the eyes had been established between the beautiful gypsy boy and the gaunt man from New York. Eventually, even the teenagers realized with some confusion that their presence was superfluous. The area was deserted except for Michel and Hillman.

"You trying to tell me something?" said Michel as he put his guitar back into its case.

Hillman felt the inevitable excitement and embarrassment. "I like the songs," he said at last, in barely more than a whisper.

Michel smiled, his eyebrows raised in a kind of defiant contempt. Hillman felt himself growing red with embarrassment. He couldn't think what to say.

Finally Michel put him out of his misery. "Where do you want to go?"

Hillman had not reckoned on instant success. "I don't know . . ." he stammered, thinking wildly.

"You don't know?" mocked Michel. "Well, if you don't know, I'm sure I don't."

"The beach . . . we could go to the beach. "There's a place down there . . . a changing room . . . you know?"

"Yes. I know," said Michel, the mockery unchanged.

They moved away into the shadows and headed toward the beach hut.

"Where do you score in this place?" asked Michel about half an hour later as the two men trudged back through the sands and into the pine grove.

"Score?" asked Hillman, though he understood exactly.

"You know . . . dope . . . maybe a toot here and there."

Hillman swallowed hard. "The new chief of the village is an antidope freak. If any of the staff get caught with anything, we're out."

"So I hear," said Michel, as though he hadn't heard at all. "That doesn't answer my question. Where do you score in this place?"

"I don't really know," said Hillman.

Michel looked at him disbelievingly. "Come on. You had a good time, didn't you?"

Hillman nodded yes.

"So?"

There was a long silence. They had stopped walking. "So, maybe I could find you a little snow," said Hillman.

"Tonight?" asked Michel. "I'd like a little toot tonight."

Hillman began to unfasten his belt. To share his personal supply with someone as desirable as Michel was no hardship. Hillman opened the concealed compartments on the underside of the belt.

Michel looked inside, then whistled softly. "I can see I found the right man," he said.

Hillman didn't reply.

Michel took the belt from Hillman and strapped it to his own waist. "Tell you what, Matt. You keep the supply coming, and you and me are gonna have a real good time together. You know what I mean?"

Hillman nodded silently. He understood exactly what

Michel meant. But Hillman was in love. What could he do?

There was no way he could tell Brummer. Brummer would never understand. Hillman would have to play this game by himself and hope to God he could get out before he was discovered. Standing there gazing at Michel, the wrath of his Colombian employers seemed very far away.

Piebald Jane liked to think she had a talent for uncovering dope, and since she had grown accustomed to quantities of confections, this was particularly fortunate.

Quite obviously, her roommate, Cassandra, was going to be no use in that regard, but several of the CVs, including Hector, the disgraced picnic organizer, looked promising. She approached Hector first.

"Sorry, honey," he said, while his fingers lewdly traced the outline of her spine down to her bottom. "I'm out. This place is so isolated that getting supplies is pretty difficult. Now, if it's a screw you're looking for . . ."

Piebald Jane pushed his hand away. She certainly didn't need this gorilla. She had heard about Hardin's antidope lecture, and she decided that all the employees were keeping a low profile.

Michel, on the other hand, looked promising. She had come across half a dozen men in her life like Michel; men of uncertain sexual proclivities who used their wits and charm to whatever advantage they desired. His face was pretty and his body beautiful, but somewhere in his eyes was the shadow of dissipation, the hardness of the opportunist, the wilderness of the loner.

His loneliness held the key. At a glance she could see that his sexuality was of the consenting nature. He could be straight or gay depending on what the moment called for, but Jane was pretty certain that neither choice held any real attraction for him. He used sex.

161

Jane understood him. She talked to him, spent long hours with him by the pool, on the beach, and in the shade of the thatch-roofed sun shades. She listened while he bragged of his exploits. She never once suggested that her body was for bargaining.

And because she held off in this way, Michel opened up to her as he did to nobody else. For once, he had found someone who did not wish to exploit him, who listened to him, who made him feel good, and he was flattered. She didn't believe more than a tenth of what he told her, and he guessed that, but it didn't matter. He told her that his family were Romanies who had roamed Europe before settling in Montreal, and then that his grandmother had been a full-blooded Mohawk. He weaved stories of deprivation and sumptuous wealth, hardly seeming to realize that his every word contradicted another.

He was rootless, lonely, and greedy for an affection he was incapable of giving and did not deserve from others. But he sang like a dream. Although he preferred bittersweet, lonely songs, he could just as easily ape Gordon Lightfoot or David Gates or Billy Joel. And when he sang the Paul McCartney line "don't go chasing polar bears," Piebald Jane felt a shiver of regret that such talent was wasted on a man as shallow and cruelly promiscuous as Michel.

His sexuality was cold and his eyes were mirrors, reflecting exactly the emotions with which they were faced. The rank desire of the Club Village groupies saw a lascivious carnality in Michel. Matt Hillman recognized his own needs. But Jane saw just the loneliness of a beautiful boy who was too dumb to use his attributes for more than instant gratification.

But then, that was all Jane had ever done, too.

Michel liked her. And when she hit on him for a toot he could hardly help but say, "I know there's a shortage in this place, but there's no shortage where that came from."

Piebald Jane smiled, snorted, and then took a little supply for next time. Back in her cabin she offered Cassandra some.

"Absolutely not."

"Why absolutely not?" asked Jane, bemused, trying to recall the last time anyone had refused coke.

"I am here to fill my lungs full of good clean Caribbean air instead of London murk. The last thing I want is to sneeze, like Woody Allen in *Annie Hall*. Where did you get it? I thought they were running an antidope campaign in this place."

Piebald Jane smiled. "You know Michel, the singer? He's plugged himself into a main supplier here. Useful to know these people, you know. I brought only Quaaludes and blues and amyl with me."

Cassandra mused. Tales of orgies and drugs would make wonderful magazine reading, but it would hardly do Hardin any good. Not for the first time in her life, she felt the divided loyalties that faced all good reporters. She put her head down on her pillow, turned off her bedside light, and determined not to start writing her story until the middle of her second week in the village. By then her attraction for Hardin probably would have faded, she assured herself.

_____*PART IV*

It snowed heavily in Paris during the last week in January, bringing that familiar muffled silence to the city, throwing the Métro into chaos, closing down the airports for a time, and even restricting Quatre Bras. He detested snow because it interfered with business. Snow was for the mountains; the city was for work. The fortunes of Club Village were at a critical stage, and the last thing he wanted was interference.

At eight-thirty on the Monday of the blizzard Girardot called, prompt as usual, though six inches of snow covered the city.

Quatre Bras was in his office reading the Telexes from the previous night as Girardot entered.

"Sit down," said Quatre Bras without looking up.

Quatre Bras stared at the Telexes. There were fourteen, ranging in subject from a flu epidemic in Kenya to a suspected shark killing in the Bay of Islands in the far north of New Zealand. Quatre Bras flicked through them. At the moment he had time only for the American zone. The most important message had, therefore, come directly from Elixir and Hardin.

"Our friend Hardin says he has no immediate problems other than a group of lazy CVs," Quatre Bras told Girardot while the latter sipped a cup of coffee. "He says there is absolutely no news on the death of Pagett, but he would be surprised if it turned out to be a complete accident. He wants the London bureau to make discreet

167

inquiries about a woman called Cassandra Mallinson. He thinks she is probably a journalist trying to uncover a dirty story."

"We've nothing to be ashamed of," said Girardot indignantly.

"We may not have, my friend, but someone down there in the islands certainly has." He looked back at the Telex. "He also wants information on the comic there, someone called Hamlet Yablans. With a name like that he certainly needs investigating."

Girardot had been uncertain when Quatre Bras decided to send Hardin to Elixir. There were more experienced people in Club Village, and the rumors about Hardin's romantic attachments, particularly the latest one with Beta Ullman, were constant sources of amusement to the secretaries and discomfort to the senior staff.

But Quatre Bras had refused to be dissuaded. He wanted someone who could act on his own, who was not owned body and soul by the club and would not be afraid to come up with unorthodox solutions.

Quatre Bras stared out at the falling snow. "Perhaps the weather in New York will be better," he said.

"New York?"

Quatre Bras nodded: "It's time for serious discussions. We'll go tomorrow."

"Concorde?" asked Girardot with some misgivings. He distrusted the superplane, convinced that sooner or later the great Anglo-French folly was certain to crash, and that the passengers would be immortalized in jokes, the way the band on the *Titanic* had become famous.

"Of course," said Quatre Bras. "Come on, don't be so suspicious, Corporal, remember how we began."

"We were young men then . . . boys," said Girardot. "And everything was fun. Nothing seems like fun anymore."

Quatre Bras looked sharply at Girardot. "Well, maybe not to you. But this trip to New York will be the biggest adventure of my life."

"But that's only business," retorted Girardot. "Rich

men sitting around a table smoking cigars and talking in numbers isn't *fun.*"

"But that's the real adventure," said Quatre Bras. "Don't you see? Only power can provide true adventure."

Girardot shook his head. "No, I don't see," he said. Club Village had become so big that it was too big for him to comprehend. Now, against all advice, Quatre Bras was going to make it even bigger.

It would be more fun, thought Girardot, if they went back to picking pockets.

Beta Ullman used the Paris blizzard as an excuse to keep Ernst Ronay in bed for an extra hour that morning. She needed to, for his peace of mind and for her future.

She awoke first at the small, bijou apartment Ronay provided for her in Rue Winterman, a small Left Bank street popular with students. For a while she enjoyed looking out at the city in snow. It reminded her of her childhood in Helsinki.

Ronay was just waking as she reentered the room, carrying the morning papers and a pot of coffee. He glanced at his watch, but she quickly covered it with her hand.

"It's late, I must be going," he insisted, running his free hand up her thigh and under her nightgown.

"There's been a blizzard. The radio says that Paris is in chaos, and if you look out the window you'll see that your car is buried under snow," she said, handing him a large cup of coffee and climbing in bed alongside him. "No one will be working in the Bourse until at least lunchtime."

"Quatre Bras will," said Ronay. "If Paris were covered by a ton of volcanic ash that old bastard would still be at the office, scheming."

"Do you love me, Ernst?" Beta asked after a moment.

Ronay hesitated, suspecting a trap. "What kind of a question is that?"

"A lover's question. I mean, I'd like to know if you're getting bored. People do get bored with each other."

For the first time that morning Ronay looked closely at her. "But of course I do, Beta. Would I be here if I didn't?"

"Probably," said Beta.

Ronay considered that for a moment before answering. "Yes, that is possible. But I do love you. It just happens that there's no way I can show you. If I weren't married . . ."

Beta stopped him. "I wasn't angling for a proposal. Marriage doesn't come into it. I just like to hear you tell me." And with that she began a slow ritual with her tongue and lips, starting high on his bronzed, stern forehead and working downward.

After they had finished making love, Ronay stared at the ceiling for several minutes. At last he spoke. "This man Hardin, the one Quatre Bras sent out to Elixir, I think you know him. Don't you?"

Beta kept her eyes closed. She decided it was best to be as honest as possible. "Yes, he was in Val d'Isabelle last week."

"And would you say he was a good *chef de village?*"

"Yes, I think so. He was very popular."

Ronay went quiet again, musing. His interest in Hardin was strictly business. "You know, Beta, I think you and I could do with a small vacation in the sun. What do you say?"

"I've only just come back from the mountains."

"Yes, but we should spend more time together. I'll make arrangements for us to go to Elixir next week."

"Elixir?" Beta heard alarm bells ring.

"Yes," smiled Ronay. "We can go see whether Quatre Bras is right or not about the American adventure."

Beta thought quickly. "I did have a job here next week," she said, which was true. She had been booked by David Bailey to do a fashion spread for the September edition of *Italian Vogue*.

"I'm sure you can cancel it."

Beta bit her lip. Bailey wasn't the sort of photographer that you canceled just like that, and Elixir was the last place in the world she wanted to go with Ronay. But if she didn't go it might make him suspicious. She made one last effort. "Does it have to be so soon?" she asked.

"Of course, if you don't want to come . . ." Ronay was playing his hurt-little-man act, with just a hint of blackmail.

"No. I want to come. I'll get Olga to call Bailey and tell him I'm ill."

"Good girl." Ronay smiled, kissed her, and climbed out of bed. His elegant figure looked gaunt when naked. "And now I really must get out there and face that snow and see what mischief our chairman has been up to."

Beta watched him disappear into the bathroom. An awful lot could happen during a week in Elixir. She hoped nobody was going to regret anything.

It was never John Arrowsmith's intention to get Piebald Jane into bed, but at the same time it was not his intention to ignore such an opportunity should it occur. On Tuesday, one did occur.

That morning Ruth announced that she, Joanna, and Roeg were going on a boat trip to the outer cays. Since this would be a six-hour trip in the burning sun, Arrowsmith turned down her invitation to join them. He played tennis all morning, feeling younger and bolder with every winning shot. The idea that Ruth was going to be away for the whole day gave him an illusion of freedom.

At lunch he accidently-on-purpose found himself sitting next to Piebald Jane. She was now extremely tanned, and had come to lunch in the briefest of white crocheted bikinis.

"Having a good time?" he asked, as he had done on the five or six occasions he had bought her a drink.

"The best," she replied with a dimpled, sensuous smile.

"Where is your roommate today?" asked Arrowsmith. In the past couple of days he had seen Jane talking a great deal with a tall, snobby English girl.

"She went on the boat trip. She'll probably fry out there," said Jane.

"Oh. My wife went too," said Arrowsmith.

"That's nice," said Jane.

What she intended to be interpreted by that remark

Arrowsmith had no way of knowing, but it sounded friendly, perhaps even encouraging.

"Do you like my roommate?" Jane asked.

"I hardly know her," said Arrowsmith, which was true.

"But do you want to screw her?" asked Jane as she sawed a steak in half.

Arrowsmith's jaw sagged.

"Well, I think the chance would be a fine thing," he said weakly.

Jane thought about this for a couple of seconds and then carried on. "If you don't like them long and lanky, then, what about little and plump like me?" she said.

Arrowsmith felt the hairs at the back of his neck begin to rise. Was this a come-on? It was so long since he had been in a position to be propositioned that he couldn't be sure, and there was no way he was going to risk making a fool of himself.

"I think you're very . . . attractive," he said. "Would you like some strawberries?"

"Oh, yes . . . thank you." Jane had given up on the steak and was fiddling with the salad.

Arrowsmith hurried over to the fruit table and piled two dishes with strawberries. It seemed such a luxury to have strawberries in January. When he sat down again, Jane was in conversation with an unattractive Canadian CV on the far side of her. Arrowsmith watched, jealousy lancing him. Piebald Jane was such a wayward spirit. She had quite captured his imagination during the past few days. He put down the strawberries and began to eat slowly. At last Jane shook off the attentions of the CV and returned to him.

"That was very nice of you," she said. Slowly she picked up the largest of the strawberries between two deliciously painted fingers. "You know, something just occurred to me," she said. "Why do people always talk about losing their cherry? I would have thought a strawberry much more appropriate, wouldn't you?"

Arrowsmith stared at the strawberry. Indeed, now that

she mentioned it, he could see there was indeed a strong similarity between a strawberry and a pudendum.

"Yes, I see what you mean," he said, feeling once again the full force of her baby-blue-eyed gaze.

Then, suddenly dropping the fruit into her mouth, she abruptly changed the subject and began to talk about the fun she'd had as a kid picking fruit in California. The moment had gone, Arrowsmith thought.

But of course it hadn't. As they finished lunch and walked out toward the sun Arrowsmith said, "Well, what are your plans?"

"Long-term or short-term?" asked Piebald Jane.

"Whichever you want to tell me about," said Arrowsmith.

"Well, long-term I want to take a trip to Nepal before it gets invaded by the Russians or Chinese, and I also want to be a Playmate of the Month."

Arrowsmith smiled. "And short-term?" he asked.

"Short-term, I want to go back to your room with you for the rest of the afternoon and fool around."

It took several seconds for her remark to sink in.

"Of course, if you don't want to, I'll go lie by the pool and think about Robert Redford."

"I didn't say I didn't want to."

"You didn't say you did."

"I—was surprised. No one ever said that to me before."

"I'm surprised, too. A good-looking guy like you? You've been married to that sports freak for too long."

Defense of Ruth leaped to Arrowsmith's mind. But at the same time he didn't want to do anything to make the lady change her mind. In the end, he said nothing.

Piebald Jane took a deep breath. "Well, what is it gonna be?"

"We're in C34," he said. Do you want to follow me up?"

"Can't we go together?"

Arrowsmith looked around. Guilt was already pursuing him. "We'll go together," he said quietly, and began to walk along the concrete pathway toward C Block.

Without further conversation they reached C Block, and climbing the outside stairs made their way to the Arrowsmiths' room. By now Arrowsmith could feel his heart palpitations slamming into his ribs beneath his tennis shirt. With one last quick glance along the balcony to ascertain that he was not being observed, Arrowsmith opened the door. Jane slipped in ahead of him. Quickly he stepped inside and closing the door tried to draw the flimsy lock. It didn't work. But it hardly mattered. Ruth was away for the day. Ignoring it, he lowered the venetian blinds.

"Exactly the same," said Jane as she promptly sat down on Ruth's bed.

"What's the same?" said Arrowsmith, wishing that she had chosen his bed to sit on. It bothered him to think that his first act of adultery would be on his wife's bed.

"The room. Exactly like mine."

"Oh, yes."

There was a momentary pause while Jane unfastened her shoes and let them drop onto the floor. They clattered noisily, and Arrowsmith wondered if anyone on the floor below would hear them. He moved nearer to her. His tennis shorts were sticking to him. He realized that the air-conditioning unit wasn't working as effectively as it might and wondered whether he should try to fix it.

"You're nervous, aren't you?" said Jane, lying back and watching him.

"No," he lied, and leaning over her, he kissed her on the forehead. She made no move to react to the kiss so he pulled himself away and went into the bathroom.

In the yellow of the bathroom lights his reflection looked pale and wan. He examined himself in the mirror, then brushed his teeth and combed his hair so that the thinning patch at the front was partly disguised. Last he sprayed some Givenchy deodorant under his arms and with Givenchy *eau de toilette* on his hands ran his fingers through his hair again so that he might not have that coiffured look. He wanted to appear tousled and virile.

God, he mused to himself, he didn't even know how to get started anymore. What did he have to do? Did he just rip off all his clothes and say, "Here it is, baby, come and get it"? Did he start necking with her and gradually ease off her bra and pants? Was he supposed to go down on her before they made love? Was that the fashion these days?

Opening the bathroom door he went back into the bedroom.

Jane was now in bed, in Ruth's bed. As he entered the room, he saw her reach for her little beach bag and swallow something.

She noticed his expression. "Just a little cocktail," she said, indicating the bag. "Whatever you want, I've got. You want some amyl nitrite . . . coke, acid?"

"Acid?" He thought that had gone out of fashion.

"I'm a walking drugstore. What do you want?"

"What have you had?" he inquired.

"Oh, this and that."

"No, thanks anyway. I think I'll just stick to the wine I had at lunch."

"Okay."

There was another pause.

"Well?" Piebald Jane was looking at Arrowsmith with mystification.

"Yes," said Arrowsmith, and suddenly began to peel off his clothes, deliberately turning away from the bed so that his slightly paunchy, middle-aged stomach was hidden. He left his shorts till the very end, and then suddenly pulled them and his underpants down together and, swinging around, climbed into the bed.

"You know, you have a nice body," Jane said. "I don't know why you're so ashamed of it."

She made room for him under the sheets. Alongside him her body felt firm and smooth, and he began to feel an excitement he had almost forgotten.

"I'm not ashamed of my body," he said quietly, running his hand across her breasts and down across her stomach.

"But you're bashful. That's okay. I can't stand those *macho* guys who are covered with hair. I hate a hairy back."

"Me too," he said, stroking her back and running his hands under her bottom.

"I bet you have a whole lot of affairs, don't you, John?" she said.

He tried to attempt a shrug under the sheets. "Oh, you know, one or two, now and again . . ." he said, and slipping his hand between her thighs he began to kiss her. He could taste the wine she had drunk at lunch.

Suddenly she broke off the kiss. "You know, I've been trying to think of a way of getting you into bed since I saw you at the airport," she said.

"That's very nice. Why?"

"I like married men. I like the way they look at me," she said. "You were like a kid looking in a candy-store window. Single guys, guys who screw everything, they just assume that all they have to do is get me stoned and I'll go down on them right there. Married men treat a girl with respect."

Arrowsmith wished she wouldn't talk about married men at all. He didn't want to think about it. He also didn't want to talk. He started to kiss her again. She was cool and silky under the sheets, a very different feel from Ruth. He pushed his head into her hair, marveling at the line around her ears where the dark brown turned into creamy blond. Slowly she pushed him over onto his back and began to kiss his body, murmuring all the time about how nice his skin felt, how free from hair he was, and how clean he smelled. He thanked God for Givenchy. He was as excited as he had been in years, but Piebald Jane was an artiste of eroticism. Slowly she washed him with her mouth, alternately exciting him and then allowing him breathing space in which to control himself. If this is foreplay, who needs the tournament? he thought. By now they had both stopped talking and he was content simply to lie there, slightly drunk, and allow his body to be manipulated. She was like a little animal, he thought, nuzzling him all over, and he wondered how long it was since Ruth had shown so much joy in exploring his body.

Very gradually Arrowsmith's shyness began to dissolve

and, given new confidence by Jane's evident pleasure, he began to take control of the situation. Grasping Jane firmly by the shoulders he turned her over, in the same action drawing himself up to a kneeling position. Her body was slightly plumper than Ruth's, almost babyish in texture, and there were none of the hardened muscles which daily exercising had developed in his wife. For some reason Piebald Jane reminded him of some delicious form of confectionary, a peppermint candy bar, perhaps, and he set to work with his tongue, savouring the sweet tastes of her skin, wandering across the plains of her body, exploring skillfully its crevices.

As his tongue drew tactile patterns around her nipples, Jane tried to guide him into her, but he wanted her to wait, and, moving back down her body, he buried his mouth and tongue inside her, his arms spread-eagling her across the bed. Then slowly he twisted and pulled her over on top of him, so that he might hide beneath her, breathing in the sweet scent of her sex. At last Jane pulled away from his arms, and moving down the bed, she very delicately impaled herself upon him.

Now that he could see her face he noticed that her eyes were no longer open, and her expression had taken on that cherubic smile he had first noticed at the airport. He had been afraid that the excitement of the encounter, and the newness of the partner, would trigger him into making a fool of himself, but, as though sensing this and being determined to keep control of the situation, Jane seemed to be subconsciously pacing his levels of excitement. She was very quiet, almost as though she were asleep and seemed to be making love to him by touch alone. And when at last she decided to release him from the game which she had devised, her expression hardly altered as the spasm stretched within him and then abruptly released itself.

For a long time afterward he lay silently, half asleep. His body was glistening with sweat, but hers appeared as soft and dry as when they had begun. He knew he ought to be feeling guilt, but he did not. In fact, it was all something of a sublime relief. Perhaps this is how the reluctant virgin felt upon being deflowered, he thought—merely grateful that it is all over. He felt comfortable and sleepy. He dozed for a while, but he knew he dared not sleep.

"Are you sleeping?" he turned on to his side toward Jane. Her piebald hair was cascading across the pillow. For the first time he noticed the lace hem of Ruth's nightdress poking out from under the pillow. He wished now he had had the nerve to insist they make love in the other bed. It seemed so deceitful. He would swap the sheets before Ruth got back, he promised himself.

"Are you asleep?" he asked again.

Piebald Jane didn't answer.

He smiled to himself. Lying there, asleep, she looked very young and he was again flattered that she had chosen him.

He shook her gently. "Come on. You can't sleep here."

Still there was no response. Arrowsmith began to feel a chill of alarm.

"Come on now, Jane, wake up. It's getting late." He shook her again, more violently this time. But she still did not respond.

He rested on one arm and deliberately forced himself to think rationally. Another shake, then a yet more violent one. "For God's sake . . . wake up . . . come on . . ." he began slapping her cheek. Then suddenly he stopped. What if she were ill and they found her face covered with bruises? It would look like assault.

He searched across her body for her heartbeat. Now all the delights of her baby flesh had disappeared.

"Come on . . . wake up . . . Jane." He was virtually shouting now.

Suddenly he remembered her drugstore. Scrambling out of bed, he pulled open the beach bag, "Oh, God," he moaned. It was stuffed with all kinds of pills and vials, half of the bottles unmarked. God knew what she'd dosed herself on. Suppose she'd overdosed? In his wife's bed. Suppose she were dying. He pulled open her eyes with probing, racing fingers, although he had no idea what he was looking for. All the time he kept shaking her and begging, pleading with her to wake up. He thought of the death of Jimi Hendrix, who had gone into a deep sleep and suffocated on his own vomit. He thought of the steak and strawberries they had had at lunch, and imagined her dying trying to breathe through regurgitated strawberries.

He had to get help. Now he regretted the puppy-dog comeliness he had admired. She was a heavy girl. Standing over her, he heaved and pulled, one arm under her armpits, the other arm under her thighs.

At that moment the door opened. "Jesus Christ!" said Ruth.

Time freezes in these situations. To an outsider, the sight of a naked man desperately trying to turn the leaden, sleeping body of a naked woman onto her stomach only to be interrupted by his wife is the stuff of farce. But to John Arrowsmith it was the culmination of all his dreads. It was a judgment of God. All the guilt of fifteen years' frustrated fidelity burst out of him in an eruption of invective directed unfairly at his wife. All this was her fault, he told himself irrationally.

"Don't just stand there, for Christ's sake. She's dying," he screamed at Ruth, who was slowly entering the room, her face pale.

"John!" Ruth finally exclaimed. "What . . . what the hell are you doing?"

"What?" Arrowsmith was beginning to feel violently ill, and was wondering whether he was going to vomit from panic. A nightmare had come alive and wrecked his life. Every day of the past fifteen years had seen another rung on the ladder toward just this disaster. He needed Ruth now more than ever before. "Please, Ruth, help me. I think she's dying. She's overdosed or something. Please help me."

Ruth stared at him for just one moment, seeing her husband in a new way.

"Get dressed," she snapped sharply. Then, going over

to the unconscious girl, she searched for her pulse and stared sternly at the second hand on her watch.

Arrowsmith pulled on his jeans and shirt hastily, obediently.

"Now go to the infirmary. Get the doctor. She's there now with the chief of the village. I just saw them as I came by."

Like a child on an errand, Arrowsmith hared out of the door, along the balcony, and down the steps to the infirmary. He had seen the doctor only once before. Sarojine was a plain Indian girl with a large nose. Technically speaking, she was a scuba doctor and authorized only to give medicals to people wishing to go deep-sea diving. But in emergencies, laws just had to be bent.

He found her drinking tea with Hardin. Virtually hysterical, he blurted out what had happened.

"Show us," said Hardin, pushing him ahead of them.

"She's in there, throwing up," said Ruth as Arrowsmith led the doctor and Hardin into his room. The bed was empty, and from the sound of the bathroom came a horrible retching sound. The doctor and Hardin moved quickly past Ruth and entered the tiny bathroom. Hardin threw a towel around the girl. The doctor bent over her.

Arrowsmith looked toward Ruth. "What happened?"

"She woke up," she said simply.

"She was in a coma?"

Ruth shook her head. "She was in a deep drug-induced sleep. But she wasn't unconscious. You panicked too soon."

From the bathroom came the sound of more retching. Hardin came into the bedroom and, picking up Piebald Jane's beach bag emptied the contents onto the bed. An assortment of pills scattered over the sheet.

"She's going to be all right?" asked Arrowsmith, unable to believe the sudden turn of events.

Hardin nodded, tight-lipped. "The doctor thinks so. If you don't mind, we'd like to keep her in here for a while. Perhaps you could go and have a talk among yourselves . . ." His voice trailed away. He had no idea what state their marriage was in. "I'd like to talk to you again later," he said then, directly to Arrowsmith.

Arrowsmith nodded and looked toward Ruth. Silently she turned and walked out of the room. He followed.

_____ THIRTY-SEVEN

Ruth Arrowsmith's reasons for wishing to enjoy a vacation separately from her husband had had nothing to do with him, but everything to do with the way in which she saw herself. For nearly fifteen years she had acted the role of the archetypal invisible wife, the woman at her husband's side, the person whose individuality had been completely submerged beneath his career ambitions. Now at the age of thirty-six she was beginning to rebel.

The reappearance of Joanna into her life had caused an affirmation of what she already knew about herself. Joanna had lived the heady life, had had what sounded like exciting and glamorous jobs, had traveled, and had had numerous affairs. But all that led to was a rich little realtor in New Rochelle. When Ruth had asked, as tactfully as possible, what Joanna was doing with someone like Roeg, Joanna had given her a look of contempt and said, "Listen, at the age of thirty-six with the divorce and property laws as they are, grade-one husbands-to-be are very few. Michael is rich, generous, and good at it. So if you're thinking of a change, forget it. The one you've got is as good as you'll ever get."

Bearing this advice in mind, Ruth had gone about changing her status as the invisible wife. She had decided that if she was invisible, it was because she had never allowed her own personality to develop further than through the lives of John and the children. In the future she would make a supreme effort to regain some of the individuality she had once believed she possessed. The vacation at Club Village had been one of the steps along the way.

The Tuesday boat excursion had been planned to last until four-thirty. But fate had decreed otherwise, in the shape of a squid which became entangled in two of the propellers of the three-engined boat in which she and Joanna were traveling, forcing them to limp home on the one good engine. As a day out it had been disappointing and, as she had walked up from the marina to the village, she had determined to go in search of her husband and have a nice cool drink. It had been with these simple and homely thoughts in mind that she had opened the door to her cabin.

After Hardin shooed them both from their room, the Arrowsmiths stood for some moments on the balcony, uncertain of what to do. Which attitudes should they take toward each other? Arrowsmith was sweating with fear and relief. His mouth was dry, but he did not want to drink. He tried to turn to face his wife, but it was impossible. He dared not look into her eyes. Slowly, still without looking at each other, they made their way along the balcony and down the steps toward the beach.

Blankly, Ruth walked out to the edge of the water and waded into the ripples of waves. Arrowsmith watched her. He could see that there would be no tears. Her face was dry, her expression perplexed. He fought for words but found none.

At last Ruth wandered out of the sea and began to meander along the beach. Arrowsmith dragged himself after her, a pace or two to one side, two or three yards behind.

"John . . ."

Arrowsmith swallowed. His eyeballs burned from wanting to cry. He just wanted to be forgiven, but nothing was ever that easy.

Ruth began again. "Was it nice, John?"

This was the one question for which he was not prepared.

"I mean, was it worth it? Did you enjoy it?"

"I don't know what to say."

"I'm sorry," Ruth said.

"You're sorry?" Arrowsmith was having difficulty following.

"I mean, that's probably an impossible question to answer. But I really want to know. Is it so much nicer with her? I know you've done it before, but it was easier then because I didn't find out . . ."

"Done what before?"

"You know, been with other women."

"I haven't."

"John." Ruth half-glanced over her shoulder, a sad glance of regret that he should still think it necessary to lie to her.

Arrowsmith shook his head. "I promise you, Ruth . . . today was the only time. The first ever . . ."

Ruth was puzzled, but she believed him. "Why?" she asked. "Why did it take you so long? Don't tell me it was loyalty, either, John. And don't talk about love, either."

Arrowsmith thought hard. For years he had tried to congratulate himself on his fidelity, but now he saw the lie to that. He had been faithful because he had been too lazy, too settled in his ways to go looking. It wasn't that the occasions had never arisen; it was more a matter of being too much involved with himself to give them opportunity.

"I guess I never got around to it," he said miserably.

Ruth nodded. That was an answer she could understand. "So, was it nice?" she asked again, after a few seconds.

Numbly, he nodded, tears welling in his eyes.

"Don't cry, John," she said.

"I'm sorry," he said.

She shook her head. "Don't be. It could easily have been me. I suppose we're both in pretty much the same position. You feel that you've devoted your life to me and the kids and building up a home, and that somehow all the ideas you once had about doing something worthwhile have gotten lost along the way. If you'd been a single man you might have had a brilliant career and a great life as well, John. I know that. It could have been an exciting life, instead of pension plans and a place in suburbia."

"No, that isn't true. We both know that," broke in Arrowsmith. "Maybe that's what I'd like to be able to tell myself, to make an excuse for taking the easy way out, and going after promotions instead of the things I used to think were worth doing. But I'm just bullshitting myself. Being a family man made it easier for me to justify going the way I would have gone *any*way. I used to talk about working in politics. Do you remember that? And all that stuff I said I wanted to do for the East Village . . . that was when I lived there. I never think about those things anymore. I used to try to tell myself that my career was for the good of all of us, but I was really lying to myself. I really wanted to make it in the firm. That was the real reason. I *wanted* all the things I've worked for. They became important. Now they don't look very exciting, maybe, but on the way up I've been glad to take everything that's been offered."

"Do you love me, John?" Ruth asked suddenly. "Honestly, do you?"

Arrowsmith shook his head. "I don't know, Ruth. I don't know what the word means, not the way I used to know. I don't love anybody else, and I never have. But I can't honestly say I feel the way I did when we first began dating."

Ruth didn't answer for a while, but began drawing with her shoe in the sand, writing her name in big letters. Arrowsmith watched her. She looked younger than he had noticed in years, something like the girl he had married, but he felt more distant from her than he had ever had. For the first time he realized that he was seeing her as other men must see her. At last she turned back. "So, was it nice?" she said for the third time.

He nodded. "Yes, it was . . . wonderful," he said.

She smiled. "I'm glad, John. You deserve some fun. Too bad about the way it turned out."

Hardin would have liked to have begun his investigation of Piebald Jane right away, but Sarojine, the Indian doctor, advised against it.

"It is very difficult to investigate a nauseous person," she said, in that peculiarly formal way which Indians inherited from the British Empire. "I think it would be most advisable for us to get her back to her own room for the rest of the day. I will stay with her there, and then perhaps this evening she will be able to give us an account of the events of the day."

Hardin shrugged. "I'll send up a couple of CVs to help you get her back to her own room, then," he said. As he heard retching coming from the bathroom, he stepped out onto the balcony and headed back toward his office.

On the way past the boutique he almost bumped into Cassandra, who was deep in conversation with Homer Wolford about her possible participation in the week's tennis tournament. She blushed slightly as he excused himself. He looked harassed and angry.

"Sorry," he snapped as he almost stumbled over her long, outstretched legs, which were propping her body against the boutique window.

"My fault," she said quickly, and stood upright.

"You room with the girl with the strange hair, don't you?" he asked.

Cassandra nodded. Hardin explained, ending with, "If it kills me I'm going to clean every last goddamn drug out of this village."

Cassandra knitted her eyebrows and watched him lope away. He was being totally unrealistic. Wherever you got a large crowd of young people you were inevitably going to find all kinds of dope. She wondered what it was that made him so completely antidope.

"I never saw a man so obsessively hostile to dope," said Homer Wolford. "He's sure as hell pissing into the wind if he thinks he's gonna be able to clean up this village completely. Every charter brings its quota of pillheads."

Cassandra nodded and changed the subject. She didn't want to think about Hardin and his crusade at that moment. "What were you saying about this tennis tournament anyway, Homer? I promise you I haven't played seriously since I was at school."

"That's okay. I watched you yesterday. I would figure that you're at least quarterfinal standard. Tell me you'll put your name down for this Friday."

"Well, if you insist."

"I do insist. And so do all the tennis coaches. We discussed seeding the players last night, and they all gave you a pretty high rating."

Cassandra was flattered. At school she had played well, and during the past couple of days she had found all her old confidence quickly returning to her. That was the really seductive thing about Club Village. Everything about it made her feel youthful and confident. Despite her earlier reservations, she knew she was having a great time. She hoped she wasn't going to feel compelled to write a condemnatory article about it.

THIRTY-EIGHT

In keeping with general Club Village policy as decreed from Paris, the CV quarters were scattered throughout the village. When Quatre Bras had first devised the Club Village system he had had special quarters built for the employees, but over the years he had become firmly in favor of a more integrated system. By splitting up the CVs into units of two throughout the whole village the possibility of a CV ghetto was avoided, and the danger of a CV elite was mitigated. That CVs had exactly the same accommodations and food as guests also meant that the chief of the village was likely to hear complaints from the CVs should things not be running well.

Like the guests, the CVs were required to double up, with the exception of the chief of the village, who, because this was the American zone, had a small three-room bungalow set in the pine glade between the beach and the restaurant. Even Sarojine, the doctor, was expected to share. She roomed with Sharon Kennedy. Florinda from the boutique and Chloe from reservations made a dazzlingly beautiful couple in one room, while Hillman and Brummer lived together in dour mutual spitefulness. Homer Wolford, the head of sports, roomed with Paul Chow, a pint-sized deep-sea-diving expert from Hong Kong, while the beautiful Sacha shared with Henry, an English boy from Gloucestershire.

Although the formation of a CV elite was strictly frowned upon, there was nothing to prevent the employees of Club Village getting together after the nightly revue, when most of their work was done. Since the bar and disco were always packed with vacationing guests, the covered seats in between courts one and two, outside the tennis pavilion, had become their unofficial meeting place.

Tuesday night was sharp and chilly, and there were fewer off-duty CVs relaxing in one another's company than usual. The revue that night had been a fifties pastiche, with Homer Wolford miming to Fats Domino records, and Chloe and Florinda and a blond, bottom-heavy girl from California called Esme miming to "Short Shorts," accompanied by half a dozen male CVs, their hair slicked back, cigarette packs stuck in the short sleeves of their T-shirts. It was probably one of the worst revues Elixir had ever seen, and Hardin's bleak stare had not gone unnoticed, especially by David Le Parmentier, who was in charge of entertainments.

"He's an asshole, David. Forget him," said Hector, the picnic lecher, who had done a particularly unsuccessful impersonation of John Travolta impersonating Elvis Presley.

There was a murmur of agreement from the twenty or so other CVs. At the far end of the tennis courts, three couples were spread out, necking heavily. Everyone ignored them. Every night a little quiet screwing went on down here. The tennis courts were the places couples got to know each other. At Club Village it was almost a rule that sex came before affection.

Miguel, the chief assistant on picnics, a Mexican whose pleasures in life were totally carnal, sucked on his teeth noisily and thoughtfully. He and Hector had both been given strict warnings that unless their conduct improved there would be no home for them in Club Village next season. "He's a eunuch," Miguel said contemptuously. Miguel considered that anyone who did not wish to take part in the beach party sex games he and Hector had devised was of doubtful potency.

"He'll turn Elixir into the most boring island in the Bahamas," someone else suggested. "What do you say, Henry?"

The English boy didn't want to say anything. He had had more than his share of coconut punch at that night's cocktail party and had staggered his way through the revue, helped along by the ever-solicitous and smiling Sacha. "I think he's probably a good sort in his way," Henry volunteered vaguely. "Bit of the old school sort, though. Pity really . . . bloody shame."

Someone passed him a bottle of rum and he took it. Since he was already drunk, he might as well get plastered. That was another of the dangers of Club Village. Since CVs were paid partly in bar shells, they quickly developed a taste for alcohol. Every year at least half a dozen slipped quietly out of villages around the world when their local chief had decided that their drinking habits were more important to them than their work. Even so, Club Village continued to pay in shells.

Hector put an arm around Florinda's waist. She stepped to one side and made a face at Chloe. Chloe shrugged. Sacha watched them.

"We never had any trouble with Pagett," said Paul Chow, the Chinese scuba chief.

"Pagett understood this village," replied David Le Parmentier. Pagett had never criticized his revues.

"Pagett's dead," said Sacha bleakly.

There was a moment's silence.

"Any more from the police about poor old Dick?" Lucien asked, looking toward Homer Wolford, who was the most senior CV present.

Homer was lying on his back, drinking from a can of Lowenbrau. He shook his head, finished the can, and then, crumpling it up in his giant hand, tossed it into a litter bin. "Nothing. No sign of the boat. Nothing."

"It's pretty easy to disappear down here," said Hector. "The police can't keep check on thousands of square miles of ocean. It's the easiest thing in the world to make a man disappear."

For a few moments the CVs were busy with their thoughts. Then suddenly the sound of a low moaning filled the night. The group froze. Hector put his hand to his lips. Silently they all turned to gaze down to the far end of the courts, but it was too dark to see the couples lying there. The moaning increased. "Yes . . . yes . . . yes . . . yes," came the low muffled cry of a female voice, followed by a sudden deep intake of breath and a scratchy, high-pitched whinny of excitement.

A ribald guffaw and then applause arose from the rest of the CVs.

"Someone just scored," said Le Parmentier, peering through the gloom. "I think it was Joe."

"The earth moved," said Esme. "Seven point five on the Richter scale, or else she was faking it."

"Who would want to fake it with Joe ?" said someone else.

"I had to," said Helen, a girl whose favors had generally been shared among most of the male CVs. "It was the only way I could get him to come. He's like a goddamn piston engine when he gets going."

"How would you like to try a jet-propelled superdrive, Helen?" purred Hector, reaching out and grabbing her thigh.

Helen allowed him to molest her. "You know your trouble, Hector? You're all talk."

The group laughed again, and then fell silent. Every night someone got drunk, and the rest of them talked and watched. Isolation, even in a paradise like Elixir, could get boring.

"He's a eunuch," repeated Miguel after a moment. But he didn't mean it. That was what he always said about everyone.

A hundred feet away, far enough in shadow that nobody spotted him, stood Alex the bartender, spending his midevening break watching the CVs, as he did nearly every evening. The giggling, the sounds of sex from the far end of the courts, the popping of beer-can tops confirmed for Alex that these people were no good. He hated being here, but he forced himself to come and listen. It reminded him of what he had been like. It reminded him of the taste of sin.

Hardin began his interrogation of Piebald Jane straight after breakfast the next morning. Under the stern and vigilant eye of Cassandra, Jane had slept soundly, and she awoke at seven with little more than a hazy memory of the events of the previous day.

Quickly, while the two women dressed, Cassandra filled in the gaps in Jane's memory.

"His wife came in and caught us . . . ?" Jane echoed, aghast. "Oh, Jesus. I'm almost certain it was his first time."

Cassandra had nodded balefully. "If there's one thing certain in this world it's that every time a nice, decent married man strays off the straight and narrow, his wife is bound to find out. When the good guys are just a little bit bad, they always get caught."

Hardin was waiting for Jane in his office at nine o'clock. She tapped on the door, rather like a schoolgirl going to see the principal, and stepped inside.

"Sit down," said Hardin as Jane appeared meekly around his door.

She did as he suggested. On his desk in between them were the pharmaceutical contents of her beach bag. She looked at them with mild embarrassment. Spread out like that they looked like such a lot. She had no idea she had been carrying so much around with her. She wondered whether he had had a sly toot from the little silver snuffbox in which she had stowed Michel's gift.

199

Hardin spread his arms across his desk and surveyed her closely before speaking. At last he started. "When you arrived here in the village on Saturday, Jane, you broke two laws. You broke the laws of the Commonwealth of the Bahamas by bringing dope into the country, and you broke the rules of Club Village. In the rules and regulations, a copy of which you were given when you became a guest member of the club, there is a section about drugs. It specifically mentions grass, cocaine, hallucinogens, and heroin. We don't want dope in Club Village, Jane, and the government of the Bahamas doesn't want it in this country, either.

"Yesterday you caused a lot of people a great deal of trouble, and you behaved very badly. Now I could, and I probably should, turn you straight over to the local police and let them deal with you. But it might be possible for you and me to come to some arrangement."

Jane listened in open-mouthed amazement. Was this going to be some kind of sexual proposition?

"If you'll point a finger at the source of the stuff, I'll give you your plane tickets back to New York, refund you the cost of your vacation, and forget all about it."

"Come on," said Jane, almost wanting to laugh at him for believing her to be so naïve. "I brought the stuff in myself."

"I don't believe you," said Hardin. He didn't actually disbelieve her either, but even if she had brought it in by herself she almost certainly had a good idea of which other village residents had their own caches. He was baiting her because she might just know something.

"Honest to God, I don't know anything. And even if I did, I wouldn't tell you. You're acting like some kind of Gestapo blackmailer in a B movie. What do you think I am?"

"How old are you?" ashed Hardin quietly.

"I'm twenty-two going on forty," said Jane.

"Twenty-two," repeated Hardin. She looked older. "Listen, I know you think I'm some kind of *schmuck*, don't you? Old-fashioned? Isn't that right?"

Piebald Jane didn't say anything. She was noticing, not for the first time, just what a handsome man he was. What was wrong with Cassandra that she hadn't grabbed him instantly?

"Well, I might be," continued Hardin. "But I've got an education in dope as well. You know I was a pro tennis player for a while, and moving in those circles you get to meet a lot of rich and sophisticated people . . . people who can afford more or less whatever they want. Tennis is a fast life, and a relatively short one, unless you happen to Bjorn Borg."

Jane didn't answer. She had no idea why he was telling her all these things, but his style was beginning to take on some of the aspects of a cautionary tale. She had heard dozens before, so she knew she was immune to them.

"Well, for every Bjorn Borg there are five hundred other players. Right? And some of them care more about having a good time than playing tennis. It's a good life. Lots of girls, travel, parties, money. I was one of those players, and I had a great time. I screwed around a bit, went to a lot of parties. And then one day when I was in Rome I met this girl. She was twenty-one. She wasn't a player, but she was going through a time in her life when I suppose you could call her a tennis groupie. So we began an affair, and because I needed some time away from the circuit I stayed on for a month or so after the tournament, and got to know the kind of life she was into. She was French and had been living with a rich Roman socialite and his wife for a couple of years. It was what you'd call an open marriage, I suppose. The guy was some kind of papal prince and he had a big villa . . . maybe it was a small palace, I don't know . . . just outside Rome."

Hardin stopped speaking. His voice trailed away and he swiveled around in his chair and gazed at the sea. Piebald Jane waited. She had no idea why he should be telling her this story. Cassandra would have been much more interested in hearing about his past love life than she was.

"Anyway," said Hardin at last, "I'd been used to dope on the circuit but never in the quantities that these people used it. The guy and his wife seemed to have a built-in resistance to it. Nothing hurt them. No matter how much they took they always seemed to breeze through it. But the girl was different. She slept a lot, and then she would get up in the evening and go looking for the nearest party and the best dope. She never used a needle, but she liked to try new things. So she got through a lot of stuff, a lot of speed, opium . . .

"After a time I got bored and went off to earn my living playing tennis. I last saw her at the Rome airport. She was beautiful, and yet somehow tawdry. She had grown up to be a rich kid in Paris society, and then for some reason she became mixed up with these older people. They could handle themselves, but she couldn't. They kicked her out a few months later.

"She's dead now. She went back to Paris and into a hospital. She was really straightening her life out again, and then one night she slipped back into her old ways. Whatever resistance she might once have had was gone. She was found dead in a bathroom at her parents' home . . ."

Hardin stopped speaking. Piebald Jane stared at him. She had heard similar stories from her parents, her teachers, even the personnel officer who had eventually fired her from her job as an airline stewardess. What they didn't seem to understand, any of them, was that she was different. She could handle what she took. There was no way she was ever going to move into heroin. Only idiots did that.

Hardin guessed what was going through her mind. "I suppose you're saying to yourself, 'What has all this to do with me? I don't have that kind of problem,' Am I right?"

"Yes," said Piebald Jane, "that's exactly what I was thinking."

Hardin picked up the snuffbox containing the coke and opened it. Then very carefully he spooned some onto the end of a silver paper knife, and, raising it to his nostrils, he snorted. "Not bad, not bad at all," he said, sniffing. "You get this in New York?"

Jane nodded. "I told you I did," she said.

"Oh, yes, that's right." Hardin stared at her.

Now it was Jane's chance to talk. "Listen, you might be the chief of the village around here, and that may mean quite a lot in Club Village, but you're behaving like a fucking dictator. I mean, for Christ's sake, you're like the Narcotics Squad, Juvenile Hall, and King of the Island all rolled into one. Now, if you don't mind, I'll leave you to your reminiscences about your friend."

"And I'll call the police," said Hardin.

"But I've already told you I brought everything with me."

"And I've already told you that I don't believe you. Just point the finger for me. I know there's a lot of stuff in the village, but I don't know where."

"Why should I tell you?"

"Self-preservation. If you don't, I'll pick up the telephone and you'll probably spend the next month trying to explain to the local police just how you came to be in possession of so much junk. Believe me, it won't be a fun ride. This isn't New York. They take these things seriously down here. They're very straight people, very religious, these Bahamians."

"You wouldn't do it. You wouldn't risk the bad name of the club," said Jane, beginning to believe for the first time that he might just do it.

"I would . . ." The reply was flat and genuinely menacing.

"You know, you're crazy," she said, beginning to feel the ground slide beneath her. God knew how long she might have to rot in some stinking Nassau prison before they even worked out what to charge her with, she thought. "You're like some crusader, trying to put the world right. You can't do it, you know."

"I know that. But at least I can do my best to make sure that this village isn't a bolt hole for every druggie kid out of New York."

Piebald Jane tried to change the subject. "Did you know that my roommate Cassandra is hot for you?"

Hardin simply stared at her, his eyes totally impassive.

"Just give me a name," he said, "one name, or the police can take care of you."

Jane caved in. For God's sake, she told herself, it wasn't as though she were snitching on a friend. What did it matter? If this lunatic wanted to run his island like some dictator, let him. She would be better off out of it. "There's a guy called Michel," she said. "French-Canadian. He wears a belt with special pockets. He says there's a main supplier here. One of the staff. That's all I know. Okay?"

"Okay," said Hardin. "Guy on the travel desk will give you your airline tickets and refund you the cost of your vacation, less the five days you've been here. You'll find you're booked on the noon plane to Nassau, and then on to New York. I'm sorry your vacation ended this way, Jane."

"How do you know I'm telling the truth?" asked Jane, surprised at the speed with which the whole thing had been terminated.

"I can't be certain, can I?" replied Hardin. "But I'm prepared to take the risk. And, Jane . . . remember my story. It's true."

With that, he jumped to his feet and, walking to the door, opened it for her.

Hardin found Michel telling the story of his life to a couple of lady bank clerks in the tropical gardens which ran between the tennis courts and the pool. He was sitting in a bamboo rocking chair and was dressed in white cotton trousers and shirt. A large straw hat protected his eyes from the sun. His guitar was spread lazily across his thighs and chest. The women sat on the grass. They were both plain and in their midtwenties, and were employed by the Bank of America in Paso Robles, California. Hardin had a memory for this kind of detail. They knelt at Michel's feet like disciples, their arms, pink from too much sun, propping them up like sticks, flowered sun dresses spreading out from their bodies.

"I hope you don't mind if I interrupt you, ladies," said Hardin, with a smile that would have won a war. "I need to have a chat with Michel."

The two women climbed to their feet. "Not at all, James," said the more forward of the two. She, too, had learned the importance of memorizing names.

"Michel sure has had a fascinating life," said her companion.

"Perhaps I can buy you a drink this afternoon sometime," said Hardin, anxious to be rid of them. Michel was looking at him with surly derision, the expression of the delinquent who knows he's been caught but isn't quite sure at what.

"That would be very nice, wouldn't it, Linda?" came the reply.

Linda smiled. "Well, we'll see you later then, Michel. Perhaps you'll sing us some more of your songs."

"I'm sure he'd love to," said Hardin.

Still smiling, the two women wandered away.

"Well, this is indeed a rare pleasure, James," said Michel, mimicking the intonation of the Paso Robles girls.

Hardin towered over him, staring down into the insolent face. "Let's take a walk, shall we, Michel," said Hardin. "Let's take a walk along the beach. I think we have some talking to do."

"We can talk here," said Michel, slowly reaching for a cigarette and lighting it.

Hardin kept his voice steady. "Let's go."

Michel pulled himself to his feet. There was no reason why he should obey Hardin; after all, he had paid for his vacation. But Hardin had a way about him.

The two of them set off across the gardens, through the trees, and on toward the sea. Whenever anyone wanted a really private conversation in Club Village, the beach was the place. Only when standing on the open beach, with the sound of the Atlantic smothering all else, could you be sure of privacy.

"Show me your belt," said Hardin simply once they were safely out of earshot.

They were standing along the edge of the ocean. "What would you do if I said 'go take a fucking hike'?" asked Michel, without looking at Hardin.

Hardin grinned. "I'd grab you by the neck, take you into the sea, and push your head under until you came to your senses," he said.

"You know, you think you're a pretty tough guy," said Michel.

"The belt," Hardin insisted.

Michel shrugged and, unbuckling his belt, slid it out of his trousers and passed it over.

"Oh, very clever," said Hardin as he undid the pockets. There was a trace of coke in one. He tasted it, and then smiled. "You know, Michel," he said with a bonhomie he was not feeling, "I think you're going to be very helpful to me."

"Like fuck I am," replied Michel.

Hardin didn't even bother to look around to make sure that he wasn't being observed. With one large hand he grabbed the French-Canadian by the neck and, hurling him across the beach, dragged him into the sea and forced his head under the water. Michel kicked maniacally with his hands and feet, but Hardin held on, counting slowly to ten. At last he released him. Michel staggered out of the sea, coughing and spluttering, holding his throat and gasping.

Hardin looked around the beach. It was so huge that the other guests were hardly more than colored specks. No one appeared to have noticed the fracas. Hardin advanced on Michel. Hardin now had the belt flung carelessly over his shoulder. Michel lay like a broken bird in the burning sand.

"Now," said Hardin, "let's have a little talk, shall we?"

Michel fed the unfortunate Matt Hillman up to Hardin with hardly a whimper. Half an hour after the conversation on the beach Michel was packing his bags under the eyes of two security guards, preparing to leave Elixir on the same flight as Piebald Jane, while Matt Hillman was sweating it out in Hardin's office. By twelve o'clock Hardin had the information he wanted, and Hillman was showing him the loose floor board in the library.

"Lift the bags out," said Hardin, standing over Hillman and blocking his escape route.

"For God's sake, Brummer will kill me," sniveled Hillman.

"If he doesn't, I will," said Hardin. "Lift them out."

He had carefully made sure that Brummer was kept busy on an errand down at the marina while his questioning of Hillman had been taking place. He had had a series of lucky breaks by picking on the weaker links in the chain, but he knew that he would never have been so fortunate had he had to deal with Brummer. The Dutchman was a different proposition altogether. Hardin doubted if he would ever have found a way to break him. He had used a tried and tested method on Hillman. Once he had been apprised of the way the system worked, he had promised Hillman an airline flight out of the Bahamas if he cooperated and showed him where the dope was stored. When Hillman had realized he could be out of

Elixir and back on his way to the States before Brummer realized what had happened he jumped at the opportunity. Hardin was giving him the chance he wanted to get out of the racket and away from his Colombian partners before there were any holes in his head. So it was that Hillman gratefully joined Piebald Jane and Michel on the one-o'clock flight out of Elixir.

Hardin didn't doubt that were he to go through every single person's belongings, he would find all kinds of illegal things in the village. But that was not his purpose. He believed in doing everything as quietly as possible. Getting the police involved would be unnecessary. The publicity would ruin the club.

When Brummer arrived back from the marina at three-fifteen Hardin was waiting for him, sitting in the room which Brummer had, until that morning, shared with Hillman.

Brummer sized up the situation in an instant. If he was shocked to find Hardin lounging on Hillman's bed, and he must have been, he never for one moment betrayed his feelings.

"I hope you're making yourself at home," said Brummer, hurling himself into the one easy chair in the room while his eyes raced around the room, ending up on the two large bags of cocaine lying alongside Hardin on the bed.

"Hillman had a plane to catch," said Hardin. "He asked me to make his apologies to you." Hardin had purposely let Hillman have a head start on Brummer. To have allowed Brummer to get close to Hillman after he had so easily blurted out the truth about their operation would in all likelihood have led to violence.

"Tell me about Pagett," said Hardin. "Did he know what you were into?"

"I don't know what you're talking about," said Brummer.

Hardin had guessed right. Brummer was not the kind of man who was ever going to do a deal. He decided to level with him. "Listen, I'm not going to turn you over to the Coast Guard or police or anyone. We both know that I couldn't afford the bad publicity for the village. The Bahamian government might even decide to close us down. Certainly, they'd begin to interfere a great deal in our affairs. So let's forget all about that. You're leaving here this evening. But since we have some hours to kill, I might as well start learning something about what's been going on here. Okay?"

"How did you find out?" asked Brummer, not bothering to deny anything, but not confirming anything either.

"Does it matter? I did."

"How much did Hillman tell you?"

"Enough to make me certain that neither of you two were involved in Pagett's death."

"Would he have told you if we had been?"

Hardin smiled. "You know Hillman, Brummer. He's a squealer. If there had been anything to tell it would have come pouring out."

"What are you going to do with the bags?" asked Brummer.

"Well, I can't toot all that by myself, and I'm not about to start dealing, so I think I'll have to find some way of disposing of it."

"Have you any idea how many hundreds of thousands of dollars that stuff is worth in the States?" asked Brummer.

Hardin nodded. "I've a pretty good idea, and with inflation the way it is these days I don't doubt it's increasing in value while we're sitting here. But tell me about Pagett. I know he wasn't involved, and I know that you two guys didn't kill him. Neither of you left the village on the day he went missing. I checked that out. But I have to know how much he knew."

Brummer shook his head. "Pagett didn't know anything. He was a good guy. He kept his nose out of things that didn't concern him."

"But he was killed," said Hardin.

"Well, he's dead, for sure," said Brummer, helping

himself to a panatella from his top pocket, "but I heard the sharks got him."

"I think maybe someone got to him first."

Brummer shook his head. "Why? No one had any reason at all to kill Pagett. Do you have any evidence for thinking that?"

"None at all," said Hardin. "I was hoping you might have some ideas. It just seems so unlikely for an experienced boatsman to go down on a perfect day."

"Let me tell you, Hardin. So long as Pagett was here I was running a good business and a lot of people were doing okay. He was good news for everyone. You're the one who's heading for trouble."

"Not from you, I'm not," said Hardin.

"How did you get Hillman to talk?" asked Brummer after a moment.

"I panicked him. He was scared of the cops."

Brummer swore quietly. "Goddamn stupid faggot. I knew he couldn't be trusted."

"You make much money?" asked Hardin.

Brummer shrugged. "Some. Not enough. It's in a safe place. Not here, if you're wondering. I banked it."

"If you take my advice," said Hardin, "you'll get the hell out of this part of the world as quickly as possible. When your friends find out that you've fallen down on your part of the trade they'll come after you with dum dum bullets."

"Did you tell Hillman that?"

Hardin nodded.

"Why do you care so much about our welfare?"

"I don't. I just don't want your corpse turning up in Nassau Harbor. It's bad for business."

Brummer guffawed. "You know, you're a pretty cool guy. What has Club Village ever done for you that you're so worried about business?"

"It's nothing to do with the club," said Hardin. "To me it's all about trying to do the best you can in the situation in which you find yourself. I happen to have been sent here to clean out Elixir as quietly as possible. That's what I'm doing. If I don't, I'll feel I've failed, that I've lost, in a way. I've never been a good loser."

"What are you going to do with them?" Brummer pointed to the two bags.

Hardin checked h.. watch. "Come on, I'll show you," he said. "You've plenty of time. You aren't leaving until eight."

Standing, Hardin picked up the bags, one under each arm, and walked out of the room. Brummer followed him along the balcony, down the steps, and out into the main concourse area and across toward the pool. The sun had now gone behind some heavy rain clouds, and the pool was empty other than for a group of snorklers who were practicing. Hardin walked to the diving board, climbed the steps, and tiptoed along the springboard. When he reached the end he sat down, his legs straddling the board. Brummer watched him warily.

"If you see your Colombian friends again I want you to tell them what I did. Okay?" said Hardin. Taking a penknife from his pocket, he slit the first of the bags wide open, holding it high over the pool and allowing the five pounds of white powder to fall into the water. He did the same with the other bag, as people began edging toward the pool, watching.

Brummer watched in disbelief. "Holy shit, man," he moaned. "Do you have any idea what you've just done? You've just signed your own death warrant."

Hardin sauntered slowly back along the spring plank, carrying the two empty bags in his hands. The waters of the pool now bore no trace of the valuable treasure they had just consumed. "I don't think so, Brummer," he said. "You're the guy who let them down. You'll be the one they want to get even with. I was just doing my job. If I were you, I'd keep my head well down for a long time. Because if you don't, the odds are that you won't be living very long. Now you might as well go and pack your things. You and Hillman are both going to be wanted men. You failed to deliver. You'd better start running."

Brummer didn't wait to argue. Hardin was right. Without a word he headed back to his room. He was on his way back to Holland, grateful to have escaped the situation so easily.

Hardin watched him go. At the edge of the pool groups of CVs were watching him, open-mouthed. Now they all would know just how serious he was about keeping dope out of the village.

Cassandra was sorry to see Jane leave the village, although not exactly surprised.

"Your lunatic friend is in love with some corpse who took an overdose in a Paris toilet," Jane explained when she met Cassandra by the pool immediately after her interview with Hardin. "He's become a screaming necrophiliac because he doesn't think he did enough to save the dear girl from her wicked ways. Jesus, you should have heard him."

"So?" Cassandra had asked.

"So he's giving me a one-way ticket to Palookaville."

"To where?"

"Palookaville . . . that was one of my old man's favorite sayings. It's been nice knowing you, Cass. We'd have made a great team here, you know that?"

"I'm sorry, Jane."

"Forget it. All these palm trees give me the creeps, anyway."

"I'll help you pack."

"That's okay. Hey, Cass, next time you're in New York, look me up, okay?"

"I promise."

"And one last thing: If you ever do get that crazy dictator in the sack, fuck him once for me. Okay?"

"I can't promise."

"See you, then," said Jane, and with a quick kiss she walked off back to their room to gather her belongings.

She was going to miss Jane, thought Cassandra, but it was only later that afternoon when she returned to her room that she realized just how sorrowful was the parting.

Two of her prettiest Zandra Rhodes dresses were missing from the closet, and lying on her bed was a note scrawled in lipstick on a yard-long length of toilet tissue. It read, "Hope you don't mind, Cass, but I'm borrowing a couple of your dresses. You'll never wear them here. They're a bit big for me, but I can pin them up. I'm leaving you two of my bikinis in return, as I won't be needing them for a while. Thanks. Love, Jane. P.S. Club Village sucks."

But despite this, despite everything, Cassandra found it impossible to stay mad at Jane. At least while Jane had been with her she had not been disturbed by faces at the window. She would miss her during the rest of her stay at Elixir.

For her part, Jane left Elixir without any particular regrets. She was sorry that she had not been given the chance to apologize to Arrowsmith, but, on consideration, she thought it was probably for the best.

She met Michel and Hillman on the airstrip. Michel was particularly upset and hardly spoke, but she detected a sense of relief in Hillman.

By the time they arrived at Nassau an hour later, the three of them were quite friendly. And, prompted by Jane's encouragements, Michel disappeared into the men's washroom just a couple of paces behind a very rich dude who had made several deliberate passes at him across the bar. Michel returned five minutes later with a fresh supply of coke, enough for several toots each.

"It's good to have friends, isn't it?" said Jane to Hillman as they waited for the five-o'clock flight back to New York.

"That's what Club Village is all about, isn't it? Making new friends . . ." said Hillman, delivering the first funny line he had spoken in his entire life.

Six months later Hillman was found with his throat cut, on a houseboat in San Francisco Bay. He hadn't run far enough from his Colombian connections.

Piebald Jane developed a career in soft porn movies, and bought a tenth share in a house in Taos.

Michel worked as a singer in a Paris bar. Willem Brummer was last heard of fighting as a mercenary with the South African Army in Namibia.

You meet all kinds of interesting people in Club Village.

FORTY-TWO

Despite her prettiness Karen Sorensen was not an immediate romantic lead in Elixir. She was a shy girl, and was virtually overwhelmed with the hit-and-run tactics of most of her contemporaries in the village. She was from Colorado and had arrived alone and exhausted on the Sunday evening, feeling immediately that she was an outsider.

Twenty years old, five feet, six inches tall, with long slender legs, a delicate, almost shining complexion, and dark brown hair which she wore in pigtails, she was definitely eye-catching. But she was not that easy to get to know.

Naturally enough, all the male CVs had immediately noted her arrival and begun to buzz around her hungrily. But, since she was so obviously not interested, she was left to her own devices. She was a real bore, it was quickly decided.

Karen's roommate was hardly more sympathetic. She had been paired with a divorcée from Stuttgart called Ingrid who had gone to Elixir looking for a good time, and Karen's apparent puritanism was, at best, an imposition and, at worst, a distinct impediment to her romantic adventures.

So, although she enjoyed the tennis and swimming, Karen disliked the social side of Club Village, and was beginning to resent the fifteen hundred dollars she had invested in her vacation. Then, during a ballet lesson, she met Sacha.

At first she thought that he was just another CV trying to hit on her for an easy lay, and when he complimented her on her dancing she smiled haughtily and turned an arched shoulder toward him. But the polite, almost apologetic way with which this beautiful young man moved humbly aside for her at the end of the lesson was devastating in its attraction, and she found herself giving the nearest thing to a come-on smile she ever allowed herself.

"Perhaps we could play Ping-Pong some time?" suggested Sacha as he graciously returned the smile.

"That would be nice," said Karen. This was the first CV who had suggested anything other than a walk in the dark, a drink, a dance, or, quite simply, a straightforward fuck.

There was a momentary silence as the contagion of shyness threw its tentacles around them both. Then Sacha added: "Maybe we could have a game now. I think I see an empty table."

Again Karen smiled and together they walked across the village and up the steps toward the shaded corner which housed the Ping-Pong tables.

"Are you good?" asked Sacha as he served a deliberately easy ball.

"Better than that," Karen replied as she smashed the ball off the edge of the table.

"Ah, I see, a champion," said Sacha, and began to play properly.

Ping-Pong may not be recognized as one of the great courtship games of the twentieth century, but it does have its social values. Over table tennis two people can speedily strike up a friendship based on the tenets of sportsmanship and, unlike Ping-Pong's big brother tennis, the participants are close enough to be able to exchange jokes, smiles, and words of mutual praise. For those who play it well, Ping-Pong is indeed a useful avenue for social progress in Club Village. By the end of their game Karen and Sacha were firm friends.

"I have to go to work now, but perhaps I could see you again," said Sacha as they lingered together after the game.

Karen looked at him. He was extremely beautiful, but not pushy like the other CVs. He probably wanted to get into her pants like most men did but, at least he had the decency not to make it so obvious. That pleased her. She wasn't looking for an affair, but if it happened, then that would be nice.

"I'd like that very much," said Karen, and, with another grin, hurried off toward her room to change for dinner.

After she had gone, Sacha stood for some moments in the gardens. A lizard ran like quicksilver through some leaves. Carefully, Sacha broke off a twig and tickled its tail. Once again it made a dash, zigzagging first this way and then that, trying to escape from this playful tormentor. At last it disappeared under a hut, and Sacha gave up the chase and returned to the village theater to prepare for Saturday night's ball.

Hardin had been so disgusted with the level of the revues that he had decided to introduce the masked ball, which had been such a success in Val d'Isabelle. And Sacha, who did most of the club's artwork, had been drafted to make the masks and decorations.

Quatre Bras and Girardot saw two different cities when they each looked at New York. To Quatre Bras it was the main fortress in a nation yet to be conquered, and as he sat in the back of the black Lincoln Continental which drove him into Manhattan he felt the buzz of exhilaration which he had first known years earlier when first establishing his Club Village empire in Europe. He knew he would not, could not, relax until Club Village had become as much a part of America as it was of France. To him, the back-street boy brought up on a diet of Warner Brothers gangster films, America represented the future, and he was as starry-eyed about it as he had been on his first visit nearly thirty years before. Rich, aristocratic men like Ronay would never understand the special place which the born poor of Europe held for America. To Ronay New York was a vulgar city, a place of rootless immigrants, a dumping ground where the poor of the Old World had made themselves rich but had never taught themselves the right social graces. But to Quatre Bras America was still the land of opportunity, where the less fortunate had, in theory at least, a better chance of vaulting from their depths. At heart Quatre Bras was romantic about America.

Girardot possibly should have shared his master's enthusiasms, since they were from identical backgrounds, but Girardot was not a man for adventure. Now he was as conservative in his own way as was Ronay. Mostly it was the language that defeated Girardot. Quatre Bras had seen early in life how necessary it was for an empire builder to speak the international language of the world, and had worked hard at learning English. But Girardot, tunnel-visioned in his Frenchness, had never learned more than the words on chewing-gum wrappers.

The New York office of Club Village had booked Quatre Bras and Girardot two adjacent suites in the Plaza Hotel, which was where Quatre Bras welcomed Anthony Scorcese, the president of Universal-American Airlines, to a private dinner.

Contrary to popular belief, multimillion-dollar deals are rarely put together in vast boardrooms, chic villas, or ritzy restaurants. All of that comes later; the building blocks to the merging of capitalist empires are almost invariably set up over sandwiches and coffee. Room service dinner at the Plaza was slightly more elaborate than a sandwich, but the gastronome in Quatre Bras noted with satisfaction that better meals were served in virtually all his villages.

Anthony Scorcese was an austere, middle-aged New Yorker, of recent Italian descent, who had built a career in several of the larger corporations by being a brilliant accountant, and who was convinced that the best future for Universal-American Airlines lay in expansion into the leisure and vacation fields. His hair was thick, and iron-gray in color, and his suit was of a determined sobriety. Quatre Bras had met him before, and liked him, despite his careful conservativeness and his refusal to touch even a drop of alcohol while doing business.

"As I understand it, *monsieur*," said Scorcese as Quatre Bras passed him a Perrier water, "you may be in a position to allow us to buy heavily into Club Village in return for our help in extending your organization in the American zone."

"That is correct," said Quatre Bras, "subject, of course,

to the approval of my board, who, as you know, can be somewhat Gallicly chauvinistic at times."

Scorcese nodded, a little gentle movement of his head downward, which intimated that he too had trouble with the less farsighted members of his own board. "Of course," he said.

Quatre Bras watched Scorcese closely. Quatre Bras knew that the other man would have made massive, although discreet, inquiries into the running of Club Village, just as he had done on the viability of Universal-American Airlines. The very fact that the two men were meeting at all meant that each thought there was the basis of a deal which would suit them both.

Suddenly Scorcese smiled and pulled off his jacket. "Okay, Monsieur Quatre Bras," he said, "let's see if there's a way of making a marriage out of this thing, shall we?"

At two o'clock the following morning, Quatre Bras rang down for champagne. The basis of a deal had been reached. Both men had argued, fought, and pushed each other toward the brink before conceding so much as an inch. The details would be long and complex, and would involve the efforts of dozens of lawyers on both sides of the Atlantic, but the foundations were well laid.

"Tell me, do you think that at my time of life a Club Village vacation would have any appeal for me?" asked Scorcese as the two men celebrated. "Or am I too old for it, perhaps?"

"Too old? Of course not," said Quatre Bras. Scorcese was younger than he was, and if he didn't accept aging in himself, there was no way he could accept it in others. "What are you doing this weekend?"

Scorcese shrugged. "Nothing exceptional," he said.

"In that case, why don't we both go down to Elixir. We have a very nice village there. Our guests don't live in palaces, but I think you might enjoy a few days in the sun of the Bahamas. After all, seeing is believing, isn't it?"

Scorcese grinned. "An excellent idea. It's a long time

since I took a vacation in January. I'll have the Lear made available for us from tomorrow."

"Excellent," Quatre Bras boomed, and shook the hand of his prospective business partner very firmly, hoping desperately that Hardin would have sorted out all the Elixir problems by the time they arrived.

The news that Ernst Ronay, together with Beta Ullman, was due in Elixir on Saturday was the sort of surprise that Hardin could well have done without. Quite apart from seeing Beta again so shortly after his tryst with her in Switzerland, he needed much more time to get the village running efficiently before being visited by the top Paris brass.

Throughout the first week he had tried to concentrate on the enormous amount of work to be done at Elixir, but the presence of Cassandra Mallinson interfered with his concentration. He would have liked to have been able to ignore her, as she appeared to be finding it so easy to ignore him. But that was impossible, and he wondered, among other things, whether the arrival of Beta would exorcise her from his mind.

On Friday, at lunchtime, Winston Johnston, the senior of the two Bahamian police on the island, called at the village for a chat.

Johnston shook his head emphatically when Hardin suggested there was something suspicious about Pagett's death. "No, man, nothing suspicious at all. I've known people live all their lives in these islands, then one day they go out in a place they've been a thousand times before, get a little bit careless, catch their boat on a sharp piece of coral, and down they go before they've even had time to grab a lifebelt," he said as he drank a tall glass of rum and fruit cocktail in Hardin's office. "These waters can be treacherous even to those who know them well. I'm always surprised there aren't more accidents with people from Club Village."

"But Pagett was a first-class boatsman and swimmer," argued Hardin.

The black man grinned widely.

"Even Mark Spitz couldn't swim the Atlantic," he said. "If your boat goes down, even if you survive the cold and exposure, the sharks will get you."

Hardin knotted his hands and frowned. He could not imagine that Pagett could be the victim of such a simple accident. Perhaps he should have told the police about Brummer and Hillman and the Colombian connection, he mused, but just as quickly he dropped the idea. It wasn't his job to patrol the seaways of the Caribbean. The supplies of dope that had gone into the States by this route were totally insignificant when measured against the billion-dollar industry between Colombia and the United States. All he wanted to do was to keep dope out of Club Village, to keep Elixir as clean as possible.

For the twentieth time that week Hardin crossed his office and consulted the giant sea chart covering one entire wall. Pagett's body had been found about thirty miles southwest of Elixir, in an area where the general current was in a north-to-south direction. With his forefinger Hardin traced a northerly direction from the cross that marked the site where Pagett had been found. Fifteen miles away was a small group of islands known as Dutch Cays.

"What do you know about Dutch Cays?" he asked of Johnston, who was nearing the end of his drink.

The chief of police wrinkled his nose. "There's nothing there now. They're just dots on the map. One time there were a couple of good houses, but the owners left twenty or thirty years ago. Cays ain't good for nothing. Just a lot of swamp, I understand."

Hardin nodded and let the matter drop. There was no

way he could go sailing around the whole Caribbean looking for clues to Pagett's death.

At that moment Sharon Kennedy walked in, carrying a Telex message. "Excuse me, but I thought you ought to know," she said, passing it to Hardin.

Quickly he read it. "Well, well, it never rains but it pours," he said. "Not only are we to be blessed with the extremely unlikable Ernst Ronay and his guest, but also Quatre Bras and party are jetting down from New York. It looks like an exciting weekend."

Homer Wolford had been overgenerous when he had suggested to Cassandra that she might make the quarterfinals in the tennis tournament. In fact she was beaten 6–0, 6–0 in the third round by a tornado of a woman from Belgium. The standard of tennis at Club Village was far higher than Cassandra had imagined, and, as her opponent's serves swerved and spun past her outstretched, flagging arm, she wished desperately that she had never allowed herself to be placed in such a position. Nor had off court distractions helped. At one point, when she had been 40–30 up on her serve, Cassandra had noticed Hardin watching her from the back of the spectators. Instantly, her concentration was broken, the game went to deuce, and then, in quick succession, she served two double faults and dismissed herself from the competition.

The spectators applauded her politely, while the little Flemish whirlwind, all plaits and legs like molded steel, prepared for her next victim by going to an adjacent court and getting in some practice killing overhead smashes as the hydraulic tennis cannon lobbed balls to her.

Relieved that the ordeal was over, Cassandra made her way back up the grassy slope toward the village. A figure slipped into step alongside her.

"Goodness, you startled me," she exclaimed as she found herself looking into the deathly white features of Hamlet Yablans.

Yablans tried a smile, but succeeded only in grimacing.

"You want I should carry your tennis racquet for you?" he asked, reaching to grab it.

Cassandra snatched it away. "No, thank you," she snapped, feeling a shudder run down her spine.

"I was just trying a joke," said Yablans. "You know, like the kid who wants to carry the girl's books home from school."

"That's not funny."

"It's funny because I don't look funny. *That* makes it funny. Understand?" he said.

"No," said Cassandra, walking on as fast as she could.

"You know, I've seen you before," said Yablans, catching up with her.

"I don't think so," said Cassandra.

"I know so. I've seen your picture. You're a writer, aren't you?"

"I work for a publisher."

"You work for a New York magazine called *Night and Day*," said Yablans.

It was no use denying it.

"Am I right, or am I right?" he asked.

"What I meant was I worked in the London office of a publishing company," said Cassandra lamely. "Anyway, I don't see of what possible interest it is to you."

"You're a reporter. You do investigations. I read one of your pieces last night, something about art forgeries in Europe. Your picture was in the magazine."

"I'm taking a holiday now."

"Maybe."

"What do you mean, 'maybe'? I'm on holiday, and I shall be extremely grateful if you will kindly leave me alone and allow me to enjoy myself."

"I think you came here to do a story."

"I think you are being extremely offensive."

"I also think you came here to find out what happened to Dick Pagett."

Cassandra slowed her pace just a little. It did not look as though the weird little comic was about to molest her. "I understood that Dick Pagett was drowned in a boating accident."

"If you'll believe that, you'll believe goldfish wear roller skates," said Yablans.

"You're saying he didn't die in an accident, are you?" said Cassandra.

"I'm saying there's a crazy man in this village."

Cassandra looked at him sharply. With his porridge-colored face and dull, black-dyed hair his lips looked blue and his false teeth yellow. His black blouse had stain marks under the armpits and his leotard clung vulgarly around his crotch. He was disgusting. "And who is that crazy man?" she asked.

Hamlet grinned at her, but said nothing. At that moment Hardin appeared around the corner of the infirmary. For a frozen second she looked at him.

"Everything all right?" asked Hardin.

"Everything is fine. Hamlet here tells me he thinks there's a lunatic in the village. Isn't that right, Hamlet?"

Both Hardin and Cassandra stared at the clown. He faltered, as though unsure how to behave under their gaze. Then suddenly he laughed wickedly. "Hey, nonny, nonny-no," he said. "Not me, Cassandra. I am but mad north northwest; when the wind is southerly, I know a hawk from a handsaw." And with that he slithered away and back up toward the village.

"What the hell's he talking about?" Hardin asked.

"I think you'll find he was just living out his name," said Cassandra.

"That face you saw at your window the other night . . . was it Hamlet, do you think?"

"I don't know," said Cassandra. "I don't think so. It may have been. He told me he thought there was some madman loose in the village."

"I think it's about time I had a little talk with Hamlet. I'm sorry you were bothered by him."

"That's all right. He didn't bother me, really."

"I'm sorry that you had such a tough draw in the tennis.

I just haven't had time to get around to playing with you, have I? Look, this weekend all the top brass are coming down here, so perhaps we could have dinner together tonight, before all my time gets taken up looking after them. That is, if you've nothing else arranged."

Cassandra grabbed her moment. "I've nothing at all arranged."

Hardin smiled. "Okay, so let's say dinner in my bungalow at eight-thirty. It isn't exactly Maxim's, but the chef takes a little more trouble for me."

"I'll look forward to it," Cassandra smiled. And, clutching her tennis racquet, she went up to her room to shower and change.

FORTY-FIVE

"Hey, how would you like to go for a cruise today?"

Karen Sorensen opened her eyes and peered up into the sun. She had been sunbathing on the deck by the pool, and on the verge of falling asleep when the quiet, friendly voice of Sacha disturbed her.

"If you're interested, we could take one of the boats and a picnic and go visit some of the cays." Sacha went on. "There are all kinds of places not too far from here that are still uninhabited."

"Don't you have any work to do?" asked Karen.

"No. Today's my day off. We're supposed to get one day a week to ourselves, and if any of the boats are free we can take one."

"And one is free?"

Sacha grinned. "Now that you come to mention it, I do believe there is one available."

Karen sat up. Sacha had the charm of a slightly diffident youth. He might have been the best-looking man in the village, but he never showed that he knew it. He was never brash and never tried to make a pass. He was, thought Karen, the most perfect of men to spend the day with. "Just wait until I get some clothes together," she said.

"I'll see you down at the marina," said Sacha. Putting his arm down he helped her to her feet.

"Great." Karen dashed back to her room. Today could change her life, she thought, and she glowed.

Sacha was waiting for her on board one of the boats. Dressed now in a pale pink cotton sundress, and wearing a yachting cap with a wide brim which she had bought in haste and at great expense from the boutique, she clambered aboard.

"Hold tight, now," called Sacha as he cast off and pushed the boat out into the makeshift shallow harbor. Then, opening the throttle, gently at first and then wider, he steered the boat away from the wooden dock. Above them, on a terrace, Karen saw two couples she recognized as the Arrowsmiths and the Roegs sipping lunchtime cocktails and watching their departure. They didn't appear to be having a very happy vacation, she thought.

As the boat picked up speed and began to skim across the harbor, Karen idly allowed her hand to trail in the water. But although the sun was hot the January sea definitely was not, and she withdrew her hand after a moment. In the back seat of the boat was a Club Village picnic hamper.

"May I look and see what's for lunch?" asked Karen.

Sacha shook his head playfully. "It's a surprise," he said.

"Good. I like surprises," said Karen. She looked at a copy of the *Yachtsman's Guide to the Bahamas*, which was lying open alongside her on the front seat. "Where are we going?" she asked.

"I thought we'd take a look at a group of islands called Dutch Cays," Sacha replied. "They're sort of wild and beautiful, more like the islands you get farther south. No one lives there now. Sometimes I think I'd like to live there one day. A nice quiet place of my own, where no one could bother me."

Karen watched him as the boat bounced across the ocean waves. His eyes were focused on the far horizon, as though he were looking for something. Despite the tan, his features were soft and gentle, and wispy layers of fair hair fell across his forehead. For the first time in ages, she felt the heat of desire.

The island Sacha had chosen for their picnic was wild

and more verdant than Elixir, and the flowers were more tropical, but swamps lined much of the coast, and barriers of coral reef formed a natural hazard around the strip of beach toward which Sacha steered the boat.

"I can tell you've been here before," she remarked, admiring the skill with which he rounded the rocks.

"It's one of my favorite places. Just look at the angelfish underneath us. There's every color in the world down there."

Karen peered through the glass window bottom of the boat and watched the darting shoals as Sacha gently steered the boat around the hazards and in toward the beach. As they entered the shallower turquoise beach waters Sacha put the boat into neutral and, jumping into the sea, towed the craft along the beach until he found a convenient root to which it might be tethered. Then, together, the two of them waded ashore, hauling the hamper between them, Karen's sun dress tucked demurely into her bikini bottom.

Lunch was an almost sedate affair of *terrine de volaille*, cold bass with Dumas sauce, salad, crystallized fruit mousse, Camembert cheese, and fresh fruit. It had been a long, hot journey to the island, and the two ate with relish and urgency, sitting on a rug.

"This is like a scene from a movie," said Karen as she sucked on a cherry, savoring the juice. She had drunk quite a lot of wine and was feeling definitely romantic.

"Which movie would that be?" asked Sacha. He was now lying back in the sun, wearing only the briefest of swimming shorts. He had a lithe, golden, muscular body, surprisingly sinewy considering his delicate features.

"Which movie? Oh, I don't know. What about a modern-day version of *From Here To Eternity* . . . the one with Deborah Kerr and Burt Lancaster. Did you ever see that one?"

Sacha nodded. "I think I must have seen it about ten times on television."

"Well, the only part I remember is where the two of them are rolling in the surf at night."

"I guess that was pretty heavy stuff in those days," said Sacha, looking toward the surf, which was breaking along the beach, causing their boat to swing to and fro on its rope.

"I guess so," said Karen. "God, I'm hot. What do you say we go for a swim?"

"You swim, I'll watch," said Sacha. "Don't go too far out, though. I'm terrified of sharks and I'm a terrible lifesaver."

Pulling off her sundress, Karen scampered away down the beach to the edge of the water. Sacha watched her silently. Choosing her footing carefully, she waded in until she was thigh deep, before throwing herself under an approaching breaker. Squealing with shock, cold, and exhilaration all rolled into one, she swam a few strokes and then, turning, dashed back up the beach to the warmth of the huge Club Village towel that Sacha was holding ready for her.

"God. It looks inviting, but it's so cold," she cried, shivering and giggling in the warmth of the towel. She could now feel her body against the warmth of Sacha's skin and was both comforted and aroused.

"Stand still while I dry you," he said. Very methodically, he began to rub her gently all over, from the head downward until, kneeling before her, he eased her legs open and rubbed the insides of her thighs.

"That's wonderful," she said.

Sacha stayed at her feet, his hands resting gently on her thighs. The towel fell onto the rug. Slowly Karen sank to her knees, facing him. She put an arm out and ran her fingers along his shoulder. He didn't smile or attempt to grab her. She liked that. Most guys would have been on top of her by now, with one hand down the front of her bikini. It was nice to meet a man who was bashful, particularly a man as gorgeous as this one. She bent forward and kissed his mouth and he responded with a slight gasp of surprise. But he made no move toward her. This was becoming puzzling. When a man took a girl to a remote spot, gave her a splendid, sumptuous picnic, got happily drunk with her, and then made what she interpreted as a delicately sensuous pass, it was odd for him to be so slow in following up.

"What's the matter? Don't you like me anymore?" asked Karen, leaning forward again and tantalizingly pushing the tip of her tongue along his half-opened lips.

Sacha just stared at her, a hopeless, sad stare.

Why didn't he say something? Surely, he couldn't be that shy. She ran her hand down his chest, stroking his chest before allowing her hand to fall across his stomach. He flinched, but still he made no move toward her.

She took her hand away, crimson with embarrassment. She must certainly have mistaken his intentions!

"I'm sorry," she mumbled, turning her head away. "I think perhaps I drank too much."

Sacha still stared at her. His face was setting into a remote, far-off expression. Suddenly Karen felt cold. There was no longer any of the warmth which had so attracted her to him. She turned and reached for her sundress, but he caught her hand and stopped her.

"Take off your swimsuit, Karen," he said softly.

"What?" Karen hesitated. Five minutes earlier, such an invitation would have met with an instant acquiescence, but the moment had gone.

"Come on . . . be a sport," said Sacha. Slowly, a shy smile spread across his face. His hands moved upward from her thighs to her waist, caressing her as they went.

"I don't understand you," said Karen.

"What is there to understand?" asked Sacha, his fingers now exploring the insides of her bikini. Very carefully he leaned forward and kissed her softly on the cheek, moving her head until his lips found her mouth. For a long moment he held her like that, a moment in which Karen's confusions and doubts evaporated. Then, with great tenderness, he very carefully unfastened her bra strap, until the top fell away. Pushing his face down, his mouth found her breasts and he sank his face into them. At the same time he moved his fingers down her body to free her legs of the bottom half of her swimsuit.

Very slowly, Karen tumbled onto her back, pulling Sacha on top of her, their mouths still together, her legs now entwined around his. Her hands began to work at his shorts, pulling at him impatiently until her hands cupped his genitals.

Only then did she realize her mistake. There was no excitement in his body. Try as she may, the beautiful, perfectly formed Sacha remained totally unaroused.

"Is it me, Sacha?" Karen asked quietly.

Sacha didn't speak. Slowly she withdrew her hand. Sacha rolled off her onto the rug.

"I'm sorry, Sacha," she said. "I guess you don't like forward girls. I didn't think what I was doing."

She began to reach for her clothes.

"No." Sacha stopped her. "I want to look at you," he said, holding her down with one strong arm pinned to her shoulder.

She wriggled to free herself from his grip, but he would not allow it. For several seconds he stared at her body, allowing his eyes to wander across her breasts and stomach and thighs as though enchanted by the sight of her.

"I'm sorry I upset you. I thought you liked me?" whispered Karen.

"I like you very much, Karen. You have a beautiful body," he said, his voice soft and teasing.

"Can we go back now, Sacha? I think it's getting late, and it's a long way home." She was hurt, and she wanted to be away from him.

The journey back to Elixir was an eternity to Karen. The changes of mood that Sacha had displayed on the island had made her feel utterly rejected.

At last they reached the dock. Just as Karen was about to jump ashore, Sacha's hand went to her shoulder. "You won't tell anyone, will you?" he said. "Please don't."

"No, never." Karen answered.

"I knew I could trust you, Karen," he murmured

quietly, with a warm smile. He brushed her cheek with a kiss and released her.

Karen clambered onto the floating planks of the wooden dock and hurried back toward the village.

That, she vowed, would be the last time she ever went for a boat ride with a young Adonis.

Hardin's invitation to supper forced Cassandra to make a drastic reassessment of her presence in Club Village. She had now spent a week in Elixir, and with every day that had passed, with the ever-increasing deepening of her tan, the original reason for her trip had receded from her mind. During the first few days she had half expected to receive endless cryptic Telex messages from the London office of *Night and Day* giving further details of the way in which she should angle her story. But when these had not materialized, the general vacational ambience of Elixir had overtaken her, and every day had become less a matter of sleuthing her story than simply keeping up with the constant source of grownup amusements provided by the club.

Now the invitation from Hardin was placing her firmly on the spot. There was little doubt in her mind that before the evening was out he would make a heavy pass at her, and there was equally no question in her mind that such a pass would be welcome. At the same time, was it fair to any man to allow him to wine, dine, and woo her without admitting the real purpose of her visit? She already had quite a little mental dossier on the way Elixir operated, of the sexy picnics, the dope problems, the exorbitant boutique prices, the bar rip off with the shell money, and the dangers of being a CV, and she was certain she was going to write all of it. That was her job.

All of these thoughts crossed her mind as she prepared for her dinner *à deux* in Hardin's bungalow. She was by now extremely tanned, but concerned to discover a couple of small sun blisters on her shoulders, into which she rubbed Nivea Cream. For most of the week she had worn only the bottom half of the bikinis she had bought from Lucienne Phillips in Knightsbridge before dashing off on her assignment, and she now viewed her long, dark body with extreme satisfaction.

It is a matter of universal fact that no matter how attractive a woman or a man might be, the possibility of a new encounter urges her or him to painstaking efforts.

She decided on a pale green cotton dress she had bought at Harrod's Way In department. With her hair newly washed, and the week's sunshine seeming to glow from her new streaks, she looked about as good as she had in years.

Thus prepared, Cassandra made her way from her room, down the steps, across the village, and up the grassy knoll to Hardin's bungalow. It was situated on a slight rise so that it overlooked both the village and the beach.

Hardin was waiting for her, sitting in a rocking chair on the veranda as she made her way up the short pathway through the trees. He smiled as she approached and came down the short flight of steps to greet her.

"Later in the year I believe we could have had dinner outside, but in January it gets a little chilly, so I've had the staff lay the table inside," he said, leading the way past his rocking chair and through the screen door into the house.

The living room was large and airy. Against one wall was a large stone fireplace in which some pine logs sparked and crackled, while in the center of the room was a heavy oak dinner table, with two candles burning and laid for two. Low, imitation copper lanterns threw a warm glow over the varnished strip wooden floorboards, and the sparse collection of furnishings, a heavy mahogany chesterfield, a couple of Mexican rugs, two easy chairs, and a sideboard. On the varnished wooden walls hung a random collection of unexceptional prints.

"I asked for dinner to be served at about nine," said Hardin. "I thought we might have a drink before then."

Cassandra smiled and sat down on one end of the chesterfield. "That would be nice. As I'm in the islands, I feel I ought to have something with rum . . . what about one of those cocktails that were served the other night?"

Hardin nodded and began to prepare a drink from a tray laid out with an assortment of bottles, fruits, and glasses. "This time we'll put a little more rum in it," he said. "When you have to serve over five hundred people you instruct the staff to go very easy on the measures. That's why you can drink so many without getting drunk."

He finished mixing a couple of drinks and then turned to her. "Well, what do you think of my home?" he asked as he passed her drink to her.

"It looks extremely cozy," said Cassandra. "The perfect home for a bachelor, I would have thought. But I thought you told me you had hardly any belongings. What about all the prints and rugs?"

"They all come with the job," Hardin explained. "I inherited them from Dick Pagett."

"The man who drowned," said Cassandra.

"That's right," said Hardin. There was a moment's silence as he considered the fruit in his glass, and then suddenly asked, "Tell me, why didn't you want me to know that you were a journalist on a working vacation?"

Cassandra swallowed slowly. She was about to reply, but he beat her to it.

"I asked the head office in the Bourse to check you out in London. You seemed to be asking an awful lot of questions for someone on vacation."

"And are you cross?" asked Cassandra.

"Not at all. I'm amused. Did you think that we would try to hide things from you, or that we would want you to say only nice things about Club Village?"

"It has been known," replied Cassandra. "Is that why you asked me to dinner . . . to tell me all the good things about Club Village?"

Hardin poked the fire before answering. "I work for Club Village, Cassandra. They pay me reasonably well, and I have a reasonably pleasant life. For that, I work very hard to make sure that the village I'm in charge of works to the satisfaction of the guests. But my loyalty is not to Club Village. You can't be loyal to a corporation four thousand miles away. We have a business arrangement. I do my best for them, and they treat me accordingly.

"But the people who really matter to me are the people who pay their money and come down here for a couple of weeks in the sunshine. If there is a Club Village spirit, then it belongs to those people, because they are the only reason any of us is here. Now I know, I can see in your eyes, that you think this is so much garbage, but it happens to be true. I have no ambitions in Club Village other than cleaning up this place and making it work as efficiently as possible, which means giving the paying customers a good time. So if you want to write a piece condemning what goes on here, then just go ahead. I won't mind, I promise you. But at the same time, remember to add that an awful lot of people have good vacations, don't go to sex orgies, and don't get mixed up with dope."

"You make me feel almost guilty," said Cassandra.

"Don't be silly. Do your job," said Hardin. "That's what they pay you for. If you want to know anything, just ask; I'll tell you."

"Even if that means leaving yourself open to all kinds of criticisms?"

"Whatever it may mean. It seems to me that too many people think only about what is good for the company. The company can go out the window, I say. When I die and go up to heaven and tip my hat to St. Peter at the pearly gates, God isn't going to ask me what I did for Club Village. He's going to want to know what I did for my fellow man, and how I can justify having spent most of my life playing games."

"How will you justify that?" laughed Cassandra.

"Oh, I guess I'll just drop your name and hope they'll be

so impressed they'll give me a free ticket to everlasting happiness."

"I wouldn't count on my name."

"I don't count on anything. Drink up and I'll get you another."

"I'll be drunk."

"Promises, promises."

Cassandra finished her glass and passed it back to Hardin, who mixed them two drinks. At that moment there was a tap on the door. Hardin barked a welcome. A pretty, pareo-attired Polynesian CV and two Bahamian waiters entered the bungalow, carrying trays laden with dinner.

Cassandra watched silently.

They worked quickly and noiselessly, their faces ringed in what now seemed to Cassandra to be permanent Club Village smiles.

In three minutes they were finished and gone, the Polynesian girl being the last to close the door, flashing Hardin a voluptuous smile as she left.

"Doesn't the gap between the jobs the local people do here and the ones which girls like that do bother you?" asked Cassandra after a moment.

"You mean does it bother me that Club Village makes some employees more equal than others?" he asked.

"Yes."

"It bothers me very much. It happens all over the world. In West Africa it's always the local population who do the waiting on, while the rich Europeans have all the glamorous jobs. In Sri Lanka the locals do the menial tasks, and the better-off Indians, who come down from Delhi and Bombay, get to be CVs. And in Europe, Club Village employs North Africans and Turks to wait in the kitchens and scrub out the rooms. Yes, it bothers me that Club Village is a predominantly white, middle-class organization, and that we come out here to these people's countries and exploit them. I know it's a wrong and unfair system, but I don't know how to change it. Do you?"

Cassandra had not been prepared for the outburst. "No," she said. "I'm sorry if I upset you."

"You didn't upset me. But you mustn't assume because a situation exists that I condone it."

"I feel thoroughly chastened," said Cassandra.

"You mustn't. It's just that I am, above all, a pragmatist. I believe in doing only the things I know are possible. I like to choose my own battlegrounds, where I know I have a reasonable chance of winning. Then I gird my loins, so to speak. Now, we can get started before this cold watercress soup freezes over?"

After the sharpness of their first exchanges, dinner was a pleasant, mellow affair, in which Hardin and Cassandra gradually explored each other's pasts, their dislikes and likes, and their mutual range of attitudes. It was a period of discovery, a tentative time of seeking out areas of compatibility, and building on them.

Cassandra was glad that the embarrassment of secrecy was over. Hardin was perfectly happy to be honest about the activities of the club. It was refreshing to be able to talk so openly.

"Do you really think Dick Pagett died from drowning?" Cassandra asked at last.

"No. I'm as certain as anyone can be that he didn't. But I have no idea what did happen to him. That bothers me a great deal."

"Hamlet implied that there was someone in the village who might be a little unbalanced," she said.

"The only person I know to be unbalanced is Hamlet himself."

"He's certainly weird."

"Yes, I think so, too. I've requested that he be transferred somewhere else at the end of this season. I don't think I could stand another six months here with him around. I've tried to talk to him, but whenever I do he just ties himself up in riddles."

After that the subject was dropped, and at around midnight the two of them found themselves sitting on the chesterfield drinking cognac.

"Are you expecting me to make a pass at you?" asked Hardin as they both stared into the dying embers of the log fire. In the distance, the sound of the discotheque carried through the pine trees.

"I suppose so," Cassandra answered after a moment.

"If I did, would you make an excuse and demand to leave?"

"No."

"That's nice," said Hardin, and, taking her by the hand, he led her silently into his bedroom.

Cassandra awoke around six, with the sun shining through the shutters into her eyes. Alongside her was the warm, smooth figure of Hardin, still asleep. This was the first time she had slept with a man in several months, and she needed time alone now to savor the pleasures of the previous night. Slipping from the bed, she stole into the bathroom, where she showered and dressed. Then, taking one last look at Hardin, she quietly left the house, carrying her shoes in one hand. The morning was fresh and clean, and, drawn by the sound of the sea, she decided to go for a morning's stroll along the beach.

Morning in the Caribbean is a blessed time, and the wind and salt spray quickly washed away the passions of the previous night. It had been, she thought, one of those rare nights which she hoped she would remember when she was alone and depressed. A happy and tender occasion, a moment of romance. She had no illusions that it would lead to anything permanent. Holiday romances were not supposed to last. That was the joy of them.

_____*PART VI*

Elixir was not really big enough for both Quatre Bras and Ernst Ronay, but Hardin was determined that so long as the two rivals were in his village the atmosphere would be as sweet as possible.

Ronay arrived first, having spent a night with Beta Ullman in Nassau before hiring a local Trans Island Airways Piper Aztec to fly them to the island. Hardin was at the airstrip to meet them. He did not know whether or not Ronay had any suspicions about his nights with Beta in the Alps, but, from the slightly overpolite way in which she greeted him, he guessed not.

"I've put you in adjoining rooms," he told Ronay as he drove the two of them up to the village. It had occurred to him that he ought perhaps to give up his bungalow to one or other of the visiting Club Village dignitaries, but that had been no more than a fleeting thought. He was the *chef de village*, after all. Guests were to be treated like guests and have guest accommodations.

"Thank you," said Ronay.

"Tactful," murmured Beta.

"I trust you heard that Quatre Bras also arrives today," said Hardin.

"I beg your pardon," said Ronay.

"Yes, Quatre Bras, Monsieur Girardot, and someone called Mr. Scorcese from New York are coming down this afternoon. I thought you would have known that."

Ronay sighed. "That must have been a very sudden

decision," he said. "I thought the chairman was staying in New York."

"Oh, you know the way Quatre Bras is . . ." said Hardin, vaguely, smiling at Ronay's obvious discomfort. Through the rearview mirror Hardin caught a glimpse of Ronay's stern, high forehead knotted in an intense frown. Alongside him, Beta looked anxious.

While Ronay had wanted to arrive discreetly, Hardin knew that Quatre Bras would expect a traditional Club Village welcome. So, although Hardin despised it, he organized the best-looking CVs in their pareos and bands of flowers, and even arranged the singing of the traditional club song of welcome as the Universal-American Learjet bearing Quatre Bras, Girardot and Anthony Scorcese touched down.

Hardin could see instantly that Quatre Bras was delighted. Quatre Bras had always loved the theatrical aspects of village life, and Hardin believed that Quatre Bras secretly saw himself as a paternalistic South Sea island chief. Fittingly, as the guests stepped from the jet garlands of flowers were draped around their necks.

"What a nice surprise," Scorcese said quietly, trying not to look embarrassed by this display of bogus blue-eyed "native" hospitality.

Quatre Bras beamed, and led his guests into the midst of the chanting, singing along as he did so, ruffling the long sun-bleached hair of the CVs.

Girardot, for his part, stood well back and cast his dark eyes over the girls, wondering if he were still young enough to get lucky with any of the less beautiful CVs.

"So, James, how are things going?" Quatre Bras sat back in a leather chair in Hardin's office, a large Scotch and soda in his hand.

"Pretty well, I think," said Hardin. Since he had Telexed Quatre Bras in Paris with all the important details of what was happening in Elixir, he did not feel it necessary to give further accounts now.

"Nothing yet on Pagett?" snapped the older man.

Hardin shook his head.

"This weekend is very important for me, James. Mr. Scorcese is the president of Universal-American Airlines, and we, or certainly I, am hoping that that company will be investing heavily in Club Village in order to facilitate our American zone operations."

Hardin nodded.

"So if Scorcese wants a single thing that is in your power to provide, I would like it provided very quickly."

"Would you like me to give up my bungalow?" asked Hardin.

"No, That won't be necessary. You're the chief here. We are the guests . . . although not exactly ordinary guests. His room is fine. I checked it myself. And Mr. Scorcese made it very clear to me that he doesn't want any particular favors," said Quatre Bras. "He's a very abstemious man."

"Very well," said Hardin.

"Now tonight, James, I'd like you to find me a table somewhere in the corner, and have it set for eight. And also find me two of the prettiest CVs to be my guests. Give me girls who know what it is to be discreet. Also, ask the head of beverages to serve us his best wine in the regular Club Village carafes, and let the chef know that our table is special. Let's see if we can't get Ronay and Scorcese together."

Hardin nodded as he considered his list of CVs. Pretty and discreet! That would have to be Chloe and Florinda. They were the most decorative around.

Beta Ullman was disappointed in Ronay. He had persuaded her to come on a vacation to Elixir and give up a lucrative and prestigious photo session for *Italian Vogue,* but now that he had arrived he did nothing but complain. He complained mostly about the standard of accommodations, but she knew he was really complaining because he was having to share the village with Quatre Bras.

"If you don't like Club Village rooms, we should have stayed in Nassau Beach Hotel, or gone off to Mustique and hired a house so you could hobnob with Princess Margaret," she said as he lay on his bed in his small room, looking around him as though he were in a prison cell.

"I just thought that, as I am managing director of Club Village, I might perhaps have been given the bungalow," he sniffed.

"But that's the home of the *chef de village.*"

"Who works for me. Hardin is only a glorified CV after all is said and done. He's hardly that important."

"It's still his home, and I understand it goes with the job."

"He might at least have offered," he said starchily.

"I understand that Quatre Bras and his guest are staying in ordinary guest rooms," said Beta slyly. "And he is the founder *and* president of the club."

"Quatre Bras is a well-known eccentric. He enjoys behaving like a Boy Scout. I imagine it's something to do with his humble origins."

"And you enjoy behaving like a supreme snob," said Beta, suddenly bitter and angry. "Is that something to do with your origins?"

Ronay reacted as if he had been stung "A snob . . . you called me a snob," he said incredulously. "Coming from a tart like you, my dear, that's very neat."

Beta went suddenly still as she felt the chill of contempt. "What did you call me?" she whispered.

Ronay knew immediately that he had gone too far. "It doesn't matter," he mumbled. "It was nothing. I didn't mean it."

"It matters to me. And I think you did mean it," said Beta.

She was standing over him wearing a diaphanous shift over her bikini. His arms reached out to grab her thigh, but she pulled away. Ronay looked up at her in surprise.

"I was making a joke," Ronay said. "You called me a snob, and I was making a joke."

"You are a snob, though, Ernst. You must know that," she said. "And I suppose I am a tart," she finished, talking more to herself than to him.

"Look, I don't want to argue," he said.

"No." She was suddenly tired and defeated. "Let's not argue. After all, why should a man like you waste his time arguing with a tart?"

Ronay didn't answer. Sharply, he pulled himself off his bed, and began riffling through his briefcase. This was the way he always behaved when he didn't wish to discuss something. He did not ask for forgiveness. Ronay never apologized.

"Did I touch a nerve, Ernst?" Beta asked, goading him now.

"I think we should discontinue this conversation. I have a great deal of reading to do if I am to talk to Quatre Bras tonight," said Ronay.

Beta stood looking at him for a minute. Suddenly his wealth, charm, and sophistication seemed less attractive. She had to get away from him.

"Will you be coming down to the pool later?"

"Yes, perhaps," said Ronay, looking up from the report he was reading. "I'll see you later, anyway. Why don't you go and see if there's anything in the boutique you'd like?"

Beta smiled. Now he was treating her like a hooker. "No. I think I'll just go and sit in the sun for a while," she said, and, impetuously, she stepped forward and kissed him quickly on his bald forehead. It was, she thought, almost a kiss of good-bye.

Beta would have liked then to go back to her own room and cry, but something stopped her. She had always known that despite his protestations of love Ronay must inevitably despise her, but she had always managed to smother the realization. He had not been the first man she had lived on, although he was most certainly the richest and the most powerful. By profession she was a model, and a very good model, but she knew that on all those occasions when her private life had come into conflict with her professional life, the private won. She was what was known in other societies and other eras as a good-time girl.

Was that a thing to be ashamed of? She used her beauty to give her the best possible life, in the way that people with brilliant minds used theirs to get the best opportunities in life. She was only using her one asset. But was she really a tart?

It was with these thoughts in her mind that Beta went down to the pool that afternoon and, taking off her robe, ordered herself a white wine and soda and lay face down on one of the only two vacant canvas sun beds.

A moment later a quiet American voice beside her broke into her thoughts. "Would you mind if I sat down here?"

She opened her eyes and saw a dark man of about fifty. His body was pale but trim, and he had a slight down of white hair on his chest.

"Not at all," she said, and indicated that the canvas bed was free.

"That's very kind of you," came the answer.

Through half-opened eyes, Beta watched as the man sat down and, opening a John le Carré book, began to read. She had expected him to begin a conversation, and was relieved that he hadn't.

Her thoughts returned to Ronay. She had always known that the affair would end in recrimination. Probably he would try to paper over the cracks in their friendship until they got back to Paris, but there was surely no future for them. And she could no longer ignore the ugly implications of their relationship. Very quietly, she began to cry to herself, huge salt tears falling down behind her sunglasses onto the canvas.

"If you're going to cry, would you mind doing it quietly?" said the voice at her side. The American was looking at her over the top of his book.

"I'm sorry," mumbled Beta absurdly.

"That's okay. Just keep your sobs quiet and we'll get along fine," said the man and returned to his book.

What an extraordinary character, she thought, and wondered who on earth he could be.

On the far side of the pool Karen Sorensen was making friends with the two village beauties, Chloe from reservations and Florinda from the boutique. She had met them while watching a pareo-tying display in which Florinda and Chloe acted as models, and Hardin gave a running commentary in French and then English.

"The pareo has become a sort of uniform of Club Village," said Hardin as Florinda promenaded in a deep-blue patterned garment that was hung, Grecian style, over one shoulder and fastened at the side. "Basically it's just one large piece of silk, which can be tied in as many ways as you have imagination. There's just one thing to remember, though: If you tie it on the right, it means you're anybody's. But if it's tied on the left, then you're spoken for. A lot of trouble can happen when people forget this one basic rule! Of course, if the person you're supposed to be 'taken by' isn't around, then there's no trouble at all in changing the knot to the other side and seeing if you get lucky. Isn't that right, Florinda?"

With a quick swivel Florinda swung the pareo until it hung down from the other side. Then, together with the razor-cropped and equally beautiful Chloe, she went into an elaborate ritual designed to display the multiplicity of ways in which the pareo could be tied, turning it into culottes, a Mexican poncho, a Roman toga, and a mini-skirt. Karen watched in fascination. It all looked so easy.

"And now we get to the interesting part of our fashion display," said Hardin as the poolside applause for the girls died down. "We'd like two guests, a man and a woman, who think they can tie a pareo in the normal style as worn in the Pacific islands, where we borrowed the idea. Come on now, one girl and one boy."

For some reason Karen found herself near the front of the low stage. She put up her hand. At the same time, a blond-haired scientific-looking journalist from Buffalo joined her. Together they mounted the steps.

"Right, we have our two volunteers," said Hardin. "Let's see how you do."

Florinda and Chloe passed each of them a large square of silk. Karen had decided to tie hers in the simple skirt fashion. She folded it over into a triangle, tucked it in at one of the corners, and then attempted to tie it around her waist. It didn't quite fit. She tried again, and again it slipped off. The journalist was having more difficulties. He had elected to turn his into a toga, but was having even more trouble. After three minutes Karen had the semblance of a skirt around her waist. Her companion was in a state of disarray. Hardin stepped in.

"All right, that's enough. Give them both a big hand, ladies and gentlemen. As you can see, it's more difficult than it looks, but I think you'll all agree that Karen here is the outright winner, and Buffalo Bill, well, he tried hard. For being good sports we're going to give you a pareo each, so that you can practice in your own rooms and be the envy of your friends when you get back home. And by the way, our fashion experts tell us that pareos are going to be the very height of fashion this year in New York and Paris. So if any of you would like to buy one to take home, we have an abundance of different colors and fabrics in the boutique right now, which will be open until seven. So hurry now, while stocks last."

His commercial over for the day, Hardin stepped down from the stage, embarrassed. This was the part of being a *chef de village* he hated most. It was so degrading.

Karen, meanwhile, was having her pareo adjusted by both Florinda and Chloe. From the dance floor the sound of Chuck Berry singing "Sweet Little Sixteen" burst from the speakers. Amusements never stopped at Club Village.

"Do you think I could change this pareo for one in green?" Karen asked Florinda. "Or would that be asking too much?"

"Not at all. Come over to the boutique now, before we get mobbed," said Florinda, putting a friendly arm around her.

Karen didn't have much in common with Florinda and Chloe. But since they were old hands at Club Village, they knew all there was about discouraging the attentions of unwelcome males, and, in the absence of any other friends, Karen found herself gravitating toward them. She felt at ease with them.

It wasn't until just before dinner, when Karen (now

wearing a pale green pareo, tied seductively at her waist so that it hung over one shoulder, leaving the other bare) was having a drink with Florinda and Chloe, that she saw Sacha again, having carefully avoided him since their picnic. Florinda and Chloe had just been told that they were to be the guests of Quatre Bras and Scorcese at dinner, and all three girls were becoming extremely giggly when Karen suddenly looked up and found herself staring into the perfectly malevolent gaze of Sacha. For a long moment he gazed at her, as Florinda and Chloe continued to laugh. The sight of him drove any thoughts of gaiety from Karen's mind.

At that moment the ragtime music that announced dinner began to play and as she joined the crush on the steps, she found Sacha pressing against her.

"Why did you tell them?" he hissed. "I told you not to tell anyone."

"I didn't, Sacha. I didn't say a word."

"They were laughing at me."

"No . . . they were laughing at something else."

"I saw them. I saw them laughing at me. I told you never to tell anyone." And with that he disappeared into the crowd of people.

Jesus, thought Karen. He certainly was difficult. She was determined not to let him near her again.

By careful management, Ronay and Quatre Bras did not actually meet in Elixir until each went into the bustling restaurant for dinner at a quarter to nine. Ronay was accompanied by the lithesome but now subdued Beta, who had not spoken to him since their sharp exchanges of the afternoon, while Quatre Bras and Scorcese were with Florinda and Chloe.

Hardin had asked Cassandra to be his guest for dinner. He knew he was playing with fire inviting Cassandra along, not only from the point of view of his recent involvement with Beta, but also because of her story. He had therefore checked with Quatre Bras, who had largely been amused by the idea. "We have nothing to hide, James," he had said. "And anyway, nothing important is ever discussed over dinner."

So it was that Cassandra found herself being flirted with outrageously by Quatre Bras, who had always had a soft spot for journalists, particularly the prettier ones.

"You came here to write a critical story, did you?" he said, laughing. "To drag Club Village through the mud? You should have told us before you left London. We would have paid your fare."

"If you'd done that how could I possibly have been objective?" asked Cassandra. "In London we call those trips 'freebies,' and the people who pay the bill sometimes get very nasty if they don't like what one writes."

"In Club Village we don't care what you write, so long as it's the truth," said Quatre Bras, beaming and passing her a glass of champagne.

"But truth can change its shape, depending upon the perspective of the viewer," said Cassandra.

Again Quatre Bras laughed aloud. But Hardin, who was listening intently, was not taken in. Cassandra was being buttered up with the half promise of future free vacations at the club's expense, so long as she wrote a favorable story. He hoped it would have not have any effect on her.

Normally two ladies as attractive as Florinda and Chloe would have found themselves being waited on and flattered by the men to whom they had been assigned, but Quatre Bras and Scorcese did not behave predictably. To Quatre Bras they were attractive employees who helped the image of Club Village, while to Scorcese they were far too young to be of any real interest. He was nearly fifty years old, recently divorced after his wife had suddenly decided she wanted to be eighteen again and had gone off with a music and dance instructor whom she had met at a midtown Manhattan rich ladies' gymnasium. Scorcese had found himself picking up the pieces of his life, throwing himself ever deeper into the running of his business. For fifteen years he had wished that they had been able to have a family. Now he was relieved that they had not.

Scorcese liked the idea of Universal-American buying

into Club Village; it made obvious good sense for a company like his to spread its capitalization into as many areas linked with travel and vacations as possible. But, unlike Quatre Bras, he had no powers of patronage over his board. He knew that in many ways the Club Village board was like a medieval court, with all but Ernst Ronay and his banking cohorts bowing to Quatre Bras. But at Universal-American he was merely a very clever accountant who had been voted president by the board, and who could be unseated just as easily should the figures begin to go against him. If he were to recommend buying a large share of Club Village and began to set up a massive American chain of villages, then he would have to have some very convincing arguments to put before his colleagues.

Only after the group had had a drink did Ronay present himself. Presuming the aristocratic privilege of being late without excuse, he suddenly strode across the polished wooden floor, smiling graciously to left and right, like a politician on a whistle-stop tour. On his arm was the mute, though beautiful, Beta.

Quatre Bras leaped to his feet as he saw the chief thorn in his side approaching. "Ernst, we were so worried about you. We thought you might miss dinner," he cooed.

Ronay smiled and extended his hand around the table, regal in everything he did. When he reached Scorcese, he smiled warmly. "I'm so pleased to see you," he said. "I understand you're interested in diversification."

Scorcese made a noncommittal reply. His eyes had suddenly fixed on Beta, who was now standing just a pace behind Ronay, her gaze fixed firmly on the floor.

"Might I introduce Beta Ullman," said Ronay. And he went around the table, dismissing Florinda and Chloe with a cursory nod. Only when he reached Scorcese did Beta react.

"Hello again," said Scorcese easily.

"You two know each other?" asked Ronay, taken aback slightly by the warmth of their smiles.

"We met this afternoon by the pool," said Scorcese.

Then, turning to Beta, he added quietly, "I trust you're feeling a little happier now."

"Much, thank you," said Beta. And at that moment she began to feel that the loss of Ronay might not be the end of the world after all.

Dinner was a polite maze of conversational *culs de sac*, driven along by Quatre Bras' bonhomie and Cassandra's polite inquiries. Quatre Bras insisted that no business be discussed that evening, which suited everyone. Ronay was behaving like a pompous ram, bearing down on both Florinda and Chloe at the same time, while Scorcese only had eyes for Beta. Hardin sat quietly, watching the elaborate game-playing that was being carried on before him.

Across the room, Sacha sat with a group of CVs who had not been assigned to assist at any of the guests' tables. He was quiet and morose. From time to time he looked up from the food he was tampering with, allowing his eyes to seek out the pretty faces of first Karen Sorensen and then Florinda and Chloe.

Karen could hardly have been unaware of his attentions. By chance she had found herself sitting with the Arrowsmiths and the Roegs, and conversation at their table was hardly lively.

"Didn't I see you playing water polo this afternoon?" she asked of Roeg, not because she was interested, but because someone had to say something.

Roeg nodded, sourly.

"He nearly drowned, didn't you dear?" said his wife, smiling sweetly.

"I swallowed a lungful of salt water," said Roeg.

"His poor little heart couldn't take the exertion," Joanna stated. "He really isn't awfully good at anything physical, are you, dear?"

Roeg shot her a look of hostility which would have frozen the Amazon.

Karen tried the other couple. "Is this your first Club Village vacation?" she asked of dark, pretty Ruth Arrowsmith.

"Yes," said Ruth, and neatly severed the head of her grilled plaice.

"And what do you think of it?" asked Karen.

Ruth paused before answering. "I think," she said, choosing her words with great care, "I think that everyone should try a Club Village vacation at some time during their lives, particularly during their married lives. There's something about this place that opens up all the wounds of a lifetime. Wouldn't you say so, John?"

"Maybe," sighed Arrowsmith, and sank lower in his chair.

Behind the bar, Alex, the bartender, watched the scene sourly. Everyone looked so nice. Everyone was so well dressed. But these were not nice people. They were gross and ugly and evil. This was a place of sin. Something terrible would have to happen to straighten all these people out. He shook his head. Yes, something *terrible* would have to happen.

Later, everyone who was at Elixir would swear they had sensed danger and violence in the air the last Saturday night in January.

Perhaps it was the masked ball, or perhaps it was simply the atmosphere shrouding the island. Whatever it was, Cassandra felt strange presentiments of anxiety, and she was the least likely person to suffer imaginings.

The ball was a huge success, all of the guests joining in with exhilaration. Sacha had done a remarkable job in preparing the dance hall and the masks. From the supporting pillars hung huge, lasciviously drawn masks, while from the crossbeams hundreds of streamers and more masks trailed thirty feet to the floor, tying themselves around the dancers as they moved in muggy confusion from partner to partner, always deliberately avoiding the one with whom they had arrived.

The face masks caused even Ernst Ronay to comment favorably. "I see we have something of an artist here," he said as he admired the intricate design of Florinda's mask.

"That's Sacha's work," said Florinda. "He's had half the CVs in the village working on them for the past four days. He's a genius at design."

Among the less exalted company, the ball was the high spot of the week, coming after a series of rather lame revues on the other evenings.

"I've wanted to hold you like this all week," said Roeg to Ruth Arrowsmith as he belly-hugged her around the floor. Normally Ruth would have held the horny little man at a distance and reminded him coldly that he was married to her best friend. But she didn't, and even surprised herself by enjoying the physical attentions.

Arrowsmith sat by the bar and watched in futile misery. Any notions he might once have had toward Joanna had been stifled by the events of the past week.

Joanna, meanwhile, was changing partners enthusiastically. Early in the week it had been noticed, by those who made it their business to be aware of these things, that Mrs. Roeg had an eye for younger men. Suitors who had been reluctant to make passes on other nights found a new confidence in hiding behind their masks. In quick succession, Joanna danced and body-flirted with Homer Wolford; Hector, the picnic chief; a photographer from Charleston; and various other men behaving like boys, and boys who thought they were men. If the air in that dance floor had not been so heavy climatically, it would have been leaden with libido.

Karen Sorensen was having no less a good time. Her friendship with Florinda and Chloe had given her confidence, and she rejoiced in her own attractiveness, keeping her suitors at arm's length, but moving from one to the other with self-assurance.

Befittingly on such a night, when the most conservative people found themselves behaving quite uncharacteristically, Michael Girardot did indeed have the good fortune to bump into Ingrid, the nymphomaniac from Stuttgart with whom Karen Sorensen had been roomed. And before the evening was out Ingrid generously agreed to spend a couple of hours in Girardot's room.

To Quatre Bras, the ball was quite the best advertisement for Club Village. He had intended that Scorcese should be entertained by one of the two CVs he had provided, but with great amusement he noticed the New Yorker moving slowly on the floor with Beta Ullman, while the streamers tied themselves around them and the lights were dimmed to a romantic low. Ronay seemed oblivious to this arrangement, and was talking animatedly to Chloe and Florinda, displaying the wealth and good breeding for which he was renowned.

"I must congratulate you, James," said Quatre Bras in Hardin's ear, speaking above the sound of the record that had temporarily replaced the reggae house band. "This is the best Club Village ball I've ever attended."

Hardin shrugged. "Sacha, the CV here in charge of design, did most of the work," he said.

"But there is also a certain ambience here tonight," insisted Quatre Bras. "And in Club Village the ambience always stems from the chief."

Hardin accepted the compliment with a mumbled comment.

"Aren't you going to ask me to dance?" asked a masked Cassandra, approaching the two men.

"I didn't want to monopolize your company," said Hardin as he led her to the floor.

The disc jockey who had been put in charge of the night's music was now playing Roberta Flack's "Killing Me Softly." Slowly they moved around the floor together, their bodies warm and close. It was the first time they had been alone since the previous night.

"You know, I came out here hating the very idea of Club Village," said Cassandra. "It seemed so vulgar. But if it is, then I suppose I must like vulgarity, because I'm having a lovely time."

Hardin held her a little closer. "You're right, it is vulgar. But it's also seductive. Somehow I have to break the habit."

"I don't understand," said Cassandra. "I thought you enjoyed the club."

"I enjoy it from day to day, but when I get to the end of the year I look back and wonder what I've done with that year. There has to be more to life than a permanent vacation."

"I'm glad you think so," said Cassandra, and allowed her head to rest on his shoulder.

On the far side of the floor, Anthony Scorcese was holding Beta Ullman at arm's length, although his inclination was to wrap himself around her. With his mask on he looked not unlike the Lone Ranger, while she looked demure and enchantingly mysterious.

"If I didn't know that you were here with your boyfriend I might suggest that we take a walk around the village, or maybe down to the beach," he said quietly.

Beta looked around and saw Ronay locked in deep conversation with Florinda and Chloe. "I think my boyfriend is trying to maneuver himself into a menage that is intended to exclude me," she said. "I'd like a walk on the beach very much." And, leading him by the hand, she left the dance floor.

At that moment the sinewy figure of Hamlet Yablans sidled up to where Quatre Bras was sitting at a corner table.

"Methinks it is a midsummer night's dream in January," he whispered breathily into Quatre Bras' ear. Quatre Bras withdrew his face instinctively as the foul breath of Yablans smothered him.

"And what is that supposed to mean?" he asked.

Hamlet raised his shoulders in an affected stage pose and lifted his eyes to heaven. "Lord, what fools these mortals be," he said. And before Quatre Bras could question him further, he danced away to where his eccentricity was better appreciated.

Quatre Bras watched him go with misgivings. First thing tomorrow he was going to fire that man. There was something obscenely unpleasant about him. Besides, he had bad breath. What sort of advertisement was he for the club?

Down by the tennis courts, those CVs who were not joining in the spirit of the ball were lying around on foam pillow mattresses, drinking beer, and sweating.

"God, it's hot," said Henry, the English boy.

Nobody answered. There was nothing to be said. At the end of the mattresses Sacha sat alone, quiet and thoughtful.

"What's wrong with him?" asked Mary.

Nobody answered her either.

Mary got up and walked down the bank of mattresses to Sacha. "You're looking pretty depressed'," she said, putting a hand on his fair hair.

He jumped, badly startled, and Mary withdrew her hand.

"My God, Sacha, you're touchy tonight."

Sacha recovered quickly and tried a wry grin. "I'm sorry, I was thinking of something," he said. "I didn't hear you come up."

"Anything you want to tell us about?" said Sharon Kennedy, who had wandered down to join Mary. Since the death of Pagett she had rarely been down to the tennis courts at night, but tonight the heat around the bar had become oppressive.

"No, nothing I want to tell anyone about," said Sacha. "Thanks for the thought, though."

"That's okay," said Sharon and ruffled his hair with her hand. He was such a beautiful boy, so clean and fair, and now so troubled-looking that he brought out the latent mother in just about every woman in the village.

At midnight the CVs began to drift away from the tennis courts in twos and threes, back to their own rooms. Life in a Club Village begins very early, and those who like to stay up late usually don't last very long.

"You coming?" asked Henry as he pulled himself unsteadily off the mattress and began to tag along behind the others.

"No," said Sacha, without looking up. "I think maybe I'll just hang out here for a while. See you later."

As the tennis courts cleared of people, Sacha stretched back on the mattress and lay down and faced the stars. Every star in the sky seemed magnified. There was absolutely no wind. The stillness was total.

It was marginally cooler on the beach as Beta walked along the water's edge, side by side with Scorcese. By now both had doffed their masks and watched them float away in the swell of the Atlantic's receding tide.

"Do you want to tell me what you were crying about?" asked Scorcese.

"It was something that Ernst said," replied Beta. "He called me a tart . . . which I suppose means a whore or a hooker."

"I can see he has a way with words."

"He can be blunt, all right," said Beta.

"Is it true?" asked Scorcese.

There was a long silence. It was on the tip of Beta's tongue to deny it, but she didn't. What was the point? It was true, and she knew it. She hadn't been crying because Ronay had insulted her, but because he had so accurately described her.

"Is it true?" repeated Scorcese.

"Yes," replied Beta at last. "I suppose it's true."

"I see," said Scorcese and began to walk on down the beach.

For a moment Beta thought that he was walking away from her, but after about ten yards or so he turned to her and shouted, "Well, are you coming, or aren't you?"

She went, and together they walked the whole length of the two-mile beach, arm in arm. They did not speak.

Quatre Bras' insistence that no business be spoken that evening suited Ernst Ronay admirably. The next day he would make it clear to both Quatre Bras and Scorcese that he would do all in his power, both publicly and privately, to stop the American adventure, but in the meantime he was determined to enjoy the evening. His tiff with Beta that afternoon had been unfortunate but inevitable. While one side of him was fond of her, another part of his conscience waved an admonishing finger at him for allowing himself to become involved with a girl who, despite all her protestations of love, was almost certainly besotted by his wealth and position.

Florinda and Chloe, on the other hand, were without ambition in his direction. For reasons known only to themselves, they appeared to be in a high, almost giddy mood, which suited Ronay admirably. Earlier in the evening he had wondered how he might best split the two, and which one he should make his most open bid for. But as the hours passed and the three of them drank, danced, and even sang together, it began to occur to him that he might be able to sample both.

At eleven o'clock he found himself sitting at a poolside table, with one arm thrown casually around Florinda, while Chloe knelt at his feet.

"Did either of you girls ever play that game we have in England where you're given the names of three people of the opposite sex and you have to decide which one you would marry, which to have a dirty weekend with, and which to tip over a cliff?"

Both girls shook their heads.

"Ah, then you've missed a great deal," said Ronay. "Let me give you an example, Florinda. Suppose I said to you Monsieur Quatre Bras, James Hardin . . . and, just for the sake of the game . . . me. What do you think your reply would be? Who would you tip over a cliff out of those three?"

Florinda laughed. "That's hardly fair. Why should I wish to waste any of you?" Florinda's Brazilian accent added a certain romantic flavor to her words.

"But those are the rules."

"Well, in that case, I think Quatre Bras would have to go over the cliff," laughed Florinda, immediately to be joined by Chloe. "He's the oldest, so he should go first. "I think I'd probably go for a dirty weekend with James Hardin, and marriage . . . well, that leaves only you, doesn't it?"

Ronay smiled. "And you, Chloe?"

"Again, Quatre Bras goes over the cliff. But I think I'd probably marry James Hardin . . . which means that you get the dirty weekend."

Ronay grinned. "What a lucky man I am. One to marry, and one with whom to spend a naughty weekend. Tell me, Chloe, what qualities do you think James Hardin possesses that would make him preferable to me as a husband?"

Chloe stuck her tongue in the corner of her mouth

cockily, as though having to think deeply about this. "Let's put it another way," she answered tactfully. "To me the very best weekends . . . dirty weekends, as you called them . . . have always been extremely dirty."

At this there was more giggling from Florinda.

Chloe continued. "And I suspect that to enjoy one to its fullest then it would have to be very, very naughty. And somehow I rather think that you might make a naughtier companion than our *chef de village*, sweet though he is."

Ronay laughed heartily at this. He wished now that he had insisted on taking Hardin's bungalow. To invite these two girls back to his little room was hardly his style. He lit a cigar and ordered another drink.

At twelve-thirty Hardin whispered something quietly into Cassandra's ear. They had been dancing, and then sitting together, for some hours now. Sadly Cassandra smiled and slowly shook her head. Hardin grinned philosophically and, bending forward, kissed her gently on the forehead. And with that they made separate ways back to their individual rooms.

At twelve thirty-five Ronay made his move. "Perhaps we could continue this conversation somewhere more comfortable," he suggested jokingly. "I understand that you room together." As he said this he grinned broadly. There was no way he could lose. If they refused him, he could pretend it had been a joke.

The two girls looked at each other before answering, and then, almost telepathically, reached the same conclusion. Stretching out their arms, they each took one of Ronay's hands and led him back toward the room they shared. Not for the first time, Ronay thanked God that he had been born rich, charming, and, most of all, handsome.

"You know the trouble with this place, Karen," said Hamlet Yablans as he and Karen Sorensen watched the departing trio. "There's too many people doing things they oughta be ashamed of. You know, sometimes the whole thing sickens me. All that screwing and, you know, the other things that go on here. I hope you aren't that sort of girl. If I thought you were that kind of girl, I wouldn't be sitting here talking to you. There's a lot of sick people here, you know that?''

"I don't think it's sick for people to want to enjoy themselves while on vacation," said Karen. She actually doubted whether there was much more screwing going on in Club Village than there was on the campus of the University of Colorado. But then, Hamlet was from another generation.

"Maybe not," said Hamlet. Then he grinned. "You want to come to my room?"

"What?" asked Karen. Hamlet was the least likely man in the village to be making propositions.

Hamlet recognized his mistake immediately. He shook his head and pulled a funny face. "The iron tongue of midnight hath told twelve; Lovers, to bed; 'tis almost fairy time," he said.

"I think I'd better go. Good night," said Karen, and getting up walked quickly away from the lonely, black-clad brooding figure of the forever rejected comic.

Florinda and Chloe shared a room in C Block, a ground-floor room that, because it was on the corner of the building overlooking the sea, had its own separate entrance and a small secluded garden. Had Ernst Ronay not had quite a lot to drink over dinner, and then several glasses of Bacardi since, he might have been more reticent in allowing himself to be led so eagerly into the room of two employees. But the combination of alcohol and a hot Caribbean night had taken its toll upon his common sense and propriety and, singing quietly to himself the one reggae Jimmy Cliff song he knew, he entered their room. "The harder they come, the harder they fall," he hummed.

It was the same as every other room in the village, comprising two single beds, a closet, a small bathroom with a shower, and a view through the pines toward the open sea. But because it was the permanent home of Chloe and Florinda it had developed a warmth of its own, a fragrance of femininity. The two single beds had been pushed together, presumably, thought Ronay, to give the girls more floor space. A single large hand-woven Indian blanket covered both beds.

"That's a very pretty print," Ronay commented as he admired a David Hamilton soft-focus picture taped to the wall directly above the two beds. It showed two naked young girls admiring each other in a large gilt-edged oval mirror.

Florinda smiled and, going into the bathroom, returned with three glasses, into which Chloe poured generous measures of Bacardi and Coke, which she had produced from a box in the bottom of the closet.

Ronay sank down on the edge of the bed and swung his feet up, kicking off his white Gucci shoes as he did. The room was lit by a single bedside lamp. To soften its glow Chloe tossed a red shawl over it, and the three of them were washed in a rosy glow. Florinda sank down beside him, lying full-length diagonally across the two beds. She was wearing a pareo, tied so that it hung over one shoulder and split deep up her thigh, a revelation that increased drastically as she pushed her knee up into the air and the pareo fell limply across her hips.

"You have beautiful legs, Florinda," said Ronay.

Florinda accepted the compliment graciously, but smiled at Chloe, who was calmly untying the knot that held her pareo together. Ronay followed Florinda's eyes to the short-haired, razor-cropped French girl, turning just in time to see Chloe allow the silken square of pareo to fall from her body onto the rug at the foot of the bed. She was naked, with a young, smooth, and supple body, shining with a perfectly even tan that showed no telltale swimsuit marks.

Even Ronay, a man of the world in all its sweetest surprises, had not been expecting anything quite so instantly provocative.

"What's the matter? Don't you like what you see?" asked Chloe.

Ronay could feel Florinda stiffen with interest as the two of them gazed at Chloe's body.

"I like it very much," said Ronay in a whisper which got

caught at the back of his throat. Then, reaching out his arms, he put his hands around the tops of Chloe's thighs and gently pulled her toward him until he was able to bury his face in her taut, brown belly. Above him, unknown to him, the two girls exchanged glances of mutual amusement.

"Let me help you," murmured Florinda from behind, as she slipped her fingers around his neck and down his chest, gently and expertly opening the buttons of his silk shirt, and unfastening the buckle on his trouser belt.

Tantalizingly, Florinda ran her hands across his stomach, sending electric shocks of excitement, and causing him to convulse involuntarily. His head burrowed deeper into the perfumed body of Chloe. Then, quickly and efficiently, the two girls slipped his clothing from him and, pinioning him across the two beds, began to lavish him with kisses and caresses, Chloe performing an elaborate body massage while Ronay tore at the knot holding Florinda's pareo together. It fell away, and she too was naked, taller and leaner than her friend and with curtains of long dark hair which rained across his body. She joined Chloe and tied her limbs around both of them in willful and delicious carnality.

Though Ronay had enjoyed some bizarre trysts in his time, he found himself having to suffocate his groans of pleasure as his companions sought out his secret, private areas, forever taking him to little peaks of excitement before deftly moving their attentions to other parts. And as they explored him, he nestled in the warmth of their bodies, anxious that they too should be pleased. By and by he found himself making love to first one, and then, as their tempting started again, to the other. By this time the effect of the Bacardi and their mingled perfumes had driven him quite heady with confusion. At last, more sated than he could ever remember, he fell into a sort of sleep, spread across the beds, his body drained.

He did not sleep long. A vicious indigestion, occasioned by the combination of his advancing years, the exertions of the evening, and the amount of wine and rum he had consumed, soon stabbed at his ribs angrily, and acute heartburn forced him to drag his buckled body to a sitting position. At first his eyes were bleary, and the room was dark, the shawl-covered light having been extinguished during his sleep.

Pulling his feet off the bed, he pulled on his clothes and, carrying his shoes, headed for the door. As he opened it, a shaft of moonlight fell across the beds. There, lying still naked, but now mouth to mouth, were the sleeping forms of Chloe and Florinda, their bodies intertwined in an embrace of mutual adoration.

Now he understood why the beds had been pushed together. Now he understood the poster on the wall. Now he understood their secret jokes, their telepathy, and their beautiful female arrogance. They had merely been servicing him as the managing director of Club Village. He would never know whether they had even enjoyed the experience.

Chloe and Florinda were complete in themselves. And suddenly he felt a dreadful embarrassment at his own redundancy. Closing the door softly behind him, Ronay looked around to find his bearings. It was still dark. Setting off through the gardens, he stole silently through the sleeping, humid village, back to his own room.

_____*PART VII*

_____ *FORTY-NINE*

The weather broke just before two in the morning. All the guidebooks to the Bahamas state categorically that hurricanes can be expected only between July and November, but climatology is a capricious science, and freak storms, with their attendant hurricane-scale winds and mountainous seas, do occasionally occur out of season.

The storm which hit Elixir in the early hours had been expected for some hours by the Nassau weather watchers, as a depression and attendant cold front had gone bowling down the eastern coast of the United States bringing gales and blizzards and finally rainstorms all the way down to Florida. When it reached the Bahamas, which had been sweltering in another weakening trough blown up from the tropics along the path of the North Equatorial Current, the result was a full-scale climatic war between the very hot air from the south and the cold from the north.

At one fifty-four precisely, the advance guards of the two systems met, lightning tongued across the sky, and a draft of air whistled ominously through the village. A paper cup, tossed into the air by a sudden gust of wind, danced across the gardens.

Ingrid, Karen Sorensen's roommate, hurriedly climbed the steps to her second-floor room. Already the first drops of rain were bombarding her, great heavy globules of ice water. The moon had disappeared behind a thick bank of scudding clouds, and Ingrid wished she had stayed with Girardot.

Small nightlights led the way along the balcony to her room, C25. She reached her door and, turning the handle, stepped inside away from the storm. The room was pitch black. She had no desire to waken Karen, so she moved carefully around the edge of the bed, to the bathroom and switched on the light. It was at that moment, just as she closed the bathroom door, that she caught a glimpse of Karen. For a second, she thought Karen must have fallen asleep on top of the bed, having spilled a bottle of wine on her pillow.

Ingrid opened the door just a fraction more, peering into the room.

It was at that moment that she began to scream.

Karen was indeed lying on top of her bed, but her head hung at a puzzling angle. What Ingrid had mistaken for wine stains on the pillows and sheets was in fact the still-warm blood which had gushed out when Karen's throat had been cut from ear to ear.

It was Sharon Kennedy who heard the screams and got to the room first. She switched on the bedside light and stared in horror at the congealing blood which had sprayed across the room and splattered all over the floor, and had then run freely and thickly down the naked breasts and stomach of the dead girl, until it had soaked into the starched white Club Village monogrammed sheets.

Homer Wolford took the news of Karen Sorensen's death to Hardin. It was, Hardin would recall later, the moment he had subconsciously dreaded ever since arriving at Elixir. Now there could be no doubt that Dick Pagett had been murdered.

Dressing within seconds, he gave Homer one simple order: The entire village was to be assembled in the restaurant immediately. If the CVs had to drag the guests out of their beds, then so be it. There had to be an immediate roll call. He took it upon himself to inform Quatre Bras.

Outside, in the village, the storm was growing. The

palm trees, which normally dipped and bowed so gracefully, were permanently bowed before the increasing gale. From the beach Hardin could hear great breakers racing up the shallow beach. Untethered shutters crashed against window frames.

Hardin raced through the swinging, howling pines to the dormitory area. Before facing Quatre Bras, Hardin had to see the body of Karen Sorensen.

On the third-floor balcony of C Block there was pandemonium. Sharon Kennedy had already posted a couple of CVs by the door, but panic was already gripping the guests who had heard the news.

Inside the room Hardin found Sarojine, the Indian girl doctor, crouched over the corpse. Hardin gulped back the bile which bubbled into his throat. He had no idea that so much blood could flow from one wound. He tried to look into the face of the dead girl, but his eyes were riveted on the gaping neck wound and the blood-soaked hair.

"Did you touch anything?" he asked.

Sarojine shook her head.

"How long . . . ?" He hesitated. "How long ago do you think it happened?" he asked, not even knowing whether it mattered.

Sarojine shook her head. She was a scuba doctor, not a pathologist. "Maybe an hour," she said. "It's very recent."

"Okay," said Hardin. "There's nothing you can do here. I think you're going to be needed out there calming people. I hope to God you've got a big supply of Valium, because you're going to need it. In the meantime, let's keep the room clear until we can get the police up here."

Sarojine needed no second bidding. Together they left the room. At the door Hardin found Homer and Eugene Waterman.

"What in the name of God . . . ?" began Waterman, but Hardin silenced him.

"Just make sure no one goes in there. Nobody at all, not even you guys. Okay?" he said.

The two men nodded. At moments like this, natural leaders are instinctively obeyed. And Hardin was a natural leader. A crowd of guests, some in pajamas, others in shorts and T-shirts, and yet others in nightdresses and sweatshirts over pants, was spreading down the balcony, sheltering from the swirling rain and asking each other what was happening. Ingrid was kneeling in a doorway and sobbing breathily into the arms of Sharon Kennedy.

Hardin raised his voice. "Listen. Everyone must go immediately to the restaurant. This is extremely urgent. Don't panic. Coffee will be served there, and I will come to talk to you all in a few minutes. I will explain the situation then. Go immediately, and take all of your families with you."

Then Hardin pushed his way through the throng, down the steps, and through the garden toward E Block and the inevitable meeting with Quatre Bras.

Hardin found him standing at his door in large blue-and-white striped pajamas. Even in such undignified dress, Quatre Bras looked extremely formidable.

In three sentences Hardin explained what had happened and of his decision to have an immediate roll call in the restaurant.

"I can't allow that. You'll panic the guests," said Quatre Bras.

"I can't afford to risk not panicking them," said Hardin. "The only way to protect the guests is to put them all under one roof until we find whoever did this thing."

"I think you're panicking, James," said Quatre Bras slowly, watching Hardin carefully.

"Okay, maybe I am. But I'm panicking to protect people. Now will you get the hell over to the restaurant with the other guests? You made me chief here, remember?"

Quatre Bras gazed over Hardin's head and stared, unseeing, into the wind and rain and swirling trees. "This will finish us in the American zone," he said quietly.

Hardin looked at him uncomprehendingly. "Are you out of your mind? This has already finished a young girl.

Do you understand? A young girl has been murdered. That's more important than your Club Village."

Quatre Bras gazed at him flatly. "Not to me. The club comes before everything in my life. Everything."

"Then I feel very sorry for you," said Hardin quietly, and without waiting for a reply he set off back across the village toward his office.

By now the village floodlights had been turned on, and groups of scantily clad guests were hurrying through the gale toward the central area. In the crowd Hardin spotted Anthony Scorcese with one arm wrapped protectively around Beta Ullman. They were both still fully dressed.

"Anything I can do to help?" called Scorcese.

Hardin shook his head and hurried on.

He was about to enter his office when he saw Cassandra coming toward him through the wind, a blanket wrapped around her head as protection from the rain, still wearing her nightdress.

"If you can make coffee, you can make yourself useful," he shouted at her as he pushed her into the office and toward a coffee percolator.

Cassandra did not argue.

Picking up the phone, Hardin began to dial Police Chief Johnston's number. The death had to be reported, although what Johnston could do about it in the middle of the night and in a storm like this he could not imagine.

The singsong voice of a local Bahamian woman answered. Hardin asked for Johnston.

"Oh, no, man," the woman replied. "Him and Clive, they gone to Nassau for the night. They having a policeman's reunion, so you can bet they be gettin' up to no good, drinkin' and runnin' around and chasin' all them young girls they got there."

Hardin hung up. Again and again his mind returned to the slashed neck of Karen Sorensen. He remembered seeing her at the pareo-tying contest, a pretty girl, full of smiles. He was already dreading having to inform her parents.

Turning to Cassandra he said, "I would say you got the story you came for."

She didn't reply. There was nothing to say.

Over in the corner room of C Block neither Florinda nor Chloe saw the extraordinary atmospherics which illuminated their sea view. They did not hear the cannons of thunder, or the howling gale, just as they had not heard Ernst Ronay leave them. As the wind outside had risen and the rain had begun to beat a tattoo on the patio in front of their room, Florinda had moved drowsily toward the warmth of her sleeping friend, but she had not awakened.

Not even when their door had opened had they stirred. And when at last Chloe had opened her eyes as she felt something warm trickling down her skin, she had only just been in time to realize that she was drowning in her own blood, while a ghoulishly painted gargoyle had stood over her, tears of frustration running down his cheeks onto the double-edged knife he was holding.

"I'm sorry," he had whispered. "I'm sorry."

But there had been no one alive to hear him.

There was no sign of panic in the restaurant. Indeed, there was hardly any noise at all. Husbands tried to murmur comforting words to wives, while the few children in the village were held close to confused, anxious parents. It was nearly four in the morning. Outside, the storm had turned into heavy torrential rain and wind, the electricity of the earlier clash having burned itself out.

Cassandra checked her watch. It wouldn't be light for another two and a half hours. That still seemed like forever. As she stared at the crowds of people who were sitting waiting for the comfort of dawn, she noticed that the faces of the other guests constantly scanned each other, as though each person were trying to find the killer.

Cassandra was obsessed with the idea that perhaps she had only just escaped attack earlier in the week when she had seen the face at the window. And she wondered whether any of the three murdered girls had awakened before the attack, and seen that insanely grinning face.

English Henry and Waterman, the accountant, had discovered the bodies of Florinda and Chloe after the girls' absence from the restaurant had been noticed. Hardin had tried to keep the news secret from the guests. But within minutes rumors began to spread and he was forced to make a brief announcement absolutely forbidding anyone from leaving the restaurant.

Just as he finished speaking the lights in the village went out as the storm hit the generator. Luckily the restaurant was well stocked with lanterns and candles, but the eerie glow that was now cast upon the assembled villagers did nothing to ease the tension.

At the back of the restaurant, near the entrance to the kitchens, the CVs served a never-ending supply of coffee. For the first time since she had been in the village, Cassandra was aware of silence. It was as though she were in church, she thought. If anyone had to speak they whispered, and an undercurrent of politeness extended itself even to the most bombastic.

Cassándra moved through the restaurant, seeing and noting everything. After the initial shock, her journalistic spirit was quickly reviving. She wanted to remember everything about this night, exactly as it happened. Seeing these hundreds of frightened people, huddled together for protection against an unknown horror, made her wish she had had the presence of mind to bring her camera to the restaurant with her. When all of this was over, the haggard expressions on the faces of Quatre Bras and Ernst Ronay would be a fascinating illustration of paradise stricken by terror.

"If you ask me, they got what they deserved," a rasping nasal voice cut through her thoughts.

Cassandra turned around. Hamlet Yablans was sitting in a corner by himself. Guests and CVs tried to ignore him, but his voice sliced through the silence around him.

"They were just hookers, let's admit it. That's all that kind deserves," he went on. Apparently Shakespeare had deserted him.

"For God's sake, will you keep your foul mouth closed?" said a voice behind Cassandra. It was Sacha. He was looking at Hamlet with loathing and anger. For a moment Cassandra thought Sacha was about to punch him.

"Methinks he doth protest too much," said Hamlet quietly, grimacing horribly at Sacha, showing his incomplete set of ugly, yellow-stained false teeth.

Sacha refused to rise to the bait. Instead he looked disdainfully at the black-clad clown. "You know your trouble, Hamlet?" he said. "You're a complete asshole."

Hamlet's face collapsed, like a balloon suddenly released of air. Loneliness covered it. "I know," he said simply.

Cassandra moved between the two men. "Could I get you two some coffee?" she asked, trying to relieve the tension.

Sacha smiled sweetly. "Let me get it, Cassandra," he said, and went off to join the line.

Hamlet sat in his corner, his legs crossed, his black tights running at the knees and his velvet smock smeared with sweat. Since the electricity had been cut the air conditioning had gone off, and, as the storm was still howling outside, it had been impossible to open the windows. Cassandra knelt down alongside him. She didn't like him. She found him repellent. But when Sacha attacked him she saw a dreadful loneliness and hopelessness in Hamlet. She felt sorry for him. He was ugly and untalented in a place of youth and beauty. His act, his talking to the skull, his comments on the dead girls, now appeared only as pleas for attention from a desperately unhappy and lonely man. People laughed at him, but no one wanted to sit with him at dinner. No one ever bought him a drink. He was a grotesquerie, the modern equivalent of the ugly little dwarf doing cartwheels on the dining table of the medieval baron.

He was a reminder to everyone of just how beautiful they were. People sometimes regressed to their most primitive urges, and poor Hamlet filled the urge to taunt the misshapen. For the first time Cassandra saw all this and was ashamed that she had been so disgusted by the strange and lonely man.

She leaned forward toward him. "I know you didn't mean that about the girls, Hamlet," she said.

Tears were filling Hamlet's large, bloodshot eyes. An unpleasant aroma of perspiration mingled with cheap deodorant rose rankly from his smock. "I don't even know why I said it," he said haltingly after a moment or two. "I guess I'm just jealous. They were so beautiful, and they could have their pick of every man here in Club Village. And they were always so arrogant . . . Chloe and Florinda, I mean. The other one, I only spoke to her for the first time tonight, you know. She sort of told me to get lost. That's what they always say. You get used to hearing it, but you never get used to being hurt by it. Silly, isn't it?"

Cassandra didn't say anything. Sacha returned with two coffees in paper cups, and handed them down to her and Hamlet. Then, with a dismissive look to Hamlet, he moved a few feet away and sat down, alone and thoughtful, at a vacant table.

"You know, all my life I've wanted to make it with a girl like that. Couple of times I paid for it. And they were pretty good. But they didn't even try to hide the expressions on their faces. Everyone wants to fuck an Al Pacino or a Robert Redford. But I got feelings, too, you know."

Suddenly Cassandra remembered something. "Hamlet, you told me a couple of days ago that there was someone who was very sick in this village. . . . Whom did you mean?"

Hamlet laughed. "You wanna know? I meant me. I'm sick. I really am. I'm so sick I sometimes hate myself. You know what I mean? You know what it really means to hate yourself? Really *hate?* I hate the way I look, I hate the way I talk, I hate the way I smell . . . yeah, sure I know I smell. God, I stink when it gets hot. But I use deodorants, and there's nothing I can do to stop my breath smelling. I seen a doctor once about it. He said it has to do with stress and bad eating habits. But it doesn't go away. That's why I always turn away from people when I'm talking to them. You ever noticed that? You want to know something? I'm a fucking lonely man. That's me. Hamlet Yablans . . . lonely and pathetic. And the thing I hate most of all is me feeling sorry for myself, and people like you coming to talk to me because you feel sorry for me. I don't need anyone feeling sorry for me. I can handle it all by myself. All right? I've always been by myself . . . always . . . and I've gotten along okay, so don't you start coming around here pretending that you give a shit, because I know your type. I seen your picture in that magazine. And you was writing about a lot of rich and good-looking people, people who wouldn't piss on me if I was on fire.

"Well, I don't need your sympathy. Because I'm okay. I get along all right. Everything's just great with me. Okay? I'm sorry that those girls got killed . . . honest to God, I'm sorry . . . but, you know, I bet they never had a bad day in their lives before. Know what I mean? Maybe the young kid was okay, but the other two—shit!—did they love themselves? I heard they got their throats cut . . . that true? I heard there was blood everywhere. Did you hear that? Shit! They didn't deserve that."

"Who do you think killed them, Hamlet?" Cassandra asked quietly.

"Holy shit, lady." Hamlet shook his head slowly. "You're asking me? Listen, I do the Hamlet act here, not the Lady Macbeth. Okay? Now please push off and get out of my light because, you know, you're beginning to bug me a little. Okay? Nothing personal. Okay?"

Cassandra moved away from Hamlet and sat down at the table alongside Sacha. She felt ashamed that it had taken a situation like this to get her to talk to Hamlet, and now even more ashamed that it should ever have crossed her mind that he might be capable of murder. All week he

had seemed sinister and frightening. But now, hunched up
in the corner, he reminded her of a frightened, shunned,
lame little animal who has been driven from the herd.

"The world is very unfair," said Cassandra to Sacha,
who was gazing at his hands quietly. "I just upset Hamlet
because he thought I might be suggesting that he was in
some way involved in . . . in, you know, what happened
tonight."

"Why is it unfair?"

"Oh, I suppose because in my mind I equated the fact
that he's ugly, and well, weird, and . . . almost deformed,
with guilt."

Sacha nodded. "God, I wish they could open the
windows in here, or something. The air is just about pure
carbon dioxide." He screwed up his nose.

"It should be dawn in about two hours," replied Cassandra. "I suppose they'll let us all go back to our rooms then.
Everyone feels safer in the daytime."

"Yes," Sacha agreed.

For the sake of conversation, Cassandra continued to
talk. "You were friendly with Florinda and Chloe, weren't
you? It's terrible about . . . I mean, I'm really sorry."

"Yes. Not great friends, you understand. They were
very much into each other. They were cute though," he
said, with that detached air of sadness, which is quite
different from grief.

Farther down the restaurant Alex, the bartender, sat
alone.

For the first time since he had been in Club Village he
felt good. The evil were being punished. Retribution had
started. God's fiery sword was burning out the cancer of
sin. Smiling secretly to himself, Alex surveyed the hundreds of frightened people. He was not afraid. With God
on his side, why should he be?

For the first time in his life Ernst Ronay understood the
experience of disorientation. He simply could not believe

what had happened to him. What had started out as a deliciously wicked evening had turned first bitter, and then poisonous.

After being told what had happened, he had gone to the restaurant and sat quietly by himself for a long time, staring out mutely at the storm, listening to the sea, which suddenly sounded as though it were about to swallow the whole island in its fury. Suddenly the life of the high-flying socialite jet-setter had lost its attraction. He looked around for Beta and saw her sitting next to Scorcese. He had an arm around her shoulder.

He looked out the window again and thought about the girls who had died. They could have been his own children, he told himself. A large lump grew in his throat as he thought about his own daughters and son back at school in England, and how hurt they would be when they learned of his involvement.

Quatre Bras was not thinking about the dead girls. He had hardly known them so he did not feel any particular loss, although as the patriarchal head of Club Village he would later issue a statement heavy with grief, claiming that it was as though he had lost a child.

In the meantime, his most important task was to save the good name of the club. There had never been a murder on the grounds of Club Village before (more by good fortune than anything else, he was prepared to concede), and he was already beginning to plan ways to introduce new security measures.

If anyone grieved deeply for Karen Sorensen, Chloe, and Florinda that night, it was not the staff of Club Village, whose reactions had been dulled by years of forced smiles and false living. Oddly it was the guests who felt the shock most deeply. John Arrowsmith summed up their feelings most accurately.

"I feel ashamed," he said to Michael Roeg and their two wives as they huddled over a corner table drinking coffee. "When I first heard all the panic, when they began beating on the doors, when I first heard that some kid had been murdered, I didn't even stop to ask her name. I was so goddamn scared all I could think was, 'Thank God it wasn't me. . . . ' And even now, I'm sitting here looking around at everybody else, thinking, 'Is it him?' or 'Is it him?' and I'm still finding it hard to feel sorry for the kids he got to."

There was a long silence, broken at last as Ruth said, "It sort of makes everything else seem so unimportant, doesn't it?" She gazed steadily at her husband.

Arrowsmith tried a wan, apologetic smile toward her. Gently she took his hand, in a gesture of mutual comfort. Alongside murder, everything else pales into insignificance.

For two people the events of the night were to act as catalysts. Anthony Scorcese and Beta Ullman talked for hours, telling their life stories. He insisted on being told everything about her. He wanted no lies, no coverups, just the truth as she saw it. They sat in a corner and she told him everything she could think of, even the bits that embarrassed her, such as her fling with Hardin. And he listened quietly, nodding from time to time, although whether the nods were intended to convey understanding, or were simply a way of punctuating her thoughts, she had no way of knowing.

At one point Quatre Bras came across to Scorcese and muttered a few words of embarrassment and frustration, but he did not persist in conversation when Scorcese suggested that it would perhaps be best if they met in New York sometime when the situation could be assessed in a less emotional atmosphere. Recognizing a polite closing of the door, Quatre Bras smiled, drew himself up as pompously as he could in pajamas, and returned to the far end of the room to the comfort of Girardot and his last remaining Gitane.

And Scorcese and Beta went back to each other.

The sight of Quatre Bras and Ronay slumped in separate corners of the room, each busy with his own thoughts, fascinated Cassandra as only a journalist could be fascinated by such a situation. Around her the oil lamps flickered on the faces of the guests, bewildered evacuees from terror. If only *Night and Day* had sent a photographer down with her! This had to be the best story she was ever likely to cover, but she needed pictures, shots of Quatre Bras, sucking on the stump of his last cigarette; of Ronay, crucified by what public opinion was about to do to him; and of the terrified guests and CVs.

She checked her watch. It was nearly 6:00 A.M. It would be dawn soon. Perhaps she could sneak across the village and get her camera. But then she thought about the bodies of the three girls, lying across their beds. She dared not go out there alone.

For a moment she considered soliciting Hardin's protection, but just as quickly she abandoned the idea. He would be the last person to want to help her take photographs. At that moment Sacha caught her eye. He was standing near a window and gazing out into the storm.

Cassandra reflected for a moment, then made her decision. "Sacha, I know this is asking an awful lot of you . . . but would you mind coming with me to my room? I have to get something," she said.

Sacha looked around at her quizzically. Cassandra decided to explain. "The truth is, Sacha, I have to get my camera out of my suitcase. I—I'm a journalist. All this is too good for a journalist to miss." With a wave she indicated the room full of people.

"They aren't letting anyone out until it gets light," said Sacha.

"I know. But they aren't paying that much attention either, are they? No one is exactly rushing to go out there."

After a moment's thought, he grinned impishly and nodded. "Okay. Why not? I like a little excitement. I'll go first. We'll go over through the kitchens. They'll assume we've gone to get something to eat."

Cassandra smiled. He was a brave kid. She hoped he wouldn't regret helping her.

Nonchalantly, Sacha meandered off toward the kitchens. No one stopped him. The Bahamian security guards walked purposefully around the room, their eyes on the guests. Most of the CVs were congregated in little groups, quietly gossiping among themselves. As soon as Cassandra saw that Sacha had gone, she stood up and wandered after him.

One of the security guards approached her. She smiled, and made a comment about being grateful when it would be light. The man nodded and moved on. Then, with one quick look behind her, Cassandra slipped into the kitchens.

Only Alex noticed as they left the restaurant. Alex always noticed everything. He was a watcher. He was God's eyes and ears, wasn't he?

Sacha was waiting for Cassandra behind a bank of vast refrigerators in the kitchens. As she entered he stepped out from the gloom and beckoned to her.

"Come on, this way; there's a window over here we can open," he said.

Taking her by the arm, he led her around the huge cold storage area.

"I never saw so many fridges in my life," said Cassandra.

"They have a problem keeping the food fresh in this

climate," explained Sacha. Then, mischievously, he pulled open a freezer door. A side of beef was hanging from a hook. "This is where they put people when they die," he said suddenly.

"What?" asked Cassandra, startled.

"In here. Just like this beef," said Sacha, grinning. "Weird, isn't it? They have to keep the bodies fresh for the coroner, you see, and it gets pretty hot here in the summer. There was a guy had a heart attack here last September. They had him in here for days until they could decide what to do with the body."

"Fascinating," said Cassandra, and pushed the freezer door closed.

Carefully Sacha opened a window over a row of washbasins. "The CVs use this window for getting in and raiding the food supplies," he explained.

Cassandra nodded and, holding her nightdress skirt around her knees, she climbed onto the basin and out into the storm. Sacha followed.

Outside, the grass was covered with an inch of water, and their feet sank into the soft turf. But it was raining less than it had been an hour earlier, and a stiff, cool breeze was blowing down from the north. Looking out toward the Atlantic, Cassandra could already see a faint, pale-gray glow in the far sky.

Quickly, they hurried across the dark and silent village. As they passed C Block, Cassandra cast fearful eyes to the end room, where she knew the bodies of Chloe and Florinda still lay. Sacha put a comforting arm out. Gripping his hand, she felt instantly stronger.

"I'm in B23," she said.

"I know," replied Sacha, but his reply was drowned by the sound of rain rushing and spraying over the balcony from a blocked gutter.

They climbed the steps of B Block quickly. It was very dark, but Cassandra now knew the steps so well that she could feel her way, holding onto the banister all the way up. Only when she reached her room did she stop. She was, she realized, afraid to enter.

"Sacha . . ." She turned to her companion almost sheepishly.

Sacha grinned reassuringly. Stepping past her, he opened the door and allowed it to swing open. Cassandra peered inside.

"Come on, it's quite safe," said Sacha and entered the room.

Encouraged by Sacha'a display of pluck, Cassandra followed him, feeling her way carefully across to the bed. Although she didn't smoke, she had left a book of matches in the ashtray on the bedside table. They had been a silly memento from her night in the Balmoral Beach Hotel, Nassau, just over a week before.

Gingerly, she groped among the objects on the table for the matches. Her wrist caught against the lampshade, and the lamp fell off the table and smashed onto the tile floor.

"Oh, God," she cried.

"Take it easy, take it easy," cooed Sacha. *"You've* nothing to be afraid of. *I'm* here, remember?"

Something about the way Sacha accentuated the word "you've" puzzled Cassandra, but she said nothing.

Groping across the table again, she finally discovered the matches. With shaking fingers she tore one off the book and struck it.

"Here, light this," said Sacha, producing a stub of a candle he must have taken from the restaurant.

Cassandra held the match to the candle. Quickly, the wick caught fire. Allowing some hot wax to drip into the ashtray, Cassandra stood the candle in the wax until it was secure.

"God, that's better," she said as the glow filled the room.

Sacha laughed and, closing the door, locked out the wind that had been threatening to blow out the flame. "You're a very nervous person, Cassandra," he said.

She turned to look at him. In the yellow glow of candlelight his hair looked even fairer. She smiled back.

She opened the closet and lifted down her suitcase. Sacha helped her put it onto the bed. Flicking open the two locks, she opened it. The Pentax was hidden beneath a scattered pile of underwear. She felt slightly embarrassed that he should see them. Quickly, she pulled out the camera and snapped the case shut again.

"I hope you have film in it,' said Sacha.

"Yes," said Cassandra. "Always prepared . . . or nearly always, anyway."

At that moment she saw a shadow move across her pillow. She looked up. Sacha had frozen at her side. "I could have sworn I saw something move," she said.

Allowing her curiosity to get the better of her she gently folded back the counterpane on her bed. Suddenly the shadow slid rapidly toward her. She screamed and jumped back.

Sacha sprang. In one movement his hand went down to his ankle and, almost before Cassandra was aware of it, a knife was plunged deep into the pillow, pinning a wriggling lizard to the bed. Cassandra felt something splash across her face. Without pausing, Sacha pulled the lizard off the end of his knife and, taking it by the back legs, savagely ripped it apart.

"In the name of God . . ." Cassandra screamed. And then suddenly she was quiet.

The benign expression had gone from Sacha's face. His features were contracted in a gaze of delicious triumph. He was high on his kill, heady with a taste of killing. His lips curled at the sides. A dimple flickered in his cheek.

Cassandra's eyes fixed on the knife. In the flickering candlelight she could see the guts of the lizard sticking to the blade. "Oh, my God," she whispered as she saw the pieces of flesh soaking her pillow.

As Sacha became aware of her again, the expression of delight drained from his eyes. He was still holding the knife.

Cassandra stepped toward the door, trying to get past him. Suddenly she stumbled and tripped over the foot of the bed that had been Piebald Jane's, falling, sprawling onto the floor. Automatically, she screamed.

"Quiet," hissed Sacha.

Cassandra looked up. Sacha was standing over her, holding the knife. He put his free hand down to help her up, but she didn't take it. Her eyes never left the knife. Gradually, she tried to slide away from Sacha across the floor.

"What are you doing, Cassandra?" Sacha asked, his voice as innocent as a little boy's. He took one step after her.

She held her hand up in front of her face. "Please, Sacha . . ." she heard herself murmuring. Everything was so clear to her now. This strange beautiful boy who had been friendly to all the girls had been possessed of an almost beatific gentleness. But now a manic savagery gripped him, and a desire to inflict pain shone on his face.

She wondered how she could have been so blind. She moved across the floor, away from him again, and found her hand resting in the wet fleshy remains of the torn lizard. She shuddered and pulled her hand away, wiping the slime on the skirt of her nightdress.

She stared at him. In the flickering candlelight she now saw another face, as his expression seemed to transform into the grinning reptile mask that had stared in at her that first night. She tried to pull herself to her feet. She wondered if she could scream, but knew instinctively that it was useless. The sound of rain was unceasing, and all help lay on the other side of the village.

Sacha stepped forward so that he was standing over her. "I asked you what you're so frightened of, Cassandra," he repeated. "Didn't you ever see a lizard killed before? There's nothing wrong with killing lizards, you know. They're not like people. Lizards don't matter. Not like people."

Cassandra tried to drag herself away, but Sacha stood on the hem of her nightdress. As she struggled, the skirt tore, revealing a wide stretch of her thighs.

"My, my, you sure have pretty legs, Cassandra. Anybody ever tell you that before?" Sacha was staring down at her. "I bet you've been told that a lot of times, haven't you? I like pretty girls. Only pretty girls. I'm a pretty guy, aren't I? Everyone says that. Good-looking Sacha. That's what they call me. All talk and no follow-through. Isn't that what they say?"

Cassandra tried to move again, but Sacha remained where he was. The nightdress tore farther, revealing the tops of her thighs.

Sacha gazed at the soft, cotton V shape of her panties. Very slowly he drew the tip of his tongue across the underside of his top lip.

"Very nice, Cassandra," he murmured.

Cassandra stared at him. Something was telling her that it wasn't happening, that she was imagining everything. Speak normally, she told herself. "I think . . . I think we ought to be getting back," she said absurdly. "They'll have missed us by now."

Sacha simply stared at her, neither moving nor answering. His grip on the knife became tighter.

Suddenly Cassandra heard herself begin to sob. "Please, Sacha, can we go back . . . ?"

"There's no going back for me, Cassandra. Not really," came the reply.

"I don't know what you mean. If we go now . . . they'll never know we've been out. And I won't tell them anything . . ." gabbled Cassandra. She had no idea what she was saying. She was talking to stay alive. Sacha's hand gripped tightly around the knife.

"What do you mean?" he asked. "What aren't you going to tell them?"

"Well . . . nothing." Cassandra tried to wrench herself away again. Her nightdress tore as far as the waist. Keeping her eyes glued to his gaze, she pulled a torn fold of cotton nightdress across her thighs, more as a diversionary tactic than as an act of modesty.

"What aren't you going to tell them?" asked Sacha again.

"I didn't mean anything, I promise you," she whispered again.

Carefully, deliberately, Sacha wiped the blade of his knife on the counterpane of one of the beds. "She told you, too, didn't she?" he said at last.

"I don't know what you mean," gasped Cassandra. "Who told me what?"

"I bet you think it's funny, too? Isn't that right? Did you laugh, Cassandra? Jesus, I bet you split yourself over that. Poor old Sacha, pretty-boy Sacha, can't get it up. I should have known you'd be just like all the others. Isn't it incredible? I could have any woman I want, and I can't have any at all! Karen shouldn't have told you. She shouldn't have told anyone. There was no need for her to tell anyone. Look at the trouble she's caused. It's all her fault. You can see that, can't you? It isn't my fault that it's broken. That it doesn't work. Jesus Christ, no one can blame me."

"I don't know what you're talking about."

"Don't tell me lies. I don't want to be lied to. Too many people lied before. They said it didn't matter. *They* told *me* it didn't matter. Don't you think that's funny? *They* told *me*. Jesus, but it matters to me. Shit, if you only knew how much it matters. If you only knew what it's like to want it so badly that you can feel the blood pumping through your skull like a fucking hammer, and yet there's no way . . . no way. It's broken, they said. The hydraulics are fucked up. You'll get used to it in time. Oh yes. In time. Maybe it's all psychological, I thought. No . . . no . . . sorry, they said. It's really broken. Never to work again. We're sorry, we can't help you, son."

He stopped talking and stared at Cassandra. Then he looked down at her thighs again and very delicately, with the tip of his blade, parted her nightdress and slipped the knife between her skin and the top of her pants, cutting the thin cotton material. Cassandra stared down at the knife, unable to move away from its gentle, terrible probing. One sudden movement and her stomach would be ripped open.

"What do you want me to do?" she murmured hoarsely, trying desperately to keep her voice from soaring.

Slowly, Sacha sank to his knees before her, spreading her thighs with his hands, until he knelt before her almost in an attitude of adoration.

"Dick Pagett . . . he thought I was some kind of freak . . ." Sacha was lying down now, his head between Cassandra's legs. She could feel his breath warm on her thighs. The knife continued to cut through the fabric of her panties. "He used to make fun of me. Maybe he guessed. One day he followed me. He said he didn't. But I knew he had. I'd made a home for myself on one of the cays. I called it my weekend home. Then he came and spoiled it all. . . ."

Cassandra flinched as the tip of the knife dug accidentally into the flesh at the top of her thigh. Sacha stopped talking. Cassandra felt a trickle of warm blood run down the inside of her thigh. She gasped. Tears filled her eyes. But she stayed quiet.

Sacha gazed at the trickle of blood, his mood changing again. "I'm sorry . . . I hurt you," he said. "I'm sorry, Cassandra. I didn't want to hurt you. I don't want to hurt anyone. I'm sorry. Please forgive me. I like you. I liked you the first day I met you. I came to look for you, but you frightened me away. God, I'm sorry, Cassandra. I don't want to hurt you."

Cassandra lay still. Sacha had become a babbling, weeping child.

"I don't want to hurt anyone," Sacha repeated. "It was Karen's fault. She made them laugh at me. I loved them . . . I loved Chloe and Florinda. They never tried to fuck me. They were my friends, until I saw them laughing at me. She told them. She shouldn't have told them. Just like you laughed when she told you."

Slowly Cassandra was pulling herself up off the floor. Sacha was now in a crouching position. His hands covered his eyes. Tears ran freely down his cheeks.

"She didn't tell me anything, Sacha," said Cassandra very quietly. "Karen didn't tell me anything. No one laughed at you. No one. It was your imagination. No one knew."

Sacha was slowly crumpling on the floor; his knife flipped out of his hand as his sobbing grew deeper.

"I didn't want to hurt them," he said. "I didn't want to hurt you. You know that, don't you? But I thought they were laughing at me . . . I thought they were all laughing at me. I couldn't let them do that . . . I couldn't let them laugh, could I . . . ?"

Cassandra was now on her feet and edging toward the door. Sacha didn't move. Very quietly, she opened the door and stepped outside onto the balcony.

Homer Wolford found Sacha shortly after eight o'clock on that chill Sunday morning. As soon as it had become light, groups of male CVs were sent to scour the village, hunting in threes, with instructions not to get too close, but to report back as soon as Sacha was sighted.

After Cassandra had stumbled back into the restaurant, Hardin and Quatre Bras decided that the safest thing to do was to wait for dawn. After all, there was nowhere Sacha could run. Even if he took a boat, which was unlikely, he could hardly get very far in an hour.

As it turned out, he didn't get very far at all, and there was no need for caution. When Homer found him, Sacha was alone in the open-sided theater, dead, swinging slowly from one of the overhead crossbeams, a length of wire tied around his neck, under his long blond hair.

Homer was tall, so tall that he almost brushed his head against Sacha's feet as he looked around the theater, still decorated with the beautifully ornate swinging masks and paper figures Sacha had designed for the ball. And there was Sacha, even more beautiful than anything he had created, hanging with them, the best-looking man anyone had ever seen in Club Village, a world of beautiful people.

The wind had dropped to nothing and the sea was now no more than a murmur. The storm was over.

Hardin and Quatre Bras were present when they cut Sacha down.

"My God . . . look at his face," said Michel Girardot as the corpse was lowered to the ground.

Hardin stared into the bulging, bloated face of the boy who had once been so beautiful. Painted all over his skin were flecks of green and black and yellow. Around his eyes were black slit marks, while his mouth was painted to stretch nearly back to his ears.

"He had a thing about lizards," Hardin said simply. "He hated them. He tried to make himself look like one."

_____*PART VIII*

_____FIFTY-ONE

A cock crowed; an amplified stereophonic Sergeant Pepper cock. "Good morning, good morning, good morning," sang John Lennon over the loudspeakers, and another day began in Elixir's Club Village. Another day. The sun shone; the gardeners tied back bougainvillea bushes that had been battered by the storm; on the tennis courts the early risers, stripped to the waist, rallied backward and forward; along the beach the joggers pounded the sand; in the pool the spartans worked up an appetite; and down at the marina the scuba team checked and double-checked the oxygen equipment that would be used that day.

In the restaurant, Cassandra helped herself to fruit juice and croissants, and made her way across to where Hardin was sitting alone, meditating into his coffee cup.

It was Monday morning, twenty-four hours after her ordeal, and inevitably the village was back to normal, burying its memories of death and terror in the sunshine smiles of another day. Another day in Never-Never-Land.

The police had arrived at Elixir shortly after lunch on Sunday, the two local policemen together with six detectives and two pathologists from Nassau. As expected, Ernst Ronay had had to give a complete account of his activities the previous night, as had all the Club Village staff. The police were polite, but when half a dozen reporters and three photographers flew into Elixir that afternoon, it was clear that the story was out. It was going to be every man for himself.

At this point Cassandra had made her one request to Hardin. "Would you have any objections if I used the Telex machine?"

"To file your story to New York?"

"Yes."

"If I say no?"

"I'll take the plane to Nassau and file from there," she had replied.

"For somebody who nearly got herself killed just a few hours ago, you're very determined. Go ahead. If Quatre Bras comes snooping around, tell him you're writing to your mother."

"Not everything I'm going to say about Club Village is going to be flattering," Cassandra had said, hesitating at what might seem a betrayal of his kindness and friendship.

"It's your job, Cassandra. If you did less than your job, you'd be letting yourself down."

And with that Hardin had led her into his office, pulled up his chair to the Telex machine and, with a parting "Don't forget to spell my name correctly," left her.

It had taken Cassandra two hours to write and file her report. It was a very long news feature, the pictures being supplied by agency photographers who were at that moment roaming all over the village.

Shortly after she had completed her final paragraph, a reply had come tapping out of the machine. The message was simple. "CONGRATS. COVER STORY. RETURN N.Y. SOONEST." It was signed by the *Night and Day* editor-in-chief.

"If I were you I'd go off to bed now and get a very long sleep," Hardin had said when he returned.

"Would you consider it pushy if I asked if I could stay in the bungalow tonight?" Cassandra had asked after a moment's embarrassed hesitation. "I mean, I know you have an extra room there. I wouldn't be a nuisance. You wouldn't know I was there."

"That's what I'm afraid of," Hardin smiled. Then, taking her by the hand, he had led her across the gardens to his bungalow, where she had quickly fallen asleep in the spare bedroom. Outside he had rocked thoughtfully on his veranda.

Cassandra had slept fitfully but undisturbed and when she had awoken at eight on Monday morning she was surprised to realize that somehow normality had descended upon the village like a heavy suffocating blanket.

"It's as though nothing ever happened here," she said to Hardin as she joined him at the breakfast table.

He grimaced. "That's the strength of Club Village. We're all brainwashed by the system. Last night, after you went to bed, Quatre Bras told everyone that their whole vacation cost would be refunded, that all the CVs would get a month's extra pay and supply of bar shells, and that the bar would be completely free until midnight. You should have seen the good times people were having. It was as though they were almost grateful to Sacha. It was frightening. It made me feel sick."

"So what are you going to do?"

"I guess I'll look for a job."

"You've got a job."

"Not anymore I haven't. Last night Quatre Bras complained about my letting you use the Telex machine. He thought he could have talked you into writing something flattering about the way we handled the crisis."

"How do you know I didn't?"

"I don't. But he assumed you'd done a hatchet job on us and he got pretty irate, so . . . so I told him to stuff his job and Club Village."

"Oh, God, you lost your job because of me?"

"No. I lost my job because of *me*. I don't believe in Club Village anymore. I think it's an okay place for people to come on vacation. They get value for money, and all that. But it does something to the people who work here. I left once before because I couldn't stand being cut off from the outside world. This time I'm leaving for good. It's dangerous to be on vacation all year round. I need some reality. I don't know what I mean other than maybe I have a more useful contribution to make somewhere else in the world, doing something else. So far my life had always been tied up with trivia . . . playing tennis, running vacations for well-off middle-class people . . . screwing a lot of beautiful ladies . . . sorry, don't blush . . . I didn't mean to say that. . . ."

"That's okay," said Cassandra. "Go on."

"Well, there's not a great deal more to say, other than that I'm hitching a ride out of here with Scorcese this morning, and I'll be looking for a job when I get to New York."

"You're going with Scorcese?"

"His Learjet is coming for him."

"Any chance of a spare seat on the Lear, do you think?"

"I'm sure. I was going to suggest it to you, anyway. But I knew you'd ask."

"I'm a journalist."

"Of course. You make your own luck, I know." Hardin paused and stirred his coffee. "Perhaps if you're going to be in New York for a few days we could meet again, before you go home to London."

"Yes," said Cassandra. "I'd like that very much."

Quatre Bras walked sternly along the beach. The Club Village massacre, as it was luridly coming to be called, was already the newspaper story of the week, even before he had managed to get his lawyers and publicists out from New York and Paris to handle the affair. Yet, somehow, it didn't all seem like failure. He knew he had lost Scorcese, and that his own plans for building a new empire in the American zone were going to have to wait awhile, but he also knew that there would be other chances. It was, of course, a major setback. But that was the fun of business, riding the waves of success and of failure. He was down now, but he would climb back, and in the meantime he was going to have to concentrate all his energies on holding the position of Club Village in the vacation world. The main rival, Club Med, was expanding every day.

There was, of course, one particularly nice consolation to all this. Late the previous evening after taking a grilling from the Nassau police over his involvement with Florinda and Chloe, Ernst Ronay had crept up to him and quietly announced his resignation. The bad publicity was sure to force him into seclusion. Magnanimous in victory, Quatre Bras had shaken his head sadly and pulled out a bottle of cognac. And for the first time since they had worked together, the two men had shared the conviviality of a quiet drink alone. Not that this sudden display of friendship would have any effect upon Ronay's decision. Quatre Bras had already accepted his resignation on behalf of the board. Once again, Quatre Bras would be the complete master of Club Village.

Contemplating this, Quatre Bras smiled to himself, standing erect, a general mulling over a small defeat, knowing that bigger victories lay just ahead. Men like Quatre Bras can and do survive everything.

James Hardin was not the only person to lose his job at Elixir that weekend. Hamlet Yablans was given six months' pay and free passage out of Elixir on the first available plane. He was not surprised. He was used to being fired. Quatre Bras had not shared Dick Pagett's bizarre sense of humor. Hamlet's sin was that he was ugly. He left at ten o'clock that morning, sweating profusely and trying to disguise his bad breath with a stick of chewing gum. Nobody saw him off, although Alex the bartender grinned gleefully as the sad little clown stumbled over his heavy suitcases.

The Monday game of mixed doubles was Ruth Arrowsmith's idea. That was how she and John had met up with Joanna and Michael Roeg at the tournament in New Rochelle, and it seemed the perfect way of loosening up after the traumas of the weekend.

"Michael and I will play against you two," said Ruth as the two couples took the court after breakfast.

Joanna and Arrowsmith nodded and retreated to the far end of the court.

Roeg smiled at Ruth. "I hope you don't mind me saying this, Ruth, but I sort of think you're wonderful," he said as she prepared to serve to her husband. "Maybe when we get back to New York you'd both like to come over some night and join Joanna and me in our hot tub."

Ruth hit the ball. It was an ace. "Fifteen–love," she shouted. Then turning to Roeg she said quietly, "Who needs John and Joanna, Michael?"

Roeg's face fell into a half smile of astonishment. Ruth served again. This time Arrowsmith returned it into the net.

"Thirty–love," shouted Ruth. Then to Roeg she added, "I'm free Thursdays. Okay?"

"Okay!" said Roeg.

"Okay," said Ruth, and winked. She wasn't going to be the invisible, dutiful wife anymore. And God, how good it felt.

Homer Wolford drove Hardin and Cassandra down to the airstrip in the red Citroën. A Club Village lifer, Homer was now acting as chief of the village.

This was the second time in two weeks that Hardin had left a village, but this time he was saying good-bye to all the clubs. At the airstrip he shook hands with Scorcese and Beta Ullman, who were waiting for them.

"We have some news for you," said Scorcese as the two couples climbed aboard the plane. "Beta and I are going to be married. She's looking for a millionaire to indulge her, and I'm looking for a beautiful woman to indulge. Sounds like a great idea, doesn't it?"

"Well, yes. Congratulations, both of you," Hardin said and, leaning forward, shook Scorcese's hand and kissed Beta lightly on the cheek.

Minutes later, as the Lear with its four passengers roared into the sky, Scorcese unbuckled his seat belt and, going to a refrigerator, pulled out a bottle of Bollinger. With the skill of a man who has spent his life opening champagne bottles on jets, he poured four glasses without spilling a drop.

"To your happiness," said Hardin as Scorcese and Beta raised and clinked their glasses.

"I'm sure you'll be very happy," said Cassandra, and meant it.

"Thank you," said Scorcese, and for the very first time he kissed the astonished Beta. He hadn't bothered to tell her about the engagement. He knew she would say yes.

As the plane banked and turned, Cassandra and Hardin settled back in their seats.

"Do you think it will last?" whispered Cassandra into Hardin's ear as she tried not to hiccup bubbles of champagne.

Hardin shrugged, grinned, and then finally shook his head. "It's just one of those vacation romances," he said. "They never last. You know that, don't you?"

But for once in her life Cassandra was not sure.

Coming in January 1982

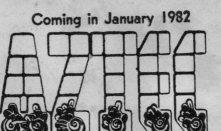

The National Bestseller by

GARY JENNINGS

"A blockbuster historical novel. . . . From the start of this epic, the reader is caught up in the sweep and grandeur, the richness and humanity of this fictive unfolding of life in Mexico before the Spanish conquest. . . . Anyone who lusts for adventure, or that book you can't put down, will glory in AZTEC!"

The Los Angeles Times

"A dazzling and hypnotic historical novel. . . . AZTEC has everything that makes a story appealing . . . both ecstasy and appalling tragedy . . . sex . . . violence . . . and the story is filled with revenge. . . . Mr. Jennings is an absolutely marvelous yarnspinner. . . . A book to get lost in!"

The New York Times

"Sumptuously detailed. . . . AZTEC falls into the same genre of historical novel as SHOGUN."

Chicago Tribune

"Unforgettable images. . . . Jennings is a master at graphic description. . . . The book is so vivid that this reviewer had the novel experience of dreaming of the Aztec world, in technicolor, for several nights in a row . . . so real that the tragedy of the Spanish conquest is truly felt."

Chicago Sun Times

AVON Paperback   55889 . . . $3.95

Available wherever paperbacks are sold, or directly from the publisher. Include 50¢ per copy for postage and handling: allow 6-8 weeks for delivery. Avon Books, Mail Order Dept., 224 West 57th St., N.Y., N.Y. 10019.

Aztec 10-81